SATREIH

7/17/08
To Caroline,
Enjoy!

Kristina Schilling

SATREIH

The Making of a Legend

Kristina Skilling

iUniverse, Inc.
New York Lincoln Shanghai

Satreih
The Making of a Legend

Copyright © 2008 by Kristina Skilling

iUniverse books may be ordered through booksellers or by contacting:

iUniverse
2021 Pine Lake Road, Suite 100
Lincoln, NE 68512
www.iuniverse.com
1-800-Authors (1-800-288-4677)

Because of the dynamic nature of the Internet, any Web addresses or links contained in this book may have changed since publication and may no longer be valid.

This is a work of fiction. All of the characters, names, incidents, organizations, and dialogue in this novel are either the products of the author's imagination or are used fictitiously.

ISBN: 978-0-595-47625-1 (pbk)
ISBN: 978-0-595-71225-0 (cloth)
ISBN: 978-0-595-91890-4 (ebk)

Printed in the United States of America

for my family, Drew Evans, and everyone else who
helped me put this together

CHARACTER AND PLACES BACKROUND

Akaidi~ (Ak'idi)

A witch skilled in potion making, fortune telling, and deciphering. She lives in a shack right outside the Rasiamoramisa Mountain. Akaidi always expects payment from the visitor, usually in vedis. However, if the visitor brings her a gift that has more value, she'll accept that instead. She was the woman who mentored and raised Yia.

Auburn~

A red dragon who lives near the village of Lupine Hills. He is the only dragon that lives on the opposite side of the Ugulaly Ocean. He keeps mainly to himself, away from the men.

Castelo~

King of the centaurs. He refuses to acknowledge that the problems in his forest are from a morith that had been placed there. Still, he agrees whole-heartedly to the strange request that King Lathik makes. He shares a never-dying friendship with a unicorn who lives in his forest.

Chikara~ {both characters share the same name}

1. Satreih's mother. She is one of the many people who fought in the ancient battle. Thousands of years after the battle, Chikara fled from her home and friends, fearing an impending attack. She had learned of her husband Airon's death a couple of months before their child's birth. Taking only their infant son with her, Chikara flees to a forest, in an attempt to lose her pursuers.

2. A powerful, golden dragoness. Satreih named her after his mother. Chikara has more wisdom than her age would normally allow. Whenever Satreih needs advice, Chikara is always the first one he asks. She becomes one of Satreih's most trusted and closest companions.

Eiéoner~ (Eon'ner)

The Leader of the Dragons. Eiéoner lives with other dragons in Seven Waterfalls. He carried an unconscious Meithoko and his father to safety after Meithoko fought a tiring battle with Verteq.

Helioff~

King of the Hasini Clan. He rules with his wife, Queen Rhenai, and his son, Kaskin. They and their clan live underground in the Sakki desert, away from the sun's rays and the cannibals. The Hasinis were ravaged by a plague that nearly exterminated them. Staying underground has a disadvantage: most everyone's immune system is weak from not being exposed to the elements.

Inuje Swemms~ (Inu'he Swemms)

A group of water nymphs who live in Kajie, led by Keelu. Their job is to hunt for the two thousand people who live in Kajie. The job has been made more difficult because giant sharks have been living in the area. Although the sharks pose no threat to the fish, they eat just about anything else.

Itimei~

King Stephenson's daughter, and the only heir to his throne. She has many years of experience with the bow. If a child is expected to become a warrior and shows interest in archery, she gladly teaches the child the art.

Jaemia~

Shamika's granddaughter. She quickly befriends Rasnir when she and her grand-mother welcome him into their home. When Jaemia is abducted by the Spies, Rasnir does everything in his power to retrieve her.

Jeshu~

A young water nymph who lives in Kajie. He has just come of age. Jeshu recently received the position of co-captain of the Inuje Swemms. The position doesn't seem to be the best job for him. Jeshu doesn't adjust well to danger, and he's manipulative. Verteq seems to have something in store for him.

Kajie~ (Ka'he)

An underwater cavern that's home to the water nymphs. It's far below the ocean's surface. The water nymphs are capable of controlling the flow of the water through Kajie. They can easily empty it to allow air-breathing guests, or entirely flood the city to keep out enemies.

Kaskin~

Prince of the Hasini clan, skilled in every form of fighting except archery. He is desperate to find some help for his clan after they are ravaged by the plague. Once he is certain that his clan will survive, he begins to travel with Satreih and Chikara, in gratitude for their generosity. He quickly befriends them.

Keelu~

Captain of the Inuje Swemms. During the middle of a hunting session, he is the first to notice that a dragon and a couple of riders were trying to make their way through a perilous storm. Keelu cancels the hunt for the day once the dragon falls from the sky. He orders Kajie to be drained to allow the dragon and her riders in. Keelu offers the strangers hospitality.

Lathik~ (La'thick)

King of the dwarfs. Once hatred between his people and the elves begins to rise, King Lathik cannot tolerate the elves. Whenever an elf is found close to his boundaries, he automatically places them in prison. Strangely, King Lathik makes a request that includes the protection of the elves.

Makue~ (Mak'oo)

An immortal unicorn. Makue shares a friendship with King Castelo. Makue is aware that a morith was placed into the heart of the forest that he lives in. The trees began to die with unnatural causes. Whenever Makue goes by a dead tree, the tree will appear alive. Makue teaches Satreih how to use some of the sword's hidden capabilities, and tells him the extent of the sword's power, along with a forgotten legend.

Meikosa~

Home of the elves. Mountains surround most of it. A sparkling, snow-fed river runs through Meikosa. The river never runs dry. There is no piece of trash anywhere in Meikosa's streets. Most of Meikosa's kings have done great deeds. They were put into legend.

Meithoko~

The king of Meikosa preceding Thuoj. Shamika is his granddaughter. Meithoko came to power after defeating Verteq in a death match. He and his friends were able to live unnaturally long lives. The legend claims that he fled from the throne as he was being chased by brigands. The brigands were possessed by a nameless and powerful evil. No one knows what happened to him. Most people believed he was killed.

Mosiania~

This dreadful place is built like a fort to keep out intruders. Mosiania is built on the slope of Mt. Ogick. Mosiania is the only area not affected by the harsh winter that Verteq cursed upon the land. All of Verteq's beasts, including the Spies and Wi'oks, claim Mosiania as their home. Aside from Verteq, the Spies are the most feared because of their brute strength.

Mt. Ogick~

A volcano that Mosiania was built upon.

Oj'yer~ (O'jeer)

A powerful black dragon who enjoys hunting with Weuh. He was the only dragon in the past to challenge the Dragon Leader, Eiéoner. He was unsuccessful. Weuh nursed him back to health with magic. Now, Oj'yer is a faithful companion to Verteq because of Weuh's generosity.

Queas~

Leader of Kajie. His main concern is to find food for his two thousand people. Once Verteq's powers begin to rise, Queas organizes more hunts with Keelu, due to the disappearance of fish.

Rasiamoramisa~ (Razi'a'more'a'miza)

Home of the dwarfs. Rasiamoramisa is filled with countless beautiful gems. The dwarfs are always working to make the gems more beautiful. Some of the gems are used for lighting purposes. Ventilation shafts are scattered throughout the mountain, to provide the dwarfs with fresh air.

Rasnir~

A man with unique powers: all of his senses are as sharp as an animal's. Many people, including his mother and uncle, turn away from him because of his abilities. After tragedy strikes him once more, Rasnir travels to a distant forest. When he comes upon the body of a dead elf, Rasnir takes the baby that she holds and buries her. The baby's mother's spirit thanks him. She decides to leave her child, Satreih, in his care.

Razij~ (Raz'ege)

A werecat who subjects himself to Yia. He is one of the only werecats left. Razij made the Rasiamoramisa Mountain his home, but the dwarfs are unaware of his presence. He has special powers and uses them to help his friends. He speaks in broken English.

Rhenai~

Queen of the Hasinis. She rules side-by-side with her husband, King Helioff. Queen Rhenai helps the doctors find cures for diseases. She gives the only ophilla—a shirt-like suit of armor that protects the arms, chest, back, and neck—to Satreih.

Sakametio~

Home of the men. Asuv is the king. Sakametio's castle soars into the sky. It can be seen from neighboring mountains. Many tiny villages surround the castle. However, the Race of Men is famed for letting their emotions control their hearts and minds. Because of that, Sakametio is one of the places that Verteq decides to directly attack.

Sakki Desert~

The Sakki Desert is a long stretch of land that is treacherous to cross by foot. Most of the inhabitants are cannibals, except for the Hasini clan. The Sakki

Desert does have a guardian that watches over it, but no one knows who or what the guardian is.

Satreih~

An orphaned young elf. The dragon egg that he discovers hatches after Satreih finds it. As soon as he befriends the dragon, his adoptive father, Rasnir, is abducted by the same villains in the legend. Satreih's only intentions are to free his father. He soon realizes that there is a war seemingly revolving around him and someone else he doesn't yet know. Satreih and the dragon are soon joined by friends who were affected by the war.

Seven Waterfalls~

Home of the dragons. This is where Eiéoner lives. Seven Waterfalls is surrounded by jungle and mountains. It has a peculiar atmosphere: anyone who suffers from altitude and motion sickness will be instantly cured.

Shamika~

The kind old woman who took Rasnir in, but never officially adopted him. Shamika is the person in charge of her village. Her grandfather was Meithoko. At first, she is the only one who knows that the ancient myth is real.

Starlitih~ (Star'lit'he)

Home of the centaurs. Starlitih is in a forest clearing. The centaurs have control of the vines from the trees, using them to attack intruders.

Stephenson~

The king of Lupine Hills, a firm believer that creatures of myth do not exist. He is aware of the land on the opposite side of the Ugulaly Ocean, but has never made the trip across.

Thuoj~ (Thu'ge)

King of the elves. He is known for his generosity and is gifted with healing powers. People of all races bring him bedridden family members for him to heal. King Thuoj gives many of them, as well as fallen warriors, another chance at life.

Ugulaly Ocean~

An ocean that separates two lands. It is rumored to be hard to find and treacherous to cross. It becomes even more treacherous to cross once Verteq discovers its location. Only a few people know of the ocean and what awaits on the opposite side.

Usthil~ (Ist'hill)

Rasnir's and Jaemia's son. Usthil narrowly escaped death as a baby. Like his father, he has a strong sense of smell. He works tirelessly to restore Sakametio to its former glory after it is attacked by Verteq. Usthil is the only man who survived the attack.

Verteq~

"King" of Mosiania. The title isn't official, but he controls the hearts and minds of his followers. He and his minions killed many people during years of war. Verteq was the original creator of the fire swords. However, one was mysteriously stolen from him, causing him to kill many people in an attempt to find it. The sword was later used against him in a death match. Verteq survived, but his magical powers were gone. He spent the next centuries trying to retrieve the sword and his magic.

Vineras~

The vampire that Akaidi saved from the stake. Vineras stays with her now, guarding her payments. He watches the ground below from the rafters. Vineras attacks any outsider who enters Akaidi's shack.

Weuh~ (Wo'oh)

An elderly wizard skilled in dark magic and creating storms. He is one of the few wizards who can change appearance at will. Weuh wasn't always evil, but he always had distaste for the Race of Men. Weuh is Verteq's most trusted ally.

Yia~

A young witch who is far more skilled than any other her age. Yia has the ability to change her appearance at will. She has placed herself in a very dangerous position. She may very soon be trusted by no one. Her intentions are mostly unknown to Satreih until Yia reluctantly tells him part of what is going on.

Yuzr Ocean~ (Yu'ser)

This is the ocean that separates Rasiamoramisa from the Sakki Desert. The Yuzr Ocean used to be bigger in the past. It carved out the tunnels that the Hasini clan claims as home. Water nymphs are abundant in the ocean, their major home being Kajie.

AN ANCIENT MYTH
REVEALED AS
REALITY

Rasnir was a child, only five years old, but he was not normal. He was born with powers. His senses were as sharp as an animal's. He had unique blue eyes and short ebony hair that was as sleek as silk. As attractive as his appearance was, people learned of his abilities. They would talk, and whisper behind his back. People would tease him, continuously telling him that he was the reason why his mother committed suicide. They knew she gave birth to an animal, and she could not bear the burden. She hanged herself. They knew that's why his father left him. Rasnir desperately attempted to hide his powers, but people found out about his capabilities. They always did.

Rasnir was sent to his uncle, who moved away during the night. Rasnir was left in his uncle's cottage, a shack, burning by day, freezing by night.

Rasnir left the shack to seek refuge in one of the villages of Sakametio. An old woman spotted him and pitied him. To her eyes, he was a weak and starving creature, with eyes that looked through you, and his rib cage showing through his skin. The old woman, Shamika, took him to her cottage, fed him, and began to nurse him back to health. Shamika had a grand-daughter, who was the same age as Rasnir. Her name was Jaemia. Jaemia looked like a queen, with piercing green eyes, and long red hair.

Rasnir was content. He quickly loved Shamika as his mother, and quickly became best friends with Jaemia. They learned of his abilities, but Shamika and Jaemia were the only people who loved him for what he was.

✳   ✳   ✳   ✳

Jaemia and Rasnir, now both sixteen years old, were playing at sunset, near the forest. They would soon head home to the cottage that they lived in for dinner. They were laughing, and tackling each other to the ground.

Rasnir looked up in the direction of home; his nostrils flaring. He smelled corpses. The scent confused him. If there had been an attack, the smell of fresh blood and fear would mix with the scent of death.

"Rasnir?" Jaemia asked uncertainly, following his gaze. "What's wrong? You smell something, don't you?"

He nodded. "We should go ba—" Her scream cut him off. He saw an unfamiliar arm wrapped forcefully around her head, muffling the scream. The smell of this new man was so revolting that it was making her gag.

"You! Let her go!" Rasnir made a fist. He attempted to punch the dark-cloaked man. He wished the bow and arrows that Sakametio's blacksmith had promised to make for him were in his hands.

Quick as lightning, the man withdrew a sword from a scabbard, and slashed it against Rasnir's chest.

Rasnir cried out in pain as he flew backwards, his back slamming against a tree.

Four other men appeared magically besides the first. As quickly as the assault began, they left, taking Jaemia with them.

Rasnir brushed his hand against his mouth, wiping away the blood that started to trickle out of it. He knew he was hurt, but he could only think of Jaemia. He stood shakily, and sprinted all the way back to the village. Stopping only to retrieve the newly made weapons from the blacksmith, he made his way back to Shamika's cottage.

Shamika looked up from the dishes that she was washing when she heard the door to her cottage open. "My word, Rasnir," Shamika said when she spotted the dark gash on his chest, "What on earth happened to you?"

Rasnir panted, "J-Jaemia ... she ... was kidnapped!"

Without a word, Shamika pushed past him, forcing her old bones into a sprint. In no time, she had gathered a bunch of young village men to help her and Rasnir.

Rasnir led them to the spot where he and Jaemia were attacked, following his own blood scent. It was now night. The area that they were attacked somehow appeared more sinister. It was colder than what normal night would have brought.

One of the village men asked him, "Do you know who kidnapped her?"

"No. I don't. The kidnappers wore dark cloaks, and smelled of corpses."

Another village man whispered softly, so that the others could barely hear, "The Spies of Mosiania."

Another said, "You are crazy! They are from the story that we tell our younglings! The Spies are from the Forsaken Land of Mosiania. They and their masters have killed many over the years, and started wars that led the few survivors to famine and disease. The good people of the land that we are from had war with the monsters, and we beat the evil Verteq. We all know that story! We were told it ourselves as younglings!"

Rasnir cocked his head slightly in confusion, not recognizing the Spies from any story he had been told.

Shamika said softly, "But it is not just a story."

The old woman saw all the shocked faces, and knew she had their attention. She began, "My great-grandfather fought in that war. I never knew him. He died of injuries after the battle. Later, my grandfather, Meithoko, was assassinated. He was the king of Sakametio, the land which we are from. In the past, elves used to rule Sakametio, but they made an agreement with men, giving them their land. The elves soon resettled in Meikosa.

"With a great speech, Great-grandfather convinced his fellow elves, the dwarfs of Rasiamoramisa, the dragons, and the men to fight by his side. He claimed that every race in perpetuity would lead pitiful and fear-filled lives. The speech was successful. After preparing for several months, each race, led by their king, marched up to Mosiania, declaring war upon every inhabitant. My great-grandfather's army clashed with the beasts and Spies of Mosiania. Blood was shed.

"Meithoko ran away from the fight, and climbed Verteq's tower, fighting beasts as he went. He himself fought with Verteq, while the war raged on below. My grandfather and Verteq both became weary after fighting many days. They were both bleeding heavily. Even though he had been stabbed by Verteq's fire sword many times, grandfather could never get used to the pain that associated with it. After one particularly brutal attack, Grandfather fell to the ground, quickly rolling out of the way of another.

"Verteq came up from behind Meithoko and once again Grandfather felt the burning pain from the devilish sword. This time the pain was so intolerable he felt as if he was about to fall into unconsciousness. Grandfather chanted some incomprehensible words, calling upon the power of the Ice Goddess. He stabbed Verteq with his sword, which had mysteriously turned blue. Grandfather saw Verteq freezing up with ice. The ice went all the way up to the top of Verteq's head, bursting into tiny shards of ice daggers. Verteq immediately perished. Unable to fight unconsciousness any longer, Grandfather allowed himself to black out.

"Great-grandfather had multiple wounds. The battle below was over. Neither side could claim victory. Both had suffered enormous casualties. Great-grandfather started to walk around the corpses, looking for his son, fearing he was dead. He saw blue light spewing from Verteq's tower, and ran in that direction. He climbed the stairs, hesitating to open the door at the top. Nevertheless, he had no choice. Opening the door, great-grandfather came upon the body of his son, and only traces of Verteq. He cried out as he ran to his son. He found that his son was not dead, but unconscious. Great-grandfather called to the Leader of the Dragons, Eiéoner. He and his son were carried by air to their home.

"Grandfather woke up and found that he was not in the room in which he had killed Verteq, but in his bed in his cottage. His wounds had healed. He went outside, and saw that the entire village was in tears. He asked 'What happened?' The village people told him that while he was unconscious, his father had died of blood loss. The eldest man of the village went up to Grandfather and said 'Since your father has died, you are the king of Sakametio.' The old man placed Great-grandfather's crown upon his head. Soon after, they moved to Meikosa. Meithoko ruled until he was murdered by brigands."

All of the village men stood still, not believing that the story they had told their younglings was real. Shamika waited patiently, ready for them to come out of their trance and help her find her grand-daughter.

Rasnir, who had been listening to the old woman tell the tale, grew angry. He listened to the woods about him. In the distance, he could faintly hear Jaemia cry for help. He took off in that direction, fitting an arrow onto the bowstring. Shamika followed him. The village men, finally out of their dazed trance, ran after them.

Jaemia called out for help, but the Spy that was carrying her quickly put his hand over her mouth. Again, Jaemia gagged. She winced each time they struck her. Jaemia couldn't cry out any longer. The Spies had put some sort of spell on her that prevented her from making any noise.

A herd of powerful horses appeared in the distance. The herd charged at the Spies. They caused confusion in their ranks. Jaemia fell to the ground. She could not see who the riders on the horses were; they wore dark green cloaks that covered their entire bodies. None of the riders saw the young woman. A Spy's sword struck a great horse, causing it to crash down in front of her. Jaemia rolled away just in time. The rider jumped off his horse. He landed on another horse, behind one of his comrades.

Jaemia ran away from the skirmish, climbing a tree. Soon, the sounds of the battle died away. She heard someone calling her name in the distance. She recognized the voice as Rasnir's. She climbed down the tree and followed the sound of his voice, and soon saw her friend. Jaemia ran up to him and hugged him.

Rasnir looked at his best friend, glad that she was safe. Jaemia only had a few bruises, and a cut on the side of her head. Jaemia explained what had happened after she and Rasnir were attacked. She learned that the green-cloaked people were elves from Meikosa. Everyone headed back to their cottages, happy to be out of the sudden, unnatural cold.

*   *   *   *

Four years later, Rasnir and Jaemia married. There was a celebration with food and fireworks. The fireworks were the best, since they were given to the people of Sakametio by a wizard. Everyone from Sakametio showed up, and even a few elves and dwarfs. The elves and dwarfs mostly stayed away from each other.

Shamika had died of old age before the party. The party came at a perfect time; since many people, including Rasnir and Jaemia, were still grieving.

Three years after the celebration, Jaemia became pregnant. Jaemia and Rasnir worked hard to try to get a better life for their baby. Much to Rasnir's grief, Jaemia died in childbirth. Rasnir's newborn son died shortly after. Rasnir disappeared from the village.

*   *   *   *

Rasnir sniffed the ground, searching for his prey. After his wife and son died, he had walked to a place very far from Sakametio, settling in a deciduous forest with dense vegetation. The forest itself was beautiful. Some trees were bent or fallen, offering a home for many animals. The whole forest seemed to sparkle in the sunlight.

Rasnir himself had changed. He was no longer an excited young man with an attractive appearance. His hair was long, shaggy, and dirty-looking. His eyes were full of despair. He wasn't completely stupid when he left Sakametio. Rasnir had taken his bow and arrows, blankets, gauze, a bit of food, and anything else he might need for survival.

Rasnir was hunting a bear. In his hands, he held the bow that he had received from the blacksmith. Strapped to his back was a quiver filled with arrows. He came to a clearing, and saw the bear. It was a huge grizzly. Using the thick vegetation as camouflage, Rasnir held the bow out in front of him and fitted the arrow on it. He pulled the bowstring back to his ear, being absolutely silent. Something startled the grizzly, causing it to run off.

Cursing, Rasnir tried to shoot it, but the arrow stuck into a tree harmlessly. Rasnir listened, and heard the sounds of a battle. He had been paying so much attention to the bear that he didn't smell the sweat of the attackers, the fear of the victim, or the spilt blood. He also smelled a disturbing scent, the scent of corpses.

The battle was still far away, and it took Rasnir a bit of time to get there. When he arrived at the scene, the attackers were gone. Rasnir could smell blood. A woman's body lay on the ground. He could tell that she did not survive. Even in death she was still beautiful; she had long golden hair and had deep blue sightless eyes. A silver head piece curved around her head, with a sapphire gem connecting the two ends of the head piece. The woman had extremely long ears. Rasnir could see that she had a fatal wound on her neck. *The injury that killed her,* he thought.

Rasnir noticed that she was clutching a bundle to her breast. The bundle squirmed and whimpered. With some difficulty, Rasnir pried the bundle out of the woman's fingers. A baby was wedged within the protection of the soft material. He greatly resembled his mother. He also had golden hair, and deep blue eyes. The baby reached up. He had some fuzz from the material on his fingers. The tips of the baby's fingers touched Rasnir's nose, making him sneeze. Rasnir managed to cover his nose. He was rewarded with the baby's giggle.

Looking fondly at the baby, Rasnir gently placed him down and began to bury the infant's mother.

Rasnir brought the baby to the back of the cave that he had chosen to live in. He began to care for him. But soon he fell asleep, with the baby in his arms. He didn't know if the sleep came naturally, or if someone had put a sleeping spell on him.

*   *   *   *

Rasnir woke up, but he was not in his cave. Rasnir was in a thick fog, in the spot where the beautiful woman was killed. The baby was not with him. The fog started to lessen, and he caught the scent of death. In the distance, he saw a silhouette approach him. Rasnir's adrenaline spiked. He was tempted to run. He didn't have his bow and arrows with him. He couldn't see the figure since the fog was still too thick, and the smell of death was overwhelming. The figure approached him, and laid a hand on his arm. Instantly he calmed down. Rasnir recognized the figure. It was the spirit of the beautiful woman. The fatal wound on her neck was gone.

"My name is Chikara. I am an elf from the land of Meikosa. You came upon my body after I was attacked and killed by the Spies of Mosiania. I thank you for burying me."

Rasnir nodded, his throat tightening. He remembered his best friend, Jaemia, soon to be his wife, having been kidnapped by the Spies.

Chikara continued: "You may think that the Battle of Mosiania is a tale to amuse children. It isn't. The battle was real, and it took place more than ten thousand years ago. I know, because I was there, fighting for Sakametio, my home at the time. I am not jesting you.

"I was attacked by the Spies. They cut my neck, and I was killed. The Spies wanted to kill my child as well, but you came and they ran off, apparently not wanting to bother with you. They spared my son's life. His name is Satreih. I shall leave him in your care."

Before Rasnir could say anything, the spirit of Chikara disappeared. Rasnir was left in unnoticeable darkness.

A STRANGE SYMBOL

Satreih was focused on his prey, a deer with huge horns. If he were to be stabbed by them, it would seriously hurt, like being stabbed by a spear. Not that he had ever been stabbed by a spear, but he knew it would hurt. Satreih knocked an arrow and aimed it at the deer. He pulled back on the bowstring and let the arrow fly. It hit its mark. He smiled in triumph. Rasnir's lessons had been well learned.

He made his way over to the fallen deer, but stopped suddenly when he heard a snake hiss. He looked past the deer's corpse, and he felt the blood drain out of his face. A somewhat small, two-headed cobra was staring straight at him. It had focused, angry, red eyes. The deer had fallen on it, but the weight didn't kill it. It just made the snake angry. The snake slithered out from underneath the corpse. Satreih knocked another arrow. The snake lunged, barely missing his feet. He tripped, and fell off of the small hill that he and the snake were on. The slope of the hill was covered in thorns. They continued to pull at his jacket and pants.

Satreih landed at the foot of the hill. He had an abundance of small cuts, and he was a little dazed. He looked up at the devil snake, smiling. It wouldn't be able to make its way down the hill; there were too many thorns. He said a few taunting words to the snake, for his own amusement. It tried to get to him, hissing again in frustration. The two-headed cobra turned around and started to head to its home.

Satreih laid there for a few minutes, trying to catch his breath. *What a freaky cobra!* He sat up, and looked around. He was in a clearing. Everything about the forest here was the same, except in the middle of the clearing there was a small mound of dirt with a stone placed on top of it. *I'll ask Father about this later.* Then he saw something strange. At first he thought it was gold, but he quickly proved himself wrong. Gold was not perfectly round. This odd thing was. It was just colored gold. Satreih cautiously walked up to it, his bow held out in front of him for protection. It didn't look dangerous, but he had learned his lesson time and time again.

Satreih warily watched this thing for nearly ten minutes. After the time was up, Satreih was convinced that it wasn't going to hurt him. He picked the thing up and his curiosity spiked a little higher. He heard sounds coming from it. He dropped it in surprise. *There's something inside this thing!* Hitting the ground, however, didn't seem to hurt it. Instead, it seemed to help it.

It started to shake. There was a blinding light spewing from the top, which had cracked a little. The light got so bright that Satreih had to cover his eyes. There was a splitting sound. Satreih felt parts of the stone hit him. The light stopped. Everything seemed normal. Satreih cautiously removed his arms from his face. He blinked once, then twice. The thing was gone; its remains were scattered throughout the clearing. He realized that the thing had been an egg. Standing in its place, blinking in the sunlight, was a golden baby dragon.

The dragon squeaked and walked up to him. It had sharp ridges snaking down its back. The dragon had bright green eyes. It was a little wobbly, and it plopped down on his feet, instantly going to sleep.

It's so cute! But, what should I do with it? I'm already attached to the dragon. Hey, my injuries from the fall are completely gone! Satreih picked up the baby dragon, who was already fast asleep, and put it into one of his coat pockets. The pocket was plenty big enough. *I have to hide any clues that the dragon was here. I wonder what I'll tell Rasnir.* Satreih picked up all of the eggshell pieces, which became very fragile now that the dragon was not using them. He crumbled up all of the pieces and made them even more miniscule. He tossed the golden dust into the nearby river.

Satreih climbed up the hill that he had fallen from, using his bow to knock the thorns out of the way. The thorns seemed somewhat magical. They seemed to shiver whenever they were hit, and shrank back down like well-trained puppies.

Satreih remembered the two-headed cobra that had attacked him earlier. *I hope it went away. I don't want it attacking me or the baby dragon.* When he got to the top of the hill, he saw the corpse of the deer that he had slain. There were already flies on it. *Good, no snake.* Satreih knocked the flies out of the way with his bow. They fell down, dead. He wiped the fly guts off of the deer. He picked up the deer's corpse and carried it back to the cave that he lived in with Rasnir.

*   *   *   *

Satreih was very close to the cave. He could feel the spray from the waterfall that guarded it. The waterfall was spring-fed. The water was crystal clear and crashed into the deep lake a hundred feet below. During the summer, the water was gorgeous. He loved to swim in it during that time.

The only way to get to the cave was to swim. Without thinking, Satreih placed the deer's corpse on the surface of the water, holding it up. He put the still sleeping dragon on top of it. It was nearing winter. Shivering somewhat, Satreih held his arms over the baby dragon, protecting it from the water of the waterfall. He pushed the deer's corpse through the waterfall, and was soon on the other side. He replaced the baby dragon in his pocket.

The cave was enormous, in both width and length. Anyone who entered had to walk a mile to get to the end of it. Satreih and Rasnir lived at the very end of the cave. The cave itself was beautiful. There were unique structures of stalactites and stalagmites. The rushing water above slowly eroded the rock. The water dripped down the stalactites and formed a small pool. They could hear the steady sound of it dripping. The sound was soothing at night. There was enough light throughout the cave to see. The lighting was always the same; a small gloom. Just enough to see, but not too bright to have trouble trying to sleep.

Satreih finally made it to the back of the cave, with water droplets still dripping off of him, and found his father building a fire. Next to him there was a single squirrel.

Without looking up, Rasnir asked, "Catch anything good?" He knew he shouldn't have bothered answering. His nose already told him. The scent was making his mouth water. He was slightly curious about a charcoal-like scent, but the smell of the deer was overpowering.

"Yup."

Rasnir glanced up to see what his son had brought. "Oh, you show-off. You know that it's getting close to winter. The prey's harder to find."

"I didn't have a problem."

"I see that. Good job. My lessons were well learned, I guess."

"Yeah, they were. Here you go." Satreih plopped the deer's body down next to his father. "I want to tell you something."

Satreih told his father about shooting the deer with an arrow first try, the devil two-headed cobra, his fall down the small hill with all the thorns, and finding the small mound of dirt with a stone on top. Satreih left out the part with the egg and the dragon. He didn't know what his father would think of that.

Rasnir thought, *It's time to tell him.* "That mound of dirt with the stone on top is the grave—of your mother. She was killed by the Spies of Mosiania. They smell of corpses. I found her body after she was attacked. By the time I got there, she was dead. She was holding you; you were a baby. I took you and buried her. Your mother, Chikara, came to me in a dream and asked me to care for you. I am not your father by blood. I don't know who is, or if he is still alive."

Satreih looked at the ground, thinking. He had always thought Rasnir was his father.

Rasnir let him think for a while, then asked with a raised eyebrow, "If you fell down that hill with all the thorns, why aren't you cut?"

Satreih had forgotten about that. He looked up quickly. "Um … I'm an elf. Remember, it took me a couple of hours to get back. I guess elves heal a lot faster than men do." It was mostly the truth. He was grateful that Rasnir bought the small lie.

Satreih felt the dragon squirm in his pocket and heard it squeak softly. He winced, thinking Rasnir would have heard it, dreading his keen hearing. His father didn't notice; he was too intent on eating his cooked deer's leg, hungrily gobbling it up.

Satreih breathed a sigh of relief. He got up and said, "I'm going to go outside to get some fresh air."

As soon as he was outside, he took the baby dragon out. It squeaked again, and nipped at Satreih's fingers, a move that clearly showed that it was hungry. It was nearing dusk. He knew that was around the time dragons hunt.

Satreih climbed a tree, placing the baby dragon on the highest branch. He told it, "Stay here. I'll get you some food." Satreih climbed down, and the dragon stayed. As he walked away, he felt the dragon's eyes follow him.

*   *   *   *

A half hour later, Satreih heard a voice that seemed a little unsure of itself.
I'd like a rabbit please.

It took him a while to recognize the voice, but then realized that it was the dragon's. There was a hint of power to the voice. Satreih used the same mind-speech back and asked, *Are you sure? A rabbit is bigger than you.*

The dragon said defensively, *Just because I am little doesn't mean I can't eat my food!*

Okay, if you want a rabbit, you'll get one. It might take me a little while to find one, since rabbits are in their burrows and it is getting close to winter.

I don't mind. I'll wait here.

Oh, hey, I need to give you a name. Hmmmm, how about Gorddeon?

Uhh ... no.

Hastlefast?

No.

Jannicoleo?

No.

Oh wait ... you're a girl, aren't you?

Yes, I am, thank you.

Satreih paused, thinking. *Okay, if that's the case, how about Chikara?*

Ooh, I like that.

Chikara it is then. Oh hey, I found your rabbit. Satreih had just found a burrow with a nice, fat, rabbit inside. It was fast asleep. Satreih shot it with an arrow. He started to carry the dead rabbit out of the burrow, but then he spotted a snake out of the corner of his eye. It was the same two-headed cobra. *Ugh! What is it with this snake?* Satreih didn't mean to use mind-speech, but Chikara heard him anyway.

I'll get it.

The snake coiled up, ready to attack Satreih again. A curious thing happened. The snake shot him a surprised look, and started to writhe in pain on the ground. There was a sickening snap. The writhing instantly stopped.

Chikara spoke to him again with a hint of amusement in her voice. *Still don't think I can eat a rabbit?*

It—might have been a coincidence. The snake could have had a heart attack or something.

No, you fool. That was me.

I know. I'm just teasing you. Thanks for killing the snake!

No problem. Hey, what are those weird people doing going into your cave?

What!

Chikara's voice was suddenly cut off. Satreih didn't hear any more mind-speech from her. Fearing that something bad had happened, he quickly made his way back to the cave.

*　　　*　　　*　　　*

The trees that were around the lake were burned and destroyed, including the one that the baby dragon was in. Satreih called out to the dragon, "Chikara!"

Over here.

Chikara was crouching under a fallen log, shivering with fear. Satreih moved the log and picked her up, stroking her to calm her down.

"What happened?"

These cloaked figures approached the waterfall and went inside. They smelled of corpses. They dragged a man out of the cave. I tried to kill the cloaked figures with my mind-powers, but I can only kill things my size or smaller. Besides, even if I could kill bigger things, they were too powerful for me.

"Cloaked figures that smelled of corpses?"

Yeah. Why do you ask?

"My father said that there are some insanely evil people by that description. I hope he's all right!"

Fighting his fear, Satreih placed the baby dragon back on the ground. She seemed calmer now than she had a few minutes ago. Satreih said, "Stay here and eat your rabbit. I'll be right back."

Chikara nodded. She watched her new friend go underneath the waterfall and started to devour her tasty meal.

Satreih held his bow at his side. The cave that had been his home for sixteen years seemed less inviting than it had a few hours ago. Some of the stalactites and stalagmites that had been growing for generations were broken. Satreih looked at a broken stalagmite and saw that a skull had been carved into it with unrecognizable magic.

After a while, Satreih made it to the back of the cave. "Father!" he called out. The only answer was the howling of the wind. The logs that Rasnir had used to build the fire to cook the food were scattered everywhere. There was a pool of blood on the floor. Satreih saw a small piece of paper on the ground. He picked it up. It didn't make any sense whatsoever. It looked like it was drawn hastily, and some things were cut off.

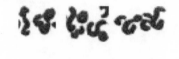

Satreih walked out of the cave with the small piece of paper in his hand. He started to walk toward the dragon, but he didn't need to. Chikara stretched her wings. She glided and landed on his shoulder. She was already the size of a small cat.

Satreih showed her the symbol and asked, "Can you translate it?" He didn't bother asking Chikara if she could read or not. Even though she was not even a day old, she could already speak fluently, kill freaky two-headed cobras with mind-powers, and fly.

Chikara stared at the symbol for a while, and mind-spoke, *No. We need to find somebody who can. Do you know of anyone?*

"Father did say there was a witch who is pretty good at translating things. But he wasn't sure. He read about her in a book. Even if she is real, she lives in Rasiamoramisa. That place is all the way on the other side of the Sakki Desert and the Yuzr Ocean. Rasiamoramisa is owned by the dwarfs." Satreih added softly, "There is some hatred between dwarfs and elves. Even if we do make it there, I doubt that they will let me see the witch."

If what you said is true, that distance is far too long to walk. We should wait three days. By then I will be big enough to carry you through the air. We will deal with the dwarfs when it is time.

It was a long three days' wait. Satreih was impatient and anxious, knowing that Rasnir could already be dead. Satreih was smart enough to know that he would need a lot of arrows if he were going to make this trip. He made more by taking the Laxuivies bark off a tree. That type of bark was very dangerous. If any-one just leaned on it, the parts of their skin that touched it would immediately bleed. When Satreih took it off, his hands bled. He laid the bark on the ground and used a sharp rock to carve it into little points. Satreih cut off some tree branches and fashioned them into arrow-sized staffs. He then tied the deadly points onto the homemade staffs with vines. He used the feathers of an eagle for the feathers of his arrows. After two days had passed, Satreih had made a total of two hundred arrows. His quiver could not hold any more than that. After he was done, Chikara leaned up against him and his hands immediately stopped bleeding.

Chikara could no longer perch on his shoulder. She was as tall as Satreih. She could already hunt for herself. Hunting for her was easy; she used her mind-powers to track prey from a distance and had already killed a good-sized boar. Chikara was a half hour flight from it, but she easily found it. At night she leaned up against Satreih, trying to keep him warm while he was making his arrows. Snow had fallen. Satreih never slept.

Finally, it was time to leave. All the preparations had been made. Satreih was excited. He had never ridden a dragon before. He was also a little anxious because he didn't know if Rasnir was all right, and because he had never left his forest and didn't know what to expect.

Chikara allowed him to jump on her back. He sat on the crest, between two ridges. Satreih held on tightly to the ridge in front of him. Even though it was sharp, he wasn't cut. Chikara stretched her wings and leapt into the air. It was the best ride Satreih could imagine. The wind was constantly in his face, and he enjoyed watching the ground far below him, watching it slip away so fast. At first, Satreih got altitude sickness, but then quickly got used to it. He was grateful that he wore his coat. Chikara and Satreih soon left the forest far behind them.

         *   *   *   *

Ahead of them, Satreih saw a village. Since the wind was raging, he used mind-speech to talk to Chikara. *We should stop at that village and ask for directions. You should hide though; people might get scared when they see you.*

"Ahh!" Satreih grabbed the ridge in front of him harder to prevent himself from falling off. It didn't take him too long to figure out that Chikara was laughing at him. *What's so funny?* He demanded.

I thought men never asked for directions!

I'm an elf.

Same thing. As she stopped laughing, Chikara landed on a plain close enough to the village so that Satreih could walk, but far enough away so the people wouldn't see her. *I'll wait here.*

Soon Satreih arrived at the village. It was an entirely new experience. When he lived in the forest with Rasnir, they were completely isolated. They had to fend for themselves. But here, the village was very busy. People were rushing about, determined to get something accomplished. There were people at the side of the street selling foods that Satreih had never seen before. Some people were doing grueling work in the fields on the outskirts of the village. They didn't look very happy. Others were herding cows.

Someone cried from behind him, "Look out!"

Satreih dove to the side just as a wagon pulled by horses barreled through where he had been standing.

The man driving the wagon looked back and said, "Watch out, sir. The street gets busy." The wagon disappeared around the corner.

Satreih moved to the side of the street and joined the other people. He whispered under his breath, "I'm way out of my league here." He walked around; looking for someone who could give him directions to Rasiamoramisa, but everyone was too busy.

A delicious smell reached his nostrils. His mouth watered and his stomach grumbled. Satreih hadn't eaten at all in three days. He was too busy making his arrows. Satreih looked in the direction of the smell. A food stand was selling very juicy meat. Satreih walked over to it and read the sign. *So,* he thought, *this meat is Calsi. Twenty vedis? What the ...?*

He asked the seller politely, "Can I have some Calsi, please?"

The person selling the meat grunted and said, "Only if you have twenty vedis."

"What's a vedi?"

The vendor looked at Satreih strangely. He shook his head and started waving at other people to come over to buy his food, completely ignoring Satreih.

Disappointed, Satreih walked away.

Chikara asked, *Any luck yet?*

No. Everyone is too busy. Hmmmm ... do you know what a vedi is?

You ask me as if I should know the answer to that.

Oh. I guess I'll keep looking.

A woman waved in Satreih's direction. Satreih turned around to face her. The woman blew past him as if he weren't even there. Confused, Satreih watched her as she fell into a man's arms. Satreih had thought that the woman waving to him. Even though he was some distance away from them, he could easily hear what they were saying.

"You're back from the desert! How are the Hasinis?"

"Not good. Their clan is dying. They were hit with a deadly plague. I didn't see Prince Kaskin, or his parents for that matter. An upper level scout has been left in charge. I gave the goods to him instead."

"You could have helped them! You're a doctor!" The woman asked softly, "How many are left?"

Her husband said sadly, "Only around fifty." He added, "I hate saying this, but no one should approach the Hasinis for awhile. They're suspicious of outsiders, thinking that we would bring in another disease that would finish them off. My old friend, Mithal, tried to attack me."

Something distracted Satreih from the conversation. A gruff looking old man was inside a cottage, beckoning to Satreih from a window. The cottage was run down, and the windows were grimy. The old man had a long and scraggly beard. His eyes were shrunken. Not knowing any better, Satreih entered the cottage.

The old man asked, "I've never seen you around in this village before. You have no idea how much you stand out. What are you doing here?"

Satreih answered, "I'm just looking for directions to Rasiamoramisa. Do you know how to get there?"

The old man snorted. "Of course I do. But, if you were smart, you would turn right back home." He looked at his guest for a moment, and then said, "I see you have no other intention but to go to Rasiamoramisa. Your face tells me."

The old man walked into another room. Satreih stayed where he was. He could hear the old man looking for something.

The old man returned, carrying a map in his hands. "The orange dots indicate the dangerous areas. Do not go there."

Satreih thought, *Great. Orange dots all the way around Rasiamoramisa.*

AN EVIL PLACE

Rasnir looked up in fear. The Spies were bringing him into a fort. The fort was on the slopes of a volcano. He had never seen it before, but he had read about it dozens of times in books after Jaemia had been kidnapped. The Spies were bringing him into Mosiania. Smoke was coming up from pits, a sign that Mosiania was indeed beginning to prepare for war once again. Rasnir tried to break free for the hundredth time. For the hundredth time the Spies held him tight with iron grips.

They entered a very tall building. Inside there was a crudely made winding staircase that they climbed. Everything about the building was crudely made. There were torches hanging on the walls. At the very top of the stairs, there was a door that they entered. Inside the room was a particular dark spot on the ground that seemed to be pulsing with an unlimited amount of evil. An old man was standing over it, with his back turned to Rasnir.

Rasnir thought, *Why is an old man here? I thought they killed every youngling and elder.*

The leader of the Spies stepped in front of the group. Without turning around the old man asked, "Did you bring him?"

The leader of the Spies replied, "Yes, master. You wanted the animal-man?"

That surprised Rasnir. He didn't know that the Spies were capable of speaking English. On the journey, they only spoke their language. Rasnir gasped as he realized that this was the very same room where Shamika's grandfather killed Verteq. That thought sent a shudder down his spine as he looked at the dark spot.

The old man finally turned around, and looked at Rasnir. Rasnir's knees went weak. A staff with a crystal on the top suddenly appeared in his hand. *So,* Rasnir thought, *He is a wizard.* The wizard had a long, grayish-whitish beard that was long enough to touch his knees. He had steely gray eyes that seemed to cut right through Rasnir. His eyes seemed to glow with an evil intensity.

The wizard drew out a dagger and said to Rasnir, "I need your blood," and started to walk toward him. Again, Rasnir tried to break free, but it was futile. The wizard cut Rasnir's arm. Rasnir bit his tongue. He did not want to appear weak.

The wizard walked back to the dark spot, holding the knife over it. He said to the cauldron, "Blood from the son of the one who wounded you, Master." He tapped the knife and drops of blood fell into the dark spot.

A hooded figure rose up and out of the dark spot. It fell heavily on the floor, as if it were weak. The wizard made a move to help the creature, but the creature roughly shoved him aside and got up itself. The wizard bowed. The Spies followed his lead, shoving Rasnir down with them.

When it spoke, its voice was terrible. It made the evil wizard seem friendly. "Take the animal-man to the cells. He will be killed when Satreih arrives." Rasnir realized who the hooded figure was. His veins were freezing up with fear. *Verteq! Wait, how in hell does he know about Satreih?*

Verteq watched with a small grin as the Spies dragged the animal-man out of the room. The animal-man tried to escape once more, but it was to no avail.

As soon as the Spies shut the door, the wizard turned to Verteq. "My Lord, is there anything I can do?"

"Yes, Weuh, there is." Verteq pulled a black circular object the size of an eye from underneath his midnight-black robe. "This is a Geom Stone. Give the Geom Stone to Jeshu, a water nymph from the Yuzr Ocean. He may seem … unreliable, but he is the exact person I need. Chikara and Satreih will be trying to fly across the Yuzr Ocean to get to Rasiamoramisa, to decipher the symbol that the worthless Spies left behind. They must not decipher it. Tell Jeshu to place the Geom Stone in the crevice between Chikara's wing and shoulder. It will be absorbed through her skin. The stone will allow me to see what they are doing. When you leave to give Jeshu the stone, get Oj'yer to carry you."

"Why must I get Oj'yer, my Lord? You know how I can disappear from here and go directly to the place where Jeshu is."

"Chikara is a descendent of Eiéoner. Oj'yer is the only one who has a chance to stand up to her strength. You will perish in a death match against her. It won't make a difference that she does not yet know the extent of her power."

"Yes my Lord, I will go summon Oj'yer to my side."

"One more thing. When Chikara and Satreih are flying over the Yuzr Ocean, create a storm to blow them off course and land them in the area where Jeshu is."

"Yes, my Lord."

Weuh disappeared without a sound.

*   *   *   *

The old wizard reappeared on a beautiful mountainside. There were seven waterfalls cascading from above the rock faces, and falling into a huge lake. In the distance, the old wizard could see the shapes of flying dragons. There was jungle everywhere around Weuh. He was at the bottom of a hill. The old wizard began to climb up it. At the top of the hill, a dragon was waiting.

Weuh said, "I demand to see Oj'yer, dragon. Move out of my way." He was tempted to spit on the dragon's forelegs, but he resisted the urge.

The dragon was suspicious of the old wizard that had suddenly appeared on his doorstep. *Who are you and why are you here?*

"Don't question me. I demand to see Oj'yer."

The dragon took a step toward the wizard, deciding that he had done enough meddling. The dragon tried to attack Weuh, but it stopped. It was paralyzed.

Weuh took out and raised his staff. "You should've known better than to attack me. You will regret your actions."

Weuh held out the staff and pointed it at the dragon. The dragon's skin was blowing off in red dust. Soon, the only thing left of the dragon was its skeleton.

Weuh walked up to the dragon and said, "Fool!" He spat on the dragon's front limbs, kicking the bones that were being used thirty seconds ago.

Weuh walked past the dragon skeleton to the waterfalls. He raised his staff once more, and the waterfalls parted, leaving a dark, gaping hole that led to Oj'yer's cave.

Weuh walked into the cave and followed it. There were bones from various creatures strewn on the floor. They crunched when he stepped on them. One arm bone still had a bunch of skin on it. Weuh picked it up. *A present for Oj'yer.*

The cave was winding and complex, but Weuh knew where to go. Soon the old wizard came into a cavern with a big pile of treasure. Weuh knew that men would risk their lives to plunder the treasure, but he also knew that their efforts would be in vain. They would lose their lives. There were vedis, gems, goblets, crowns, swords, and everything imaginable that was of value.

Oj'yer's slaves were cleaning the treasures. The slaves were men and elves. They were scraggly people, with fear always present in their eyes. They only had loin cloths to wear for clothing. The slaves were dirty, as if they hadn't taken a bath in their whole lives. Their hair was long and was tied up in their beards. To Weuh, they appeared to be over-sized dwarfs. The slaves scurried away as soon as Weuh appeared.

Weuh called out, "Oj'yer!"

A huge black shape soared down from the ceiling. *Good afternoon, Weuh. It has been a while. Is it time to go hunting again?*

"Yes, for an elf and a dragon. Oh. I forgot about something." Weuh lifted up the arm bone. "This one still has meat on it. I found it on the floor, with all the other bones." Weuh tossed it to the black dragon.

Oj'yer looked at the arm and sighed. *It is cold. You know how I like limbs warm. That's why I didn't eat it in the first place. The worthless slave brought it back late. You can very well guess where he is now.*

Weuh touched the bone with his staff. More flesh and blood appeared on it. It grew warm.

Mmmm. Thank you. Oj'yer picked up the bone and tossed it into his mouth. *What did you say about hunting another dragon and an elf?*

"The dragon and the elf are meddling with our Lord's plans. Our Lord wants me to have you help me because the dragon is a descendent of the Dragon Leader, Eiéoner." Weuh ignored Oj'yer's sudden growl. "He wants us to give this Geom Stone to a water nymph named Jeshu, who will place it between the other dragon's wing and shoulder."

Oj'yer spat the bone on the floor. One of the slaves scurried over to it, picked it up, and took it back into the tunnel from where Weuh had entered. He came back and hid in the darkness near the wall with the others.

"What about the morith? Is it safe?"

It's as safe as it could be. Oj'yer patted his stomach. *Let's go, Weuh. Don't want anybody messing up our Lord's plans.* Oj'yer called back to the slaves. *Protect my treasure! Don't you dare leave the cave, or you will join your lost brothers in my belly!*

*   *   *   *

The Spies did as they were told. They brought Rasnir to the cells. The cells were an underground prison. It was cold, dark, wet, and thrived with rats and bugs. The ground was covered with rotting bones of men, dwarfs, and elves. The Spies threw Rasnir into one of the cells. They locked the door, which was made of unbreakable steel. There was no clean running water, only the filthy, dirty water that leaked from above. There was no place to go to the bathroom. There was a bed, but there were no blankets or pillows. The bed itself was just a cold, big stone. Since the cells were underground, there was no sun. There was no way to tell the time. The whole place was very dark and very depressing.

Days passed. The Spies came in once a day to give a small piece of moldy bread and a small cup of fresh water. Rasnir thought that if this kept up, he would starve to death or die of thirst. There was plenty of time for thinking, but he still couldn't figure out how Verteq could have found out about Satreih.

Rasnir was lying on the pointless bed, trying to get some sleep. Whenever he slept, he always had nightmares, always running from some horrible fate. There were noises above, and Rasnir did not know what they were.

He heard the sound of the heavy door lock opening. He sat up, ready for his disgusting, moldy bread. They Spy came in and gave him the bread along with a small cup of water. Rasnir asked, "The other day, the old wizard said something strange. He said 'blood from the son of the one who wounded you.' What does that mean?"

The Spy didn't even look at Rasnir. It said, "In the past, your father went on a journey and collected and destroyed Verteq's moriths. They are ruby gems that pulse with evil power. There were five of them; now there are ten. They were what made Master more powerful than everything, even more powerful than the Leader of the Dragons. At first, master did not know what was going on. As time passed, Master noticed that his power was ebbing away, little by little. By then everyone else had declared war on him, and because he was so weak, Meithoko was able to kill him." The Spy looked at Rasnir and said, "Your father died of injuries after he destroyed the last morith. I was the one who inflicted the injuries on him."

With that, the Spy walked out of the cell. He slammed the door shut and locked it.

Rasnir was stunned. He only nibbled at his bread. Suddenly, he felt someone was watching him from far away. The feeling went away. He thought, *Come back!*

A voice was heard in his head. *I cannot help you. I am too far away.*

Rasnir thought, *Maybe you can help me.* He took a chance and asked, *Do you know Satreih?*

Yes I do.

Tell him to look for moriths. They are ruby gems that pulse with evil power. There are ten of them. Tell Satreih to find them and destroy them! Rasnir's excitement was growing.

I will tell him that.
Thank you so much!
The strange voice went away.

THE FIRST MORITH

Satreih left the old man's run down cottage with the map tucked into his coat pocket. It was near dusk when he got back to the plain where Chikara was waiting for him. She looked incredibly pleased with herself, and a little worried.

Satreih took the map out of his pocket and said, "We're going in the right direction. I think in a couple days' flight, we would be able to reach the Sakki Desert."

I know where your father is. He is being held in a prison in Mosiania. Verteq is back. Rasnir said to look for moriths. There are ten of these ruby gems that pulse with Verteq's evil power.

"Is he all right?"

For now. However, we now have a greater chance of rescuing him. Watch this!

Chikara opened her jaws and breathed out a stream of golden fire. After the fire ceased, Chikara had a devilish grin on her face. *I can torch any foe that comes near us!*

Satreih couldn't help but laugh. Chikara was getting cocky. Satreih said, "Let's go. Who knows? Maybe you'll enjoy the desert."

Can we go after I hunt? It is dusk.

"Yes, you can. Bring something back for me please! I'm starved!"

Chikara nodded and flew off. Twenty minutes later she came back with a cooked cow in her talons.

Satreih shook his head and thought, *I should have known. She used her fire.* He was pinned by her enormous wing beats when she landed. He said, "Let me guess, you torched the poor cow, didn't you?"

Yes, I did. She tore the cooked cow in half. *Here you go. This half is for you.*

Satreih looked at his half in amazement. "I'm not a dragon. I'm an elf. I'm not going to eat all that!"

Chikara looked at him strangely and asked, *How can you guys be as evil as the stories say and not eat this much?* She sighed. *How much do you need?*

"Probably just a fourth of that. And besides, the stories say that the Race of Men were evil to dragons, not the Race of Elves. Hmm … maybe the Race of Dwarfs, too. They feared that the dragons would take their gems."

Chikara tore off the amount and gave it to him. She kept the rest for herself. No sense in wasting good food.

"Thanks."

No problem.

*   *   *   *

After they ate their meal, Chikara allowed Satreih to climb on her back again. She took off in the direction that Satreih showed her on the map. They didn't stop until they reached the Sakki Desert. By the time they landed, it was day. Some of the sand flew in various directions when Chikara landed.

The desert was unbearably hot for Satreih. He was dismayed. The water in his canteen was already getting low. Chikara loved the heat. It made her feel more powerful.

Satreih said sadly, "I thought it was almost winter."

Chikara just shrugged as a reply.

It was time to get some rest. Chikara curled up into a ball. Satreih leaned up against her. They slept the rest of the day, and all of the night.

Chikara's nostrils twitched in the night. So many different animal scents disturbed her restful sleep, but it seemed that none wanted to do any harm. But just because they didn't want to do any harm didn't kill any of her curiosity.

Satreih woke up to feel that the sun was beating on him relentlessly again. Chikara was already awake. He said, "Maybe you should fly instead of walk. There are people in the desert. They might find your tracks."

Chikara took off into the sky. *Can't complain. Flying beats walking anytime.* She flew above Satreih, taking some of the sun's rays off of him. He was grateful for that.

Chikara was having a lot of fun flying, doing loops and steep dives. One dive was so sudden and so fast that Satreih feared that she would crash into the desert. She came out of the dive at the last second, barely missing the ground.

Satreih called up to her, "You're not going to be doing any of that when I'm on you, right?"

Depends on the situation. If we are trying to avoid an enemy in the air, then yeah, I'm going to use evasive maneuvers like these. But if we're just flying with no one following us, I won't do this. Hey, doing stunts like this is half the fun of dragonflight.

"What if I fall off when someone's chasing us?"

You won't.

An arrow flew up towards Chikara. She growled in surprise when she saw it, and easily got out of the way. The arrow completely missed her; the aim was lousy. Standing on a sand dune was a person who held a bow in his hands. Both Chikara and Satreih saw him. Chikara flew down towards him, with her talons ready.

Satreih's voice echoed in her mind, *Stop!*

That man tried to kill me. A mere arrow wouldn't do much damage to my armor, but—

Let me talk to him first.

Chikara snorted and flew back up into the air, out of any arrow's reach. Satreih walked over to the man, with his bow in hand, just in case. The man looked to be a couple of years older than Satreih. He showed no fear to Satreih or Chikara. He was very pale. He had unique light brown eyes and wavy brown hair.

Satreih asked, "Who are you? Why did you try to harm her?" He jerked his head in Chikara's direction.

"My name is Kaskin. I am the prince from the Hasini clan. The Hasini clan is one of the only civilized clans in the desert. Most of the other clans are cannibals. The land is slowly being poisoned. The food supply is growing thin. Our clan is suspicious of outsiders like you. Do you mean us any harm?" Kaskin aimed an arrow at Satreih, but waited for an answer.

Satreih took a step back. "No. We're just trying to—Chikara!"

Chikara plummeted down from the sky. She knocked the bow out of Kaskin's hands, taking some of his flesh with her as well. Kaskin fell to the ground, trying unsuccessfully to ward her off.

"CHIKARA! STOP IT!"

Chikara snorted, but stopped her assault. She landed in front of Satreih, growling.

Satreih gave her an angry look. He walked over to Kaskin, helping him up. "Sorry. She's a little—"

"Protective, I know. I'm the same way with my clan. Sorry. I shouldn't have raised my bow."

Satreih remembered the conversation between the husband and wife at the village. "Was your clan hit by a plague?"

"You're from the village?"

"No. I just overheard a conversation." Satreih offered to heal Kaskin's hands.

"No thanks. I'm fine." Kaskin cast a wary glance in Chikara's direction and sighed. "Yes. We were. There are only about fifty of us left. The plague has stopped spreading, but I fear that it has done too much damage."

"Is there any way we can help?"

"I do not know if there is any way for you to help, but you are welcome to come with me back to my clan." Kaskin turned around and started to walk away. He strapped his bow to his back. Satreih did the same. Chikara jumped up into the air again, careful not to leave tracks on the ground.

*   *   *   *

After flying for a couple of hours, Chikara observed, *Your people are a scraggly-looking bunch, Kaskin.*

Kaskin gave her a surprised look. "Those aren't my people. They're the cannibals." He growled. "I heard rumors that they were going to attack!"

We can take care of them. No sense making your people shiver like frightened rabbits when there's nothing to worry about. Chikara took out a rope that she had hidden somewhere. *C'mon, Satreih. Use this to climb up.*

Satreih asked, "Where did you get the rope?"

From the farm where I got the cow. Why does it make such a big—?

"We're not thieves, Chikara!"

Oh. Hey, give me a little credit. I'm only a few weeks old! I didn't know! We're just—um—borrowing the rope.

"Right. And I suppose that we're also borrowing the cow which has probably already passed our stomachs?"

Kaskin spoke before Chikara got the chance. "The missing rope would be no problem. That farmer is a friend of mine. I can give it back the next time he visits. As for the cow … he has plenty of others. But my clan could always supply him with extra goods from the desert if he wishes." He peered out in the distance. He could faintly see the cannibals. Some of his clan were popping out among them, taking them by surprise.

Kaskin dashed forward with the bow in his hands. *Why did I only bring a bow and arrows? I know I'm pitiful with archery!*

A dozen arrows whizzed by Kaskin's head, each hitting an unsuspecting cannibal. Satreih said, "Hey, Chikara and I are going to help."

Satreih could easily tell the difference between the Hasinis and the cannibals. The cannibals were as Chikara had said: scraggly. Their hair was long and shaggy, and was tied up in their beards. They swung their weapons wildly, unlike the Hasini's skilled training.

Satreih's stomach twisted in disgust as he fought the urge to hurl. The cannibals pounced and feasted on their fallen comrades. But others, ignoring their instinctive urge, continued fighting.

When they were close enough, Kaskin threw his bow at a cannibal who was preparing to feed on one of his injured warriors. The bow knocked the cannibal off balance. While Kaskin picked up his injured warrior, he yelled to the others that the outsiders were friends. Kaskin disappeared beneath the sand, bringing his clanmate to safety.

Satreih and Chikara fought side by side. Chikara kept torching the cannibals, always making sure that none of the Hasinis were in the way. She also swatted at some of the cannibals that were too close for comfort with her claws, but it was less to her liking.

Some cannibals tossed chains in Chikara's direction, temporarily ceasing her fire. Her mouth was wrapped up.

Satreih cursed. He saw the situation Chikara was in. He couldn't do anything to help her. He had just run out of his two hundred arrows, even though each of them found its mark. Before Satreih could reach down to take the knife out of a fallen cannibal's hand, he was struck on the back of his head by a club. Before he slipped into unconsciousness, Satreih saw Kaskin appear out of the ground.

*   *   *   *

Chikara looked at Kaskin. *Thanks for that.*

Kaskin slowly walked through the battlefield, searching for fallen warriors. "Don't mention it." He knew that she was thanking him for fending off the cannibals and removing the chains.

Chikara remained at Satreih's side. He was still unconscious. *How many have died? Before the attack, I mean.*

Kaskin replied softly, "Six million of us. There is a graveyard in one of the lower rooms."

Lower rooms? The extent of the tragedy shocked her.

"The Hasini clan lives underground. It offers more protection from the sun's rays and the cannibals. But there is a price we had to pay. Our immune systems are weak, since we are not often exposed to the elements. A simple cold can cause more damage than it should. I'm amazed and grateful that the doctors found a cure just in the nick of time."

Kaskin looked at a uniquely made arrow sticking out of a cannibal. "Are these arrows Satreih's?"

The ones with the eagle feathers? Yes.

Kaskin pulled out the arrow. "He might need them later."

After watching him for a few minutes, Chikara asked, *What do we do with the cannibals?*

"Bury them. They are humans. It would be cruel to not give them some place to rest."

*   *   *   *

Satreih opened his eyes. He was lying in a bed. He saw Kaskin. The prince's back was turned to him. He was speaking to another Hasini. Satreih could not hear what was being said. They were speaking softly. It didn't help that Satreih's ears were ringing.

Satreih grinned slightly when he saw Kaskin give the other Hasini a familiar looking rope.

As the Hasini exited the room, Kaskin said as he turned around, "You're awake. Are you all right?"

Satreih nodded. He noticed his surroundings. "Where am I?" He took his canteen that Kaskin was offering, gratefully taking a sip.

"My clan and I live underground. It offers more protection than the outside does—most of the time."

"Where's Chikara?"

"I forced her to go find something to eat. She deprived herself of food while you were unconscious."

"She listened to you?"

Kaskin grinned. "After I defeated her in a riddle contest."

Satreih chuckled. He reached up and felt the bruise that was beginning to form on the back of his head. "What happened during the battle?"

"Only five of the Hasinis died." Kaskin said softly. "Thank you. You and Chikara helped ensure our survival. Without your help, my clan would have been completely wiped out."

Chikara bounced into the room like an eager puppy. *I'm glad you're awake and okay, little one.*

"I'm the little one? I thought you were only a few weeks old." Satreih asked with concern, "Are you hurt? The cannibals ..."

I'm fine. Kaskin saved us. She gave Kaskin a sly glance. Chikara began, *Breathes in the water with no gills—*

Kaskin cut her off. "Let me say something first before you try to unsuccessfully defeat me in a riddle contest again."

Chikara growled in a friendly way as a response to the comment.

Kaskin looked to Satreih and said, "Chikara told me what happened to your father. I would like to come and aid you two in any way. It is the least I could do to repay you."

Satreih nodded with gratitude. "Thanks for the help, but it would be dangerous. Aren't you needed for the recovery process?"

"My parents will be able to take care of the clan. Also, it would be easier for you to deal with the danger if you have an extra person. I will be of some use."

Satreih looked at Chikara to see if she would have any objection. "All right. You can come."

*   *   *   *

Satreih and Chikara decided to stay with the Hasinis for a couple of days. They learned that the tunnels were all made by the Yuzr Ocean. The lights on the walls grew lighter or darker depending on the time of day outside. It didn't seem like they were underground.

Chikara took a look at the graveyard that Kaskin had mentioned. Torches were lined around the room as a memorial to those who had passed away. Kaskin had said that each torch represented a thousand people who fell victim to the plague. Chikara didn't stay long. The smell of death was overpowering.

*   *   *   *

Satreih followed Kaskin into one of the larger caverns. Unlike the other underground sections, there was only one light in this room. It was always brightly lit. The light fell on a beautiful, sparkling sword.

"Here." Kaskin said as he picked the sword up. "This sword would probably be better off with you."

Satreih gingerly took the sword. It looked fragile. The sword's hilt was made of solid glass. As soon as Satreih took it, fire erupted inside the glass, swirling in all directions. Satreih grasped the sword tighter, fearing it would break if it fell. To his surprise, the hilt felt cold. The hilt curved out to a fancy design when it met the blade. The blade seemed to shimmer. Satreih felt the edge. He drew his finger back quickly. It began to bleed immediately when he touched the blade. He could tell that the sword had power.

Satreih said softly, "I don't know if you should be giving this to me. I don't know how to spar."

"I can teach you. The sword is yours." *I'm more positive than ever that having the sword re-forged was the right thing to do. It accepts Satreih as its master. Otherwise the hilt would not have come to life.*

Satreih took a step back and raised the sword up defensively. Something had fallen from the ceiling right in front of him.

A ruby gem that pulsed with evil power was at Satreih's feet. The gem seemed to be mocking him. It filled his ears and mind with an intense and persistent ringing.

Kaskin said softly under his breath, "So *that's* what's been poisoning my clan." *Why else would so many of us die?* Momentarily forgetting that Satreih was there, Kaskin ran forward with his sword drawn. Before he had a chance to stab it, the morith erected a barrier around itself, repelling the attack. Kaskin was thrown backwards.

Satreih shook his head violently in annoyance because of the ringing. He followed Kaskin's lead. His new fire sword's blade erupted into white-hot flames. Satreih was filled with terrible agony. He didn't know if the pain was his or if it was the morith's.

The ringing intensified. Finally, the morith burst into shards, cutting both Satreih and Kaskin as it flew in various directions.

Kaskin got up from the floor. When the morith was still alive it seemed to be pressing an invisible hand on his chest that prevented him from getting up. Kaskin asked, "One down?" Chikara had also told him about the moriths.

"Nine more to go. Are you still sure that you want to come?"

"Yes, I'm sure."

SHIFTING SANDS

Satreih and Chikara met with King Helioff and Queen Rhenai of the Hasini clan. They were sincerely grateful.

The queen gave Satreih lightweight, long-sleeved, turtle-necked armor. He took it and looked at it curiously. The queen said, "The armor is called ophilla. It is stronger than most. There is only one in the entire land, and it now belongs to you."

Satreih bowed and said, "Thank you, Your Majesty."

The king pulled something out of his pocket. It was a smooth, flat stone. It looked delicate, and was glowing blue slightly.

The king held it up to Chikara and said, "This is a moonstone. I have no use for it, but who knows? It may come in handy."

Chikara bowed. *Thank you, Your Majesty.*

The queen said softly, half to herself, "Strike upon the rock." *Part of an old riddle that I never quite figured out.*

Satreih gave her a confused look but said nothing.

The king said, "Go forth with caution. Verteq is returning to this world once again. My wife and I have already seen signs on our trip."

After saying thank you a few more times, Satreih and Chikara left the room and joined Kaskin. He was already prepared and waiting outside. There was a very small hint of fear in his eyes.

Satreih noticed this and asked, "What's wrong?"

Kaskin replied, "I've never ridden a dragon before."

"Oh, come on! It's fun! I think you'll like it. That is if you're not prone to motion sickness."

Kaskin said quietly, "That's what I mean."

"You are, aren't you?"

Kaskin nodded.

Satreih added, "You can stay here with your people if you want. I'm not forcing you to come."

Kaskin said, "No. I'm coming," and climbed up on Chikara's back.

Satreih was right behind him. He used mind-speech to talk to Chikara. *Go easy this time.*

It was clear after ten minutes that Kaskin didn't enjoy dragonflight as much as Satreih did. Kaskin was paler than usual, and he was breathing somewhat heavily.

*   *   *   *

After three hours of flying, it began to get dark.

Much to Kaskin's gratitude, Chikara landed. Satreih gracefully jumped down off of Chikara's back. Kaskin wasn't as graceful. He fell off, landing heavily on the sand.

Satreih bent down to help him up. He asked, "Are you all right?"

"Y-Yeah. I'm fine," Kaskin lied.

Satreih walked away and started to find some wood or moss for a fire.

Kaskin made sure that neither Chikara nor Satreih were watching. He kissed the ground. Kaskin stood up and walked shakily behind a sand dune.

Satreih found all of the fire making supplies. Chikara blew on them, instantly catching the moss on fire. Satreih watched the sand dune that Kaskin had gone behind for a while. He looked at Chikara and said with a raised eyebrow, "I don't think he likes flying that much."

Finally, after about five minutes, Kaskin reappeared. He sat down next to Satreih, who had just finished making dinner.

After they ate their meal, Kaskin asked, "Do you have your ophilla on?"

"Whoa, how'd you know about that?"

"Mother told me that she was going to give it to you."

"Oh. Yeah, I have it on. Why?"

Kaskin said, "I promised that I would teach you how to use the sword, right?"

"What if I hit you? You're not wearing any armor, are you?"

Chikara mind-spoke, *He can just lean up against me and his injuries will heal. I think you forgot about that.*

"Sure, I'll spar. I want to improve my skills."

Satreih and Kaskin stood, facing each other, with their swords drawn. Satreih made the first move. He ran at Kaskin with his sword held high. Kaskin easily spun out of the way, and struck Satreih's chest twice with his sword. Satreih was knocked to the ground because of the force. He was stunned, but not hurt.

Kaskin bent down towards Satreih, pinning him with his knee up against Satreih's neck. "Never make the first move."

Satreih looked over at Chikara. He saw that she was trying not to grin. His voice echoed in her head, *Oh be quiet.*

Satreih stood up. Kaskin was watching him. He forgot what Kaskin said about the first move and attacked. Again, Kaskin spun out of the way. He was spinning his sword so fast that it was a blur. Still spinning the sword, he struck Satreih's back. Satreih never saw it coming. He was on the ground again. Sand flew into his mouth. He was already sweating and out of breath.

Kaskin looked a little bored and was barely winded. He asked, "What did I say about the first move?"

Satreih stood, spitting the foul-tasting sand out of his mouth. He growled, "Never make it." He asked, "Can you use your left hand, please?"

"It won't really make a difference." *Poor Satreih. He doesn't know that my left hand is my dominant hand. He thinks I'll get worse.*

"Yeah, it will."

Satreih soon found out that even though Kaskin was using his left hand, he was a little better. Satreih was frustrated from the start, but he never let his frustration give way to anger. He was knocked to the ground more times than he could count. He knew that he looked like a child trying to fight with an adult.

After being beaten to the ground again, Satreih asked in a dangerously soft voice, "How do you do that? It looks like you know what I'm going to do."

"Your eyes tell me everything I need to know," Kaskin added, sensing Satreih's frustration. "Don't get angry. It will cloud your thinking."

"Look, I'm grateful for your trying to teach me how to use a sword, but my strength is archery."

"I understand that, but it would be good to use both. We could stop for tonight, if you wish."

"Yes, I'm done."

They finally stopped being "enemies" and both leaned up against Chikara. Satreih knew that he would have a lot of painful bruises the next day.

They began to talk about different things, mainly about home. Kaskin told Satreih how he loved the nights in the desert. Not only did the humans think it was cooler at night, the animals thought so too. Most animals in the desert are nocturnal, and hide from the sun's rays during the day. The desert came alive at night. Kaskin told Satreih that the Hasinis took only what they needed, and never more than that.

In the distance, they heard a coyote howl. Satreih didn't like the noise. He thought it sounded sinister. Kaskin laughed and said it wasn't. The coyotes are territorial. They don't prey on men, or elves. The only time that they would be in danger is if they were in a coyote's territory. Kaskin told him not to worry; he knew where all of the coyotes' territories were. They were not in them. There was nothing to worry about.

In turn, Satreih told Kaskin about the lush, deciduous forest where he and Rasnir lived. It was tough for Kaskin to understand the concept of a forest, since he had lived in the desert his entire life and had never left it. He told Satreih that part of the reason he wanted to come with them was to see other parts of the world.

It was around midnight when they finally fell asleep. Chikara listened to some of the conversation, but couldn't really join in. She fell asleep long before Satreih and Kaskin did.

$$\ast \qquad \ast \qquad \ast \qquad \ast$$

Satreih awoke to find that the sun was blazing over him. All the creatures of the night had gone back into their burrows and dens under the layers of sand. Kaskin was already making breakfast. The smell wafting from the food made Satreih's mouth water. He thought he smelled this smell before, but he couldn't remember where.

Satreih walked over to Kaskin and said, "That smells good. What is it?"

"This meat is Calsi."

Satreih suddenly remembered the smell. He smelled Calsi in the village. The person who sold it looked at him strangely when he asked what a vedi is. "I smelled this in a village a while ago. Now I remember the smell! Hey, do you know what a vedi is?"

Kaskin replied, "Currency."

"That's why the guy selling the meat looked at me like I was a freak when I asked what a vedi is."

There was a hint of laughter in Kaskin's eyes. He tore the meat and gave half to Satreih.

Satreih greedily bit into the Calsi. The food was delicious. The skin was very juicy and soft. The meat was hard to chew, but that meant that more of the flavor came out. Satreih said between bites, "Mmm! This is good! You want any, Chikara?"

No thanks. I eat at dusk.

*   *   *   *

Once the delicious meal was finished, Satreih laid down on the sand, very content.

Chikara mind-spoke, *It's time to go.*

Satreih grumbled a little under his breath. He didn't want to move. But he stood up, climbing onto Chikara's back after Kaskin.

Chikara leapt into the sky. Even after fifteen minutes, Kaskin seemed completely fine. The wind was howling. Satreih used mind-speech to talk to him.

You're all right? You're not as pale as you were when you were last flying.

I'm fine. I think the Calsi helped. I've always been pale. I think living underground has something to do with that. Kaskin changed the subject. *You're right! Flying on a dragon is fun, but not when you get sick.*

Chikara's voice entered both of their minds. *We are almost to the Yuzr Ocean. I think we only have two more leagues to go. We should make it there in about a half hour.*

*   *   *   *

Chikara landed, allowing her passengers to get off.

Kaskin's eyes were wide and he said, "Wow. I've never seen so much water!" He added sadly, "Too bad I can't swim."

"I can teach you."

Soon dusk came. Chikara flew off to hunt. While she was away, Satreih taught Kaskin how to swim, float, and tread water. Kaskin caught on quickly, mastering the basics within a few hours. He wasn't a strong swimmer.

After giving Kaskin swimming lessons, Satreih checked the map that the old man had given him. He had a sick felling in his stomach when he looked at it.

Still dripping wet, Kaskin walked over and asked, "What?"

Satreih replied quietly, "We're in a bunch of orange dots."

"Right. And that means what?"

"It means we're in a dangerous area."

"That can't be. I know this desert by heart and where its dangers are."

Satreih asked, "Do you know the parts of the desert around the ocean by heart?"

"Erm, no. I've never been this close to the ocean before."

Satreih called out to Chikara with mind-speech. *Chikara! We landed in a bunch of orange dots on the map!*

We did? All right, hang on. I'm coming.

Kaskin saw the sand in front of him and Satreih moving. He lightly tapped Satreih on the shoulder, pointing at the shifting sand. Satreih grew tense and knocked an arrow onto his bow.

Two two-headed cobras erupted out of the sand. They were both about the size of Chikara. They had angry red eyes.

One of the snakes lunged, making Satreih and Kaskin scatter. Satreih shot the snake with an arrow with perfect aim, but it didn't have much effect.

The other snake attacked Kaskin, who attempted to dodge aside, also making a successful attack with his sword that hurt the snake. He managed to avoid the fangs, but the coils wove around him. Stabbing the coils with the sword didn't seem to have much effect. He needed to stab close to the necks to hurt it.

Out of the corner of his eye, Satreih saw Kaskin being lifted into the air. Withdrawing the fire sword out of his its scabbard, Satreih threw it, striking the snake in the back of one of its skulls.

Kaskin instantly felt the coils slacken as he was released. He moved to Satreih's aid after quickly retrieving the sword. The snake's corpse was alight with an incredible blaze. If he had stayed anywhere near the snake, he would have burned as well.

Even though many arrows were protruding out of the other snake, they didn't seem to help. At the last second, Satreih held his bow up to defend himself from an attack. But the snake's fang pierced through the bow, utterly destroying it. Satreih's arm was pushed back from the force, but the ophilla he was wearing underneath protected him until the snake's venom seeped through the tiny holes of the armor.

Ignoring Satreih's scream of pain for the moment, Kaskin jumped up onto the snake's back, slicing at both of its necks with his sword and the fire sword. The snake died, but the sword hadn't erupted into flame as it had when Satreih used it.

Kaskin jumped off the dead snake, returning the sword. Satreih took it with a grateful nod. Kaskin asked, "Are you all right?"

"Yeah, yeah, I'm fine." Satreih hastily removed his shirt and armor. He wiped the venom away. It left a nasty red gash, a sign that showed it was going to get infected.

The sand in front of them started to move again. Another two-headed cobra erupted out of the sand. Somehow, it looked even more deadly than the first two.

Kaskin went for his sword, but he didn't have to bother. The snake was ripped apart by huge, eagle like talons. Chikara had come to their rescue.

We should leave now, before any more snakes come. Are you okay, Satreih?

"I'm fine."

Satreih and Kaskin climbed up onto Chikara's back. They were soon flying over the ocean. Satreih kept checking the map to make sure they were headed in the right direction.

After a few hours, the clouds got dark; the wind was fiercer. All three of them could smell the scent of rain.

I cannot land. There is only water. We're going to have to fight the storm. Hold on tight.

The storm was unforgiving. The dark clouds were so thick that even Chikara had a hard time seeing things. Kaskin couldn't see anything until lightning flashed.

At first, Kaskin welcomed the coming of the storm. Rainstorms were limited in the desert. He loved watching them. Whenever one formed, Kaskin sat in the protection of one of the entrances to the underground, watching it. But he was never in the middle of one until now.

All three of them were pelted with freezing rain and hail. Satreih and Kaskin were struggling to hold on. Satreih's arm was still stinging from the snake venom. Chikara's wing beats were strained. Lightning was flashing all around them. The sky rumbled with thunder.

After what seemed like an hour, Satreih felt Chikara's strength draining away. Her wing beats were more strained than ever. All of Chikara's strength completely drained away, causing herself, Satreih, and Kaskin to plunge into the churning black water far below them.

THE WATER NYMPHS

Chikara woke to find that she was in an underwater cavern. Most of the rocks were cut away, and in their places were unique coral formations. There were decorative stained glass paintings of ocean scenes; beyond them was open water. The little bit of light that filtered from the ocean's surface leaked through the paintings, making the area dance with colorful specks. Chikara seemed to be in a hospital of some sort. She was on a padded floor between the beds containing Satreih and Kaskin.

There was a man watching them. Satreih and Kaskin were still unconscious. The man did not realize that Chikara had awakened.

Chikara growled at him. *If you harm them, I will kill you.*

He jumped in surprise. "I will not harm you, or your friends, dragon."

The man's voice was strange. It flowed, like the water. Chikara noticed that he was not a normal man. His skin was scaly; he had webbed fingers and toes. He had gills near his neck that were always rippling. The man's eyebrows and hair were a unique shade of green. He wore a rubbery, blue suit.

Chikara looked at him, not sure if she could trust him, and asked, *Who are you? Where are we?*

"My name is Keelu. I am a water nymph. We saw you trying to make your way through the perilous storm. When you fell from the sky, we took you here, to our home. You are inside the city of Kajie. You are safe and protected here. So are your friends. Are you hungry?"

Chikara nodded. She was still wary of him.

"Then I will retrieve some food." Keelu walked away.

Chikara noticed that there were other beds around, but they were empty. Satreih's map was on a table next to his bed, already dry. So were the mysterious symbol, the moonstone, and Satreih's newly repaired bow. Satreih's arm—the one that had been wounded by the snake's venom—was bandaged.

Kaskin was starting to stir. He was no longer cold, but he had a pretty big headache. Everything was slowly coming back to him. He remembered that he and Satreih were nearly ripped off of Chikara's back many times. Kaskin remembered that they fell into the ocean, but couldn't remember anything after that.

Kaskin opened his eyes. Chikara was watching him. He saw the relief on her face. Kaskin groggily asked, "What happened?"

We fell into the Yuzr Ocean. We were being watched by water nymphs. They rescued us and brought us here. Apparently, we are in a building below the surface of the Yuzr Ocean. Keelu, one of the water nymphs, was in here, watching us. He went out after I woke up to get some food. They call their city Kajie. The water nymphs are a weird race.

At that moment, Keelu came back in carrying a huge plate of food. Two other water nymphs followed him; they, too, carried food. The other water nymphs cast wary glances over in Chikara's direction.

The smell wafting from those plates was making Kaskin's mouth water. Keelu placed the biggest plate in front of Chikara. He said something in his own language to a water nymph following him. The water nymph nodded and placed his plate of food on the table next to the map and the symbol. Keelu took the plate of food from the other water nymph and gave it to Kaskin. Kaskin thanked him.

"You don't need to thank me."

Kaskin gratefully ate the food. It was delicious. He had never eaten fish before, but it was good. Keelu told them that the type of fish that they were eating was a Lemorse fish. That type of fish was found only in this part of the ocean. They were disappearing along with the other fish that they used for food. Very soon the water nymphs would die of starvation.

Kaskin nodded. He looked worriedly at Satreih.

Keelu spoke. "I recognized the wound on his arm to be the mark of an O'kiy cobra. The cobra's venom is fatal when it is not treated. But the venom works slowly and it is no match for the medicines that we have here. The injury will be gone within a couple of days. Satreih will be fine when he wakes up."

Keelu got up. He started to head out the door. He added, "I'll leave you to rest. Call for me in the morning." Keelu walked out. He left Satreih's plate of food on the table.

Kaskin watched Keelu leave with a raised eyebrow. He thought, *How did he know Satreih's name?*

Kaskin shook his head in confusion. As he looked over to Satreih, he said, "I bet I know how to get him up."

Really? How?

"Watch and learn." Kaskin leaned over, picking up Satreih's plate of food. He held it under his friend's nose. After a few minutes, Satreih was still unconscious.

"Oh well. I thought it would work. He really must be out of it."

You thought that would get him up? Chikara was grinning.

"Yeah. I did. If he were anything like me, he would have immediately woken up, no matter how far he was in dream land. Well, good night, Chikara. I'm going to sleep."

'Night.

*   *   *   *

Satreih's eyes slowly opened. He sat up as he looked to his right. Chikara and Kaskin were asleep, not unconscious. Kaskin moved in his sleep. He had the slightest hint of a satisfied grin on his face. Apparently he was having a good dream.

Satreih didn't recognize the cavern. A delicious smell caught his attention. He saw a type of fish on a plate waiting for him. There was a note next to the plate in Kaskin's handwriting, which said the food was for him.

Satreih took a greedy bite. He chewed thoughtfully. He liked it. Satreih realized that his arm was bandaged. The bandage wasn't like the white gauze that he was used to. It was blue and rubbery. *I don't think I'm in any danger. If I were, Kaskin and Chikara would be awake and alert.* He laid back down and went to sleep.

*   *   *   *

Kaskin yawned and sat up. There was a tiny bit of sunlight streaming in through the ceiling. The coral was mostly blocking it out. He heard a familiar voice.

"Morning, Kaskin. Had a nice sleep?"

Kaskin jumped. He looked over to Satreih and said, "Yeah. What time did you wake up last night?" He noticed that Satreih was admiring the repairs to his bow.

"No idea. What happened after we fell into the ocean?"

*   *   *   *

Keelu had already been awake for a few hours. He was the captain of the Inuje Swemms. It was their job to go out into the ocean and hunt food for the two thousand people that lived in Kajie. The job had gotten more dangerous recently. Giant sharks had begun to live nearby. The sharks had killed his co-captain, Vaa, the other day. The co-captain that he had now wasn't as good as Vaa was. He was easily frightened, and was not that good at fending off the sharks. He had also just come of age.

The co-captain, Jeshu, ran up to him. He was excited. "Captain, are we going out to hunt?"

"Yes, we are. Get the other Inuje Swemms members and bring them here. We'll leave once everybody's ready."

"Oh. Okay. Hey, is the hospital really harboring a dragon?"

"Yes, and also an elf and a man."

Jeshu exclaimed, "Really?"

"Yes. What did I say about the other members?" asked Keelu, trying not to get annoyed.

"To go get them. I'll be right back!" Jeshu ran off.

Keelu mumbled under his breath, "I really need to do something about that boy."

A voice came from behind. "Hi, Keelu."

Keelu jumped. The voice was Kaskin's. He, Satreih, and Chikara were being led by his daughter, Manika.

Manika said, "Father, they called for you." She giggled a little and added, "It was fun seeing everyone look at Chikara."

Keelu said, "Thanks Manika. You can go now if you like."

Manika nodded and ran off.

I don't understand. The water nymphs were not afraid of me. I thought you said that this was the first time they had seen a dragon.

"They were not frightened because I had already told them at a meeting."

Out of the corner of his eye, Keelu saw the members of the Inuje Swemms approach. He said, "I'm sorry, but I have to leave. I'm the captain of the Inuje Swemms. It's our job to hunt for the people that live in Kajie."

Satreih offered, "We'll come with you."

"It is a dangerous job, especially since the giant sharks have appeared. If you do come with us, you will need to be a strong swimmer."

Chikara mind-spoke, *Danger! Hah! We've looked danger right in the eye millions of times and survived to tell the tale!*

Satreih shook his head and laughed. *Millions of times? Hah, I don't think so. Maybe just a couple.*

Kaskin looked up and said to Keelu, "She gets cocky sometimes. We'll still come with you." He didn't mention anything about just learning how to swim. He knew that either Chikara or Satreih would help him if he got in danger.

Keelu sighed and said, "Well, all right, if you really want to come, you can. But remember that old saying, 'dead men tell no tales.'"

First off, I'm a dragon, not a man. Secondly, I'm a dragoness.

DANGEROUS FISH

Satreih, Kaskin, Chikara, and the Inuje Swemms ventured out into the water. Jeshu stayed behind. Keelu gave Satreih and Kaskin spears. He also gave them a suit that covered up their whole bodies. The suit insulated them. It had webs between the fingers and the toes. The material sucked in oxygen from the water. The suit had scales all over it and false fins, which made Satreih and Kaskin look like fish. Chikara didn't need one. She could hold her breath for long periods of time, if need be.

Keelu motioned for Chikara, Satreih, and Kaskin to follow him and the other Inuje Swemms. They traveled underwater for a long time, never seeing any fish. One of the members of the Inuje Swemms said something to Keelu in the water nymph's language. Keelu's facial expression grew dark.

Chikara's voice entered Keelu's head. *What's going on?*

Like I said, the fish have been disappearing. All of the waters of the Yuzr Ocean are charted. The area where we have to go to get the fish is a major shark territory. The sharks are smart. Unlike most fish, they patrol their borders, which we're about to enter.

Why would all the fish be inside the shark's borders?

The sharks don't eat fish, but just about anything else that's stupid enough to come close.

Chikara turned and told Satreih and Kaskin what was happening through mind-speech.

Satreih's voice appeared in Keelu's head. *We can go get the fish. All of us are good fighters.*

Are you sure?

Yes.

Everyone entered the shark's territory. They stayed close together. Keelu stayed in the front of the group, Chikara in the back.

A fish swam by a few feet away. Satreih hurled the spear, striking it. The fish was pinned by the spear and the coral behind it. Its struggles drew weak, then stopped altogether.

From behind Satreih, a shark was watching. It saw Satreih throw the spear and hit the fish. The shark attacked Satreih, knowing this was the time when he was most vulnerable.

Satreih heard something approach from behind. He spun around in surprise. A devilish shark was hurtling toward him. Satreih swam to the side just as the shark barreled past. Satreih withdrew his fire sword and struck it on its flank. He drew a little blood, but the sword didn't set the shark on fire like it did with most enemies.

Chikara heard Satreih's voice. *The sword doesn't work in the water very well!*

Chikara turned around and saw Satreih fighting the shark. A second later she couldn't see. The shark's enormous tail thrashed about. It kicked up a whirlwind of sand and silt.

Chikara felt pain in her abdomen. She looked down. Another shark decided to attack her. It was bigger than the one that was attacking Satreih. Chikara twisted around, biting it on its head. She used her talons to rip apart the lower end of the shark. The shark let go. It fell down to the bottom of the ocean and didn't get up. The water was now swirling with blood, sand, and silt.

*   *   *   *

Jeshu was in his chamber. He didn't know why he had decided to stay, but he felt as if he had to. Jeshu sighed and sat on his bed, with nothing to do until the Inuje Swemms returned.

An unfamiliar old man materialized out of thin air.

Jeshu jumped up in surprise. He asked, "Who are you? What are you doing here?"

The old man acted quickly. He grabbed Jeshu by the front of his rubber clothing, slamming him hard against the wall. Jeshu cried out in shock and pain. The old man raised a staff and jammed it under Jeshu's neck, making him look up into the cold, steely-gray eyes. The staff gleamed with an evil intensity.

The old man seethed, "Verteq has returned to this world. He needs your help. Has a dragon and an elf arrived yet?"

"Y-Yes. A day ago. There is also a m-man."

The old man blinked. "What is his name?" he hissed.

"K-Kaskin."

The old man took a circular object out of his robe. He hissed, "This is a Geom Stone. At night, when the dragon, elf, and man are sleeping, place this in the dragon's skin in the crevice between her wing and shoulder. The dragon's skin will absorb the stone. Do *not* fail me, or I will kill you, understand?"

"U-understood, c-clearly."

The old man drew the staff across Jeshu's neck. With a swish of his cloak, the old man vanished.

Jeshu drifted over to the bed and sat down. He fingered the little black stone that the old man had given him. He felt his neck. There was a small cut, just big enough to require bandaging.

*   *   *   *

Satreih stabbed the shark again with his sword, this time on the neck. It was harder to see, since Chikara had made a kill. There was blood everywhere. Satreih's shark was finished. He swam a little, and touched Chikara on her side.

Chikara jumped, but then calmed down when she heard Satreih's voice. *It's only me. Where's Kaskin?*

Fighting a shark over there somewhere. I don't know how he's doing. I can barely see.

Kaskin struck the shark with his spear. He had made a few holes in the shark, but all it seemed to do was make it mad. It spun around, trying to get a bite. The shark didn't get a chance. Strong jaws clamped around its throat. For a second, Kaskin thought it was another shark, but then relaxed when he realized that it was Chikara. He nodded thanks.

The sand and blood was starting to settle. It was getting easier to see. Keelu spun around to see if Chikara, Satreih, and Kaskin were okay. They were. Keelu watched as Satreih swam over to get to the fish he had speared.

Keelu looked around to see if the Inuje Swemms members were okay. Most of them were, except for Sakuri. She was lying on the ocean floor, breathing heavily. Both of her legs were bleeding. The other members were fine, and trying to help her. There wasn't much they could do.

Keelu swam over, checking the wound. He felt horrible, not only because Sakuri was wounded, but also because the wound was too big to get her back to Kajie. They would have to leave her there. Right before Sakuri joined the Inuje Swemms, her fiancé promised to seriously injure Keelu if he let anything happen to her. Her fiancé had good intentions; he was just a little over protective at times.

Off to his right, Keelu saw something moving, fearing it was another shark. He relaxed when he realized that it was Chikara. She laid down next to Sakuri, and her flank touched Sakuri's wound. Miraculously, the wound healed. There was no sign that the injury had ever been there.

Chikara backed off. She, Satreih, and Kaskin watched as Keelu soothingly spoke to the other water nymph in their own language. Sakuri got up, but was a little unsteady from the shock.

Everyone swam back to Kajie. There would be no more hunting today. Only one fish was caught; the one that Satreih had speared. After a while, they made it back to the underwater city. Once inside, Satreih and Kaskin started to take off their suits.

Sakuri turned to Chikara and said, "Thank you very much for saving me."

No problem.

Queas, the leader of the city, came over to the Inuje Swemms. "Any luck today?"

Keelu answered, "No. It was worse than yesterday. We only got one fish."

Satreih heard the conversation. He held up the fish that he had speared.

Keelu continued, "Sakuri was bitten by one of the sharks. Chikara has amazing healing powers. She just brushed up against Sakuri's wound. It healed itself."

Queas nodded. He sighed and said, "The situation is getting worse. We used up a tenth of our food supply for dinner. We desperately need to find more food. I might need to send you and the Inuje Swemms out more often."

*   *   *   *

Chikara, Satreih, and Kaskin were in the room that Keelu had prepared for them. It was in the highest part of the cavern, which made Chikara happy. Satreih and Kaskin had beds. Chikara didn't need anything.

Satreih was quiet for a while, thinking. "There might be a morith around here somewhere. Kaskin, remember when there was one in your home?"

Kaskin growled, "Yes, and I'm glad we got rid of it."

"Right, but you said your food supply was getting short. Same here."

"I don't know, but maybe we can ask Keelu if we can look around Kajie. We won't say why; we just want to check out the wonders of the city."

Chikara mind-spoke, *Yeah, true. I do sense some evil vibes coming from in the city, somewhere. Maybe it's the morith.*

After talking about the morith for a few more minutes, Kaskin asked, "Sparring lessons, Satreih?"

"Uh, sure. I think I'm getting a little better. I'm not on the ground nearly as much as I was at the beginning."

Satreih and Kaskin began to spar. Satreih had his ophilla on. He was doing better. Satreih wasn't making the first move any more, and he was blocking most of Kaskin's attacks. He still couldn't cut Kaskin though.

Finally, near the end of the sparring practice, Kaskin came at Satreih with his sword held high. Satreih dropped down, and rolled out of the way. He popped back up, and cut Kaskin's back.

Kaskin turned around and said, "Ooh. Nice one. I think we're done for tonight." He leaned up against Chikara and his cut healed.

*   *   *   *

One by one, Chikara, Satreih, and Kaskin fell asleep. Outside the room, Jeshu waited patiently. He was watching the sparring practice through the door crack. He tried not to breathe. He knew elves and dragons have very keen hearing. He admired Kaskin's swordsmanship.

At last, all three of them fell asleep. After two hours, Jeshu quietly snuck in. He had the Geom Stone in his hand, ready to use it. His hand was shaking. He dropped the stone, and he shut his eyes. He thought for sure one of them heard it. After a few minutes, Jeshu took a cautious peek from between his fingers. He expected to see Chikara's teeth. He didn't. She was still asleep. Jeshu sighed inwardly, and slowly bent down to pick up the stone. He snuck over to Chikara, placing the Geom Stone between her wing and shoulder. He knew that her skin would absorb it, but didn't expect it. The stone sunk beneath her skin. Jeshu took a step back. Chikara grunted a little in her sleep, making him jump. The dragon changed positions and didn't wake up. Neither did Satreih or Kaskin. Jeshu smiled and quietly exited the room. That was a job well done.

ENCOUNTER WITH WEUH

Chikara's eyes slowly opened. She stretched and yawned. She felt something weird. Chikara had an itch between her wing and shoulder. It was maddening. She rubbed it, over and over, but it didn't stop.

Satreih yawned and sat up. He noticed that Chikara was uncomfortable, trying to get at something. He asked, "What's wrong?"

Just an itch. Nothing to worry about.

After five minutes, Keelu poked his head into the room. "Breakfast is in ten minutes. Be down before then." He left.

Satreih stretched and walked over to Kaskin's bed. He tried to shake him awake. "C'mon Kaskin, time to get up."

Kaskin batted Satreih's hand away and rolled over, determined to get a few extra minutes of blissful sleep.

Satreih added, "Breakfast is in ten minutes."

Kaskin's eyes shot open. "All right, all right, I'm up."

$$*\qquad*\qquad*\qquad*$$

Soon Chikara, Satreih, and Kaskin were in the dining hall eating with the other water nymphs. Chikara was still itching, but did her best to ignore it. Satreih felt the eyes of someone on his back. He turned around. Jeshu was staring at him. As soon as Jeshu realized that he was being watched, he quickly looked down and started eating. Satreih noticed that his neck was bandaged.

Satreih nudged Chikara. He nodded in Jeshu's direction. "What do you think he did to his neck?"

Chikara shrugged.

The meal was good. Chikara, Satreih, and Kaskin left with all the others. Out of the corner of his eye, Satreih saw Jeshu sneak away from the others and turn down a different corridor.

Satreih's curiosity spiked a little higher. He thought, *What's he doing?*

He told Chikara and Kaskin that he would be right back. He took off and followed Jeshu. Satreih didn't want Jeshu to know of his presence. He hid behind various items that were lined up against the walls whenever Jeshu looked back to see if anybody were following him.

Jeshu was leading him deeper into the city. The usually well-kept walls had fungi growing on them. Some water leaked from above. Jeshu came to a door and opened it.

Satreih caught a quick glimpse of what was inside. There was nothing except an old man. The old man had his back turned to Jeshu and Satreih. He didn't notice that Satreih was there. Jeshu went inside and closed the door.

Satreih quietly made his way to the door and put his ear up against it. He heard the old man's voice. It sounded evil.

"Did you complete the task?"

"Y-Yes. I did."

The old man's voiced hissed, "Did you place it where I told you to?"

"Yes. B-But the dragon s-suspects something. She itches in the spot where I placed the s-stone."

"She itches? You fool! That was not supposed to happen!"

Satreih heard a slap. Jeshu yelped in pain.

The old man seethed, "Does the elf or the man suspect something?"

"I think the elf might. He didn't say a-anything though."

There was a pause. Satreih barely heard the old man. "Is the morith protected?"

"Morith?"

"The gem I gave you to keep in the storage room."

"Y-Yeah it is. I put it under one of the loose floor boards in the room."

Ha! I was right! There is a morith here! And Kaskin didn't believe me.

The old man hissed, "Leave, now. Get out of my sight."

Satreih heard footsteps approaching the door. He panicked, looking around for something to hide in or behind. He found a large barrel that was big enough for him to climb into. He ran over to it, and lifted the lid. Satreih glanced back behind his shoulder. The doorknob was starting to turn. He quickly got inside, pulling the lid shut. He heard the sound of Jeshu's footsteps fade away.

Through a hole in the barrel, Satreih saw the old man leave the room. The old man looked towards Satreih's hiding place. Satreih felt the blood in his veins freeze. The old man had cold, steely-gray eyes. His beard went down to his knees.

The old man walked over to the barrel and tried to lift the lid. Satreih grabbed onto the bottom of the lid, pulling it down. The old man drew a staff with a crystal on the top from underneath his cloak. He tapped the lid with the staff, and it popped off.

The wizard grabbed Satreih out of the barrel by his neck. He held Satreih up by one hand. Satreih's feet didn't even touch the floor. He could smell the wizard's sour breath. The wizard kicked the barrel away.

"So," he seethed, "you thought you could deceive me. What Verteq said was right. You *do* carelessly cast away the dice of your life."

Satreih struggled, trying to get away. The old wizard was choking him. If he couldn't break free he would perish. The wizard brought the staff up to Satreih's face. The crystal glowed with an evil intensity. The wizard had an insane gleam in his eyes.

Satreih and the wizard both heard a nearby roar. One of the tunnels erupted in golden fire. Soon Chikara and Kaskin were in sight. Kaskin had his sword drawn. He threw it. The sword sailed toward the wizard. Spotting the projectile just in time, the wizard threw Satreih against the wall and disappeared. The sword hit the ground, harmlessly.

Satreih crumpled up into a ball, gasping, trying to get his breath back. Kaskin bent down and put his hand on Satreih's back, for reassurance.

Chikara growled, *Feh. We missed the old geezer. The look in his eyes when he saw us approach was comical. Are you all right, Satreih?*

"Y-Yeah. Yeah, I'm fine. Man, that old wizard is strong."

Kaskin asked, "What did you do to get him to attack you like that?"

"I was eavesdropping on him. He was speaking to Jeshu." Satreih smiled weakly. "I was right. There is a morith here. It is down in the storage room, under a loose floor board. We need to destroy it quickly. The wizard knows I had eavesdropped. He's going to do everything in his power to protect it. What made you guys come when you did?"

You were taking too long.

Satreih slowly stood up. "Let's go destroy that morith."

*   *   *   *

Weuh appeared in Verteq's tower.

Verteq's back was facing him. He seethed, "What happened?"

"They know of the morith. The elf eavesdropped while I was speaking with Jeshu. I found him in his hiding place, but was unsuccessful when I tried to choke him. The dragon and the man came to his rescue at the last second. I had to flee." Weuh bowed low. "I—I apologize, Master."

Verteq turned around.

Weuh winced when he saw the fiery wrath in his master's eyes. The door of the room burst open. Five Spies grabbed Weuh by his arms. Weuh looked at Verteq with a questioning glance. Verteq jerked his head. The Spies followed their order. They started to drag Weuh off.

Verteq said, "You will be put in the cell with the animal-man. Don't worry; I still have use for you. I will call for you when I'm ready."

*   *   *   *

Rasnir was sitting on the slab of stone that was supposed to be a bed. He was throwing a small rock up into the air, and then catching it when it came back down. Rasnir knew it was a pitiful game, but could think of nothing else to do. He heard the heavy lock on his door open. Rasnir looked up, curious. *It's a little early for bread.*

An old man was thrown into the room. Rasnir recognized the old man to be the wizard that stole his blood.

Rasnir jumped off of the slab of stone and scurried to the other side of the room. The door slammed. Rasnir was locked in the room with the wizard. The only good news was that the wizard's staff was gone. The old wizard got up and sat on the slab of stone.

Weuh felt Rasnir's eyes on him.

After a while, Rasnir got the courage to ask, "What happened?"

Weuh didn't answer. He seemed to be concentrating on something.

*   *   *   *

Chikara, Satreih, and Kaskin found their way to the storage room. Satreih and Kaskin went around the room looking for and removing loose floor boards. The storage room was huge. It took a half hour for Satreih to find the morith.

Satreih lifted up a floor board. He felt an incredible pain. "Found it."

The gem was pulsing with an evil power. Something strange happened. The ruby gem turned black. It stretched until it was as tall as Satreih. The gem started to take form. Soon it stole Satreih's identity. There was no difference between Satreih and the gem. The gem had mimicked Satreih's scent in an attempt to fool Chikara.

The gem copied Satreih's sword, and took it out. Satreih mirrored that move. Satreih and the gem started to spar. The fight didn't go anywhere. It was easy for both of them. They knew what the other was going to do.

Kaskin said, "Satreih, let me fight it. I know how your mind works and I would be able to defeat the gem."

"Are you saying I'm weak?" Satreih stepped aside, allowing Kaskin to take his place.

It was tough for Kaskin to fight. The gem was identical to Satreih. It was making Kaskin think that he was trying to kill his friend. Kaskin was a good fighter. He never made the first move. Normally against another opponent, he would watch the opponent's eyes. The gem was lifeless. It was a puppet. There was no way to tell what it was thinking.

The gem knocked Kaskin on his back. Kaskin's sword flew out of his hand. The gem came at him with its sword, ready to plunge it into Kaskin's heart. Kaskin instinctively threw up his leg, catching the gem in the stomach area. He flipped the gem onto its back and started to wrestle it for its weapon. His own sword flew too far out of his reach.

There is wizardry commanding the gem. Chikara looked to Kaskin. *Get out of the way. I don't want to burn you by accident.*

Kaskin quickly got off the gem. He moved to the side.

A second later, golden fire torched the gem. It shrank down and became its original shape. An unbearable ringing filled the room. The gem burst into miniscule pieces. The pieces hit the wall, and then disappeared.

Chikara grinned. *Another one out of the way. The fish around Kajie should start appearing soon.*

*   *   *   *

There was a feast in Kajie that night. Chikara, Satreih, and Kaskin learned that Keelu went on a hunt with all of the other Inuje Swemms. They were attacked by the sharks again, but in the middle of the fight, the sharks suddenly grew frightened and swam away. No one was injured. Soon after the sharks left, the fish reappeared. There were tons of fish. The Inuje Swemms had an excellent hunt. Every member came back to the city with their arms full. They went out on a second hunt, coming back with full arms. The process continued until the Inuje Swemms members were weary with exhaustion. There was plenty of food for the feast.

The feast was mostly just a social event. A few water nymph children warily approached Chikara. Chikara noticed the hopefulness shining in their eyes. She reached down, gently picked one up, and placed him on her back. Chikara was rewarded with a content and excited noise that came from the child's chest. Soon, she was covered in a wave of young water nymphs. With their parents' and Satreih's permission, she took them out for a swim.

Chikara still couldn't get rid of that itch between her shoulder and wing. She hoped it would subside when they continued their journey to Rasiamoramisa in the morning.

BATTLE IN THE AIR

Chikara was flying over the Yuzr Ocean with Kaskin and Satreih on her back. Satreih was looking at the map. He frowned. The storm had blown them way off course. Now there were orange dots all around them. They were flying over some right now. If Chikara fell from the air, they would have to deal with whatever nastiness that lurked below.

Kaskin made sure to eat some Calsi before he and his friends left Kajie.

Chikara turned around and hovered in the air, searching for something.

Satreih asked, "What's wrong?"

I smell the scent of another dragon approaching. I don't see him, though. She turned around and started flying in the original direction. They flew for a couple more hours. The strange dragon scent didn't go away.

*   *   *   *

The attack came without warning. A black dragon soared down from above, with its talons ready. Chikara saw him at the last second. She dove, making the dragon miss. There was an old man riding the black dragon. Satreih gasped as he recognized the old wizard who had tried to choke him.

Chikara turned around to face her enemies. Satreih and Kaskin felt her body grow hot, and she unleashed golden fire at the dragon and wizard. The other dragon unleashed black fire. The golden and black fire combined. There was an explosion. Both dragons were pushed backwards, spiraling out of control.

They regained control and rushed at each other, ready to tear into the foe with their talons. Satreih stood up on Chikara's back. If living in a forest had taught him anything, it was good balance skills. He could easily stand on a tree branch in the middle of a thunderstorm. The wizard was already standing, with his staff in his hand. Satreih unsheathed his sword.

He and the wizard began to spar. The crystal part of the staff struck Satreih's head. It left a big gash. Satreih struck the wizard on his chest. The old man's chest was burned. Satreih drew blood. He attacked again, but the wizard raised a blue shield with his staff to protect himself.

They were high up in the air above the Yuzr Ocean. Suddenly, both dragons dove down, trying to make fighting more difficult for the other. The wizard quickly sat down, grabbing the other dragon's spike. Satreih wasn't so lucky. He slipped and fell. He banged his head on Chikara's side. He braced himself, knowing that very soon he was going to fall into the freezing ocean.

Kaskin grabbed Satreih's arm and became a lifeline. With his other hand, Kaskin reached down. He grabbed Satreih's other arm. Kaskin pulled Satreih back onto Chikara's back.

Chikara and the black dragon splashed down into the water. Satreih and Kaskin were nearly ripped off because of the force. The wizard was fine; he erected a spell that kept him on the dragon's back.

The dragons were underwater for about a minute.

Kaskin's voice entered Satreih's head. *What I wouldn't give for a suit from the Inuje Swemms right now.*

Chikara propelled herself out of the water. She was weakening. The other dragon was strong, but both of them had lost a lot of blood. If the fight continued much longer, they would both die from their injuries. The black dragon followed her up into the air. He bit into her left hind leg.

Chikara roared, blasting golden fire at him. He let go. She tore his stomach open. More of his blood spilled, and a ruby gem that pulsed with evil power spilled out as well.

Satreih saw the morith fall out of the dragon. He let an arrow fly. The arrow pulverized the ruby in midair.

Both dragons were roaring. Chikara bit into the black dragon's neck, and heard something snap. The black dragon went limp. He fell toward the Yuzr Ocean. The wizard disappeared, leaving the black dragon to die.

Chikara hovered in the air, exhausted and bleeding heavily. Her vision was blurry. She felt an odd sensation in her entire body. She felt Satreih and Kaskin tense up. They could feel the odd sensation as well. For all of them, the world slipped away into whiteness.

*   *   *   *

Kaskin opened his eyes. It was raining, but he, Chikara, and Satreih were not over the Yuzr Ocean. They had been teleported to a jungle. In the distance, they could see something big, but could not make out what it was. The rain was too thick. Satreih and Kaskin were on their feet, beside Chikara.

Satreih asked, "What happened? Are you okay, Chikara?"

Chikara's normally razor-sharp eyes were glassy. She had numerous wounds all over her body and was breathing hard. *I could be better. I believe there was a spell on that dragon that would teleport you here once you killed him. W-We should get out of the rain.*

Kaskin looked over Chikara's body. Her wounds were terrible, and would take a long time to heal.

Lightning lit up the sky and there was a crack of thunder. Satreih and Kaskin started to walk up to the big shape. Chikara flew a little above ground. Walking was difficult. They came upon the big shape. It was a dragon skeleton.

He died a very p-painful death. Whoever did this will pay dearly for it—most likely with his life.

Satreih asked, "How do you know that?"

I can tell. This happened not t-that long ago. Maybe a month ago. That is not enough time to rot to bones. Chikara growled. *Maybe that wizard did this. Seems like something he would do. H-Have you seen waterfalls do that?*

There were seven waterfalls cascading into a lake nearby. Four of the waterfalls were to the left side of a cave, three were to the right.

Satreih and Kaskin walked toward the cave, and Chikara flew. Once inside, they discovered that there were bones from various animals strewn all over the floor. Satreih and Kaskin took out their swords.

Chikara growled. *This is the cave of the black dragon. His scent is still here. He's dead now. He will not bother us.*

"Yeah," said Satreih, "But his spirit might."

This is the only place we can use for shelter. The black dragon has slaves. Men and elves. I can smell them. Maybe they can help.

Chikara, Satreih, and Kaskin found the room with the treasure. Chikara flew in; her left back leg was in great pain. She was right: there were slaves, men and elves. They were cleaning the treasure. They scurried away into the shadows near the wall when they spotted the visitors.

Chikara plopped down on the ground. She closed her eyes. Even though flying was easier than walking, it was still an effort. Kaskin stayed with her. Satreih crouched down and made his way to the men and elves. He knew that if he stood upright, he would appear threatening.

Satreih asked, "Hey. My dragon, Chikara, is hurt. I fear she will die if she doesn't get help. Can you guys help her?"

One of the men said in a hushed whisper, "Oj'yer won't like."

"Oj'yer? A big black dragon?"

The man nodded.

"Ah. Oj'yer is dead. That is why Chikara is hurt. She was fighting with him. She killed him."

Another man asked quietly, "Oj'yer, dead?"

Satreih thought he saw a glimmer of hope in all of the slaves' eyes. "Yes. He's dead."

A brave elf reached up. He started to lightly tug on Satreih's ears.

Satreih said, "Yes, I am one of your kin. Can you help Chikara?"

The elf stood up and put his hand into a hole in the wall. He pulled out some towels and a bowl. Satreih noticed that all of the other slaves started doing the same thing. Soon they were all around Chikara, healing her.

Satreih retrieved some towels and a bowl from the wall and went over to help heal Chikara. Kaskin used some of Satreih's supplies.

The slaves were amazed. No one had ever helped them with their work before.

A slave came up behind Satreih and tapped him on his shoulder.

Satreih turned around and asked, "Yes?"

The slave held his palm up to him. In the center of the slave's palm, there was a small, black ball. Satreih held out his hand.

The slave gave it to him.

Satreih looked at it curiously. "What is this? Where did you get it?"

The slave pointed to a cut on Chikara. The cut was between Chikara's wing and shoulder.

Satreih raised his eyebrow. "Hey, Kaskin. What do you think this is?"

Kaskin looked over Satreih's shoulder at the small black ball. He said, "I have no idea."

Satreih looked at the small black ball closer—and saw Verteq's face glowering at him. "Yaaaaaaah!" He threw the ball halfway across the room.

Chikara opened her eyes. *What is that!?*

"I-I don't know! I saw Verteq in that thing! One of the slaves found it in one of your cuts, the one between your wing and shoulder!"

Ahhhh, so that's why I was itching. I know what it is, too. It is a Geom Stone. It gets absorbed by dragon skin. It allowed Verteq to see what we were doing.

"Who could have placed it there? The wizard?"

No. It was itching before we met him. I think—Jeshu! Of course! Chikara growled, which made the slaves back away from her. When they lived with Oj'yer, a growl was a warning sign that told them the dragon was going to eat someone.

Chikara turned to the slaves. *No, no it's fine. I'm growling over something else, not you guys.*

The slaves continued to heal her.

Kaskin asked, "What were you saying about Jeshu?" Kaskin looked over to Satreih. "Are you all right, Satreih?"

Satreih was banging his head on Kaskin's arm. "God, I'm such an idiot. When I was eavesdropping on the wizard and Jeshu, the wizard asked, 'Did you place it where I asked you to?' Jeshu replied, 'Yes, but the dragon suspects something. She itches in the spot where I placed the stone.'"

I'm grateful that we found it so early. We were extremely lucky. Chikara looked to the slave that found it and said, *Thank you.*

The slave nodded.

Satreih walked up to the stone that he had tossed. He took out his sword and stabbed it. The stone burst into pieces. "Good. Now we don't have to deal with that thing again."

*   *   *   *

A week passed. Chikara was now almost completely healed. Chikara, Satreih, and Kaskin were getting ready to leave Oj'yer's cave. Chikara suggested that they should leave the treasure. Oj'yer was a friend of the wizard's, so he might have had the wizard put a spell on it to protect the treasure even after his death.

Satreih asked one of the slaves where they were on the map.

The slave replied, "Seven Waterfalls."

Satreih smiled. He found Seven Waterfalls on the map. It was much closer to Rasiamoramisa, which they should reach in about a day.

Chikara felt comfortable enough flying outside to stretch her wings. She quickly learned that there were other dragons living in Seven Waterfalls. All of them were friendly, and Chikara got along well with them. They told her that

Oj'yer was the bad apple. There were only five other dragons. There used to be seven. Oj'yer and Dacllo died. They told Chikara that the skeleton she saw was Dacllo. A wizard came and killed him when he didn't move out of the way. Chikara knew who the wizard was. These five dragons, and Chikara, were the only dragons left in the world. The other dragons would bring Oj'yer's slaves back to their homes soon, now that Oj'yer was dead.

*   *   *   *

Finally, it was time to leave. The other dragons told Chikara, Satreih, and Kaskin the best direction to Rasiamoramisa. The other dragons invited them to return to Seven Waterfalls after they completed their quest. The dragons knew the witch that they were looking for. She was a friend of theirs. Her name was Akaidi. She would be able to decipher the symbol.

Soon Chikara, Satreih, and Kaskin were speeding away from Seven Waterfalls. Kaskin forgot to eat the Calsi. Remarkably, he was fine. Chikara believed that Kaskin was cured of altitude sickness by the atmosphere of Seven Waterfalls.

Satreih could see Rasiamoramisa in the distance. Dwarfs lived in the mountains. Rasiamoramisa was in a mountain valley. The trick would be to find the mountain that the dwarfs and Akaidi lived in.

Satreih started to get anxious.

Kaskin sensed this. He used mind-speech and asked, *What's wrong?*

I'm an elf. Right now, there is some hatred going on between elves and dwarfs. I'll doubt that they'll let us see Akaidi.

Well, maybe you and Chikara can wait outside, and I can show Akaidi the symbol.

That might work.

Chikara chimed in, *I'm going to stop for tonight. I'm still somewhat stiff from the fight with Oj'yer. We can arrive at Rasiamoramisa early tomorrow morning.*

They were on the ground, in a forest right before the mountain range where Rasiamoramisa was situated. Satreih was excited. Being in this forest felt like being home.

After eating dinner, Satreih climbed a tree to keep watch.

Chikara kept her eyes on tiny, multicolored winged objects, silently willing them not to come near. She and Kaskin soon fell asleep.

After a few hours, Satreih heard a twig snap, and from the sounds of it, it was too large of a snap to be an animal that lived in the forest. Before Satreih could do anything about it, there was a sharp pain on the back of his head. He was instantly knocked unconscious.

PARANOID DWARFS

Satreih slowly opened his eyes. He was bound with rope. He sat up, and saw Kaskin and Chikara. Kaskin was bound with rope as well, but Chikara was bound with chains. They were both unconscious.

Satreih looked around. He noticed that they were in some sort of prison. The prison was a tall and dirty room, possibly stretching all the way up to the top of the mountain. There were bars to keep them from escaping. There was a dwarf guarding the room that Satreih and his friends were in.

Satreih struggled to turn on his side to face the guard. He called out to him, "Hey, where am I?"

The dwarf didn't turn around and snottily replied, "You ask me that like I should answer you, elf."

"Oh, c'mon. Can't you tell me?"

"No."

Satreih spent the rest of the night to try to negotiate with the dwarf. It was futile. Chikara woke up as the hours wore on.

"Hi, Chikara. Are you okay?"

Yes. Where are we?

"Some type of prison. That dwarf won't talk to us. I've already tried." There was a hint of annoyance in his voice.

Chikara bent her head down and tried to wake Kaskin with her snout. Kaskin's eyes slowly opened. He slowly sat up. "Where are we?"

Satreih says it's some sort of prison.

The dwarf guard shouted, "Quiet!"

Chikara, Satreih, and Kaskin switched to mind-speech.

If they didn't tie my mouth shut, I could blast down those doors with fire.

Yeah, but you can't. They might let you and Kaskin out of here, but I doubt they'll let me out. Satreih growled.

Are you annoyed by any chance?

Very.

A day later, two dwarfs came into the cell and untied Kaskin. They weren't gentle about it. They started shoving him out of the cell.

Satreih asked a question that he knew was pointless. "Are you going to let Chikara and me out, too?"

One dwarf answered gruffly, "No. Just the man."

As he was being shoved out of the cell, Kaskin said using mind-speech, *I'll let you guys know everything that's happening.*

Twenty minutes later, Kaskin's voice came back to Satreih and Chikara. *They want to interrogate me. I'll keep our quest secret.*

A half hour passed. Kaskin came back, and this time there were no guards with him. "They trust me."

Four dwarfs pushed past Kaskin and untied Chikara and Satreih.

Kaskin said, "They still don't trust you, and are going to keep you in here, but I've asked them to undo your bindings."

Once Chikara and Satreih were finally untied, Satreih sat up. He sat cross-legged, with his arms folded. The dwarfs left.

Kaskin made sure that the dwarfs were out of earshot and said, "If you give me the symbol, I could try to find Akaidi and ask her what it means."

Satreih didn't say anything. He dug into his coat pocket and pulled out the small piece of paper with the mysterious symbol on it. He walked over to the bars and gave it to Kaskin through the bars.

Satreih said, "Good luck. Convince those bozos to let us out of here."

"I'll do my best." Kaskin left.

*   *   *   *

Kaskin walked down the halls of Rasiamoramisa with the small piece of paper clutched in his fist, out of everyone's sight. Rasiamoramisa was inside a mountain, which was similar to being underground. He liked that. But there were too many gems. He knew that dwarfs shared a love for gems with dragons, and often quarreled with dragons to retrieve the gems. That's why they didn't trust Chikara. They thought she was going to steal some of their precious gems. There were a lot of dwarfs, hurrying on to do their own little things that they needed to get done. Some were picking at the gems embedded in the walls with pickaxes, trying to make them more dazzling. Kaskin could see that some of the gems were used for lighting purposes.

Kaskin passed a dwarf in the halls who was not hurrying to get somewhere. He approached the dwarf and asked, "Hey, do you know where Akaidi is? I'm an old friend of hers. She would want to see me."

The dwarf grunted, "Ah, sure. Follow me."

Kaskin tried not to laugh. *Dwarfs are so gullible.*

Soon the dwarf led him to the very base of the mountain. A long hallway stretched out in front of them.

The dwarf said, "Akaidi is the hundredth door on your right. If you're an old friend of hers, then you'll know she'll want payment." He walked away.

Payment? I wonder what I'll give Akaidi. I don't have any money with me at the moment.

Kaskin counted the doors. Soon he found the hundredth one and knocked. "Akaidi? You there?" After waiting for several minutes, there was no reply. Kaskin knocked again, with no answer yet again. He slightly leaned on the door, and it swung open. "Akaidi?"

Kaskin walked inside the room. He was no longer inside the mountain. He was in a two story shack. He could see moonlight. Kaskin walked into the shack. The floor boards creaked when they were stepped on. There were spider webs all over the place. On a desk, aside from spider webs and a black widow, there was a decorated box full of vedis from people who had previously visited.

He looked around to see if anyone was watching him. No one was. Kaskin took some of the vedis out of the box and pocketed them.

Kaskin walked further into the shack. Soon he got the eerie feeling that someone or something was watching him. He turned around, but he didn't see anyone.

Kaskin was just about to head up the stairs. A huge winged object flew and landed in front of him. Kaskin took a step back. He drew his sword.

The figure was seven feet tall. Its face was deathly pale, and its eyes were red. It had fangs. The figure was a vampire.

The over-sized bat attacked Kaskin. Kaskin moved to the side, and tried to stab the vampire with his sword. He didn't get the chance. The vampire hissed as it was whacked over the head with an old broomstick. An old woman was hitting it. She had big blue eyes and thin, wire rimmed glasses. The old woman had long gray hair; some of it was tied back in a bun.

"Go away! Go away, you crazy old bat! Shoo!"

The vampire hissed as it flew up into the rafters. It perched there, looking at Kaskin with hungry eyes.

"Sorry about that. He always tries to scare away my visitors. My name is Akaidi. What were you calling me for?" Akaidi held her hand out toward Kaskin, expectantly.

Kaskin placed the vedis that he had taken in her palm. She looked at the vedis and smiled slightly. Kaskin could tell just by that smile, she knew.

"Sit." Akaidi motioned to a black couch. Kaskin sat on it. He thought it smelled like mothballs. He didn't say anything about it. Akaidi sat on a couch that was across from Kaskin's. She asked, "So? What do you need? Potions? I can make any kind you ask for. Do you need something deciphered? Your fortune told?"

Kaskin pulled out that small sheet of paper that Satreih had given him through the bars. He held it out to the witch. "Can you decipher this?"

"Let me see." She took the small sheet of paper with the mysterious symbol on it and sighed. "My friend," she said sadly, "You are going to die a most painful death."

"Um—I asked you to decipher that symbol. I don't think that has anything to do with fortune telling." *Hmmm. Crazy old bat? I think there are two of them here.*

*   *   *   *

Satreih was leaning up against Chikara with his arms folded and his head down. Chikara was asleep. He was still annoyed. He wondered if Kaskin had found Akaidi yet. Satreih also wondered if Kaskin was trying to convince those good-for-nothing dwarfs to let them out.

Satreih heard some dwarfs come to the place where he and Chikara were being held. He looked up to see that they were carrying someone. The person that they were carrying was very beautiful. She had long, braided black hair that fell to her ankles. She wore lightweight armor. Satreih noticed that she had very long ears.

She was unconscious and bleeding from numerous wounds. The dwarfs also had injuries. *So, she's a fighter. It looks like she didn't go without a fight.*

Satreih elbowed Chikara and woke her up.

Hmm?

Satreih didn't answer. He just nodded in the direction of the band of dwarfs and the unconscious elf. Chikara only caught a quick glimpse. The other elf was put into the cell next to Satreih's and Chikara's.

Do you know her?

"No."

*   *   *   *

Twenty minutes later, Kaskin came back.

Satreih went up to the bars and asked, "Let me guess. You found Akaidi?"

"Yes." Kaskin handed the slip of paper through the bars. "The strange letters show where the tenth morith lies. That one is going to be the hardest to find and to destroy."

"Well, where is it?"

"In the very heart of Mosiania."

A silence fell between them.

"Well, we still need to look for the other seven first. Did Akaidi say anything about where my father is?"

"We can kill two birds with one stone."

"He's in Mosiania, isn't he?"

"Yeah."

*   *   *   *

Night had fallen. The dwarfs had given Kaskin a room that was near the prison.

A misty figure materialized in front of the cell that Satreih and Chikara were in, with her back facing them.

Satreih opened his eyes a crack. He had been sleeping peacefully a minute before, but he got the odd feeling that he should wake up. He saw the misty figure and his eyes shot all the way open.

The misty figure spoke. "You have done well, Satreih. You've already destroyed three moriths in a very short period of time. Those three are the only ones you will destroy for a while. The trail will go cold. Verteq is aware of your presence."

"How do you know me?"

"Please. How could I not know you?" The misty figure turned around so that she could face Satreih head-on. "It has been far too long, my son."

CHOSEN ONE?

Satreih stared at his mother, not believing. He got up and walked over to the bars. "Mother?" he whispered.

The spirit nodded and smiled. "The person the dwarfs brought in will be one of your most trusted allies. Her name is Yia. It may have looked like Yia was fighting the dwarfs. That isn't the case. She was fighting a Spy from Mosiania. The dwarfs found her unconscious body. The Spy left, thinking that he had killed her. The dwarfs traveled through a severe blizzard up in the mountains. That is why they're injured. Yia's wounds are critical. Take her to Meikosa. The king there will heal her. Your friend the dragon will not be able to heal her. Yia had put a spell on herself to prevent most magic from affecting her. Later, a heavy burden will be placed on Yia's shoulders. She won't tell you what it is willingly. It is up to you to free her of that burden. If not, she will certainly perish.

"The dwarfs will never let you out of here. I will." The spirit passed her hand through the lock. The cell door opened.

Satreih walked over to Chikara and shook her awake.

What?

He smiled mischievously and said, "Time to go."

The sound of another lock opening came to their ears. Satreih sprinted out of his cell. His mother was standing outside the next cell, holding the door open for him. Satreih sprinted into the other cell, gently picking up Yia's body.

Satreih turned around. He expected to see his mother, but he didn't. She had vanished. Her voice echoed through the halls. "Wake Kaskin from his sleep. Move quickly. The dwarfs are already aware of your escape."

Satreih jogged over to Chikara and put Yia on her back. "Meet us outside." Chikara nodded and started to head for the exit.

Satreih sprinted down the halls. It didn't take him long to find Kaskin's room. Kaskin was asleep on the bed.

Satreih jogged over to him, shaking him awake. "Kaskin, get up! Now! We have to leave."

Kaskin opened his eyes and sat up. "Satreih?" he asked incredulously. "How the heck did you get out of the cell?"

"Later. Chikara's waiting for us outside."

A voice came from the doorway, "There they are!" There were seven dwarfs, each holding a crossbow. The dwarf who spoke fired.

Satreih ducked aside. The arrow barely missed. Satreih and Kaskin both dove underneath the bed, using it for protection.

After a few minutes, the wave of arrows ceased.

Satreih heard his mother's voice, "It is safe now. I am holding them back. Hurry, and make your escape."

Satreih and Kaskin cautiously climbed out from underneath the bed. There was fear in all of the dwarfs' eyes. There was fog swirling around their bodies and weapons. The dwarfs were paralyzed.

Satreih said to Kaskin, "C'mon," and they sprinted out into the hall.

On his way out, Kaskin grabbed his sword that was sitting on the desk.

Soon they found their way outside. Chikara was waiting for them.

Kaskin spotted Yia and asked, "Who's that?"

We'll tell you later. We need to leave. Where do I fly, Satreih?

"Meikosa." Satreih checked the map and pointed to the northwest. "That way."

Satreih and Kaskin climbed up onto Chikara's back. Some of the dwarfs ran outside and started to fire. Chikara jumped up into the night sky. She was soon out of the range of the arrows that the dwarfs aimed at her and her riders. They sped off from Rasiamoramisa and flew toward the northwest.

During the trip, Satreih kept his hands on Yia's side so she wouldn't fall off. Using mind-speech, he filled Kaskin in on who she was and how they had escaped. Soon the sun started to rise. They could see Meikosa in the distance. It was still very far away. It took them two more hours to get there. Meikosa was big.

*   *   *   *

Soon Chikara landed, but not in Meikosa. She landed in a forest clearing nearby.

Satreih, take Yia to Meikosa. I'll stay here. They might try to attack me.

"I'll stay with Chikara," Kaskin offered.

Why? You don't think I can fight well enough?

"Oh, no. Not at all."

Chikara gave Kaskin a dirty look.

"I'm just kidding," Kaskin said quickly.

Satreih laughed and jumped down. Kaskin handed him Yia's body.

Satreih reached a concrete wall that was surrounding the entrance of Meikosa. A voice called down from above. "Stop right there! Who are you?"

"My name is Satreih. I'm an elf. The person who I hold in my arms, Yia, is critically wounded. She is also an elf. I came here to get help."

A door built into the concrete wall opened. The voice called down. "If you have any need to leave Meikosa, be back before nightfall. If you are not back before that time, you will be locked out."

Satreih walked into Meikosa, leaving the concrete wall behind him. Meikosa was beautiful. Snowcapped mountains soared high up into the sky. He knew that if the other elves let Chikara inside she would have a lot of fun flying amongst the mountains. Forests covered the slopes of the mountains. Satreih had to cross a beautifully made bridge that crossed a river from a snow-fed waterfall. The streets were clean, and seemed to sparkle. There was no trash or dust on them. Cottages were on either side of the street. People were already outside, going about their business.

There was an elf on the street ahead of Satreih. He motioned to Satreih to come to him. Satreih obliged.

The elf said, "My name is Thuoj. I am the king of Meikosa. Let me see her." Thuoj motioned to Yia.

Satreih gave Yia to him.

Thuoj said, "She does look bad. But you got her here just in time. If you had waited another half hour, she would have been impossible to save. Follow me."

Satreih followed him. Thuoj led him to a building. Thuoj turned around and said, "I ask for you to wait out here. You can come in when I call for you."

Satreih nodded.

Thuoj disappeared into the building.

Chikara's voice entered Satreih's head. *Any luck on trying to find help yet?*

Yes. The king of Meikosa, Thuoj, is healing her right now. He said that if we had waited a half hour longer, Yia would have been impossible to save.

Two hours later, Thuoj came out of the building. "She'll be fine. You can see her. She's in the second room on the left. I'd like to stay longer, but I'm the king of Meikosa and have much to attend to. Call for me if you need me." He left.

Satreih found Yia's room. He walked inside. She was on a bed. The blankets were pulled up to her chin. She was still unconscious, but all her injuries were gone. He drew a chair next to the bed and sat down.

Satreih stayed with her for a long while. Yia still did not wake. He began to worry more. An idea started to form. Maybe he could use mind-speech to talk to her.

He focused his mind on her, and then felt a terrible pain. It felt like sharp needles were piercing his skull.

A voice entered his mind. *Get—out!*

Stop! I am a friend! My name's Satreih! I brought you to Meikosa to have them heal your injuries!

The intense pain stopped.

You're Satreih?

Yeah. Why'd you attack me like that?

I thought you were the Spy. I'm still weak from the battle. It's hard to focus. I need to conserve my energy for when it is truly important. I should wake up in a couple of hours. We'll talk then. Yia acknowledged that she was safe. Though unconscious, she undid the spell that protected her from magic.

*   *   *   *

Satreih drew away, letting her be. He heard the door to the room open, and a familiar voice. "She's still not awake yet?"

Satreih jumped in surprise and turned around. "Kaskin! What're you doing here?"

"Chikara and I met with Thuoj. He came to us and offered us admittance into Meikosa. Chikara is outside the building, since she is too big to come in."

"What do the rest of the citizens of Meikosa think of her?"

"They don't mind at all. Chikara's having fun with the children again."

Satreih and Kaskin talked for a little bit more. After a while, Kaskin went outside with Chikara.

The sun was just starting to set. Yia opened her eyes and sat up.

Satreih helped her. "Thirsty?" he asked.

Yia nodded.

He used mind-speech and asked Kaskin to get some water.

Yia spoke. "People are saying that you're the chosen one. They're saying that you'll be the one to bring Verteq down."

"What!" asked Satreih, stunned. "Who's been saying that?"

"The king and queen from the Hasini clan for one. Keelu and Queas from Kajie are also saying so. Verteq is saying it as well, which is why he's trying to kill you."

"No way! This is impossible! I'm only sixteen!" He thought for a little bit. "Seventeen in a couple of days. Just because my friends and I have destroyed three moriths, that doesn't mean that I'm the chosen one!"

Wow. He's younger than I thought. I'm a couple of years older than he is! Yia countered, "You destroyed them in a very short amount of time."

Satreih tried a different track. "When a Geom stone was found in Chikara, I saw Verteq's face when I looked at it. I screamed and threw the thing halfway across the room!"

"Most people would have committed suicide."

Satreih thought and said softly, "That still doesn't qualify me for being the chosen one. I'm too young. I don't want this responsibility."

Kaskin entered the room, holding a canteen. "What's going on?" he asked. "I heard your yelling outside."

Satreih didn't answer and looked at the floor. Tension was suddenly in the room.

Kaskin gave the canteen to Yia.

Yia nodded thanks and drank.

Satreih left the room.

Outside, Satreih saw Chikara. There were still some children climbing on her. Some heard their parents calling, got off, and went to their parent's side. They still looked at Chikara with wonder in their eyes.

Chikara saw Satreih walk out of the building. *It is all right, Satreih. Kaskin and I will be with you every step of the way.*

Satreih didn't answer. He turned a corner and disappeared amongst the buildings.

Some of the children looked at Chikara curiously. They knew that she and Satreih were friends, and knew that something was going on. Chikara shrugged in reply. She knew what was happening, but didn't want the children to know.

Kaskin came out of the building. "Where'd Satreih go?"

He disappeared amongst the buildings. She jerked her head in the direction.

"Do you know what's going on?"

Some of the children expectantly looked up.

Chikara used mind-speech, so that only Kaskin could hear. *Yia told him that he's the chosen one.*

Chosen one?

He'll be the one to kill Verteq.

No wonder why he was suddenly like that. I already knew. Akaidi told me. The letters says where the morith is; the symbol represents the area where they'll fight. I was just waiting for the right time to tell him.

Thuoj approached them. "Dinner is in the dining hall in an hour. It's big enough for you, Chikara. All of you are invited. Where's Satreih?"

Again, Chikara used mind-speech. *He's somewhere. At dinner, please don't say anything about him being the chosen one. He's taking it badly.*

Thuoj nodded. "I won't. Can you find him and let him know that dinner is in an hour?"

Kaskin nodded.

"How's Yia? Did she wake?"

Kaskin answered, "Yes, she did. She's back asleep right now. Shall I wake her?"

"Yes. Please do. She'll be a guest as well." Thuoj left.

Yia came out of the building.

Kaskin said, "Wow, how'd you know to come out? I was just about to wake you."

"I just had a feeling that I should come outside."

Kaskin turned to Chikara and said, "I guess I'll try to find Satreih." He left Chikara and Yia and walked the path that Satreih took not too long ago.

Kaskin found Satreih. He was sitting on a tree branch, with his back up against the trunk. He was staring off into nothing.

"Hi, Satreih. Dinner is in an hour."

Satreih blinked.

Kaskin tried to climb the tree. "How did you climb this thing? It doesn't have any foot or hand holds."

"I lived in the forest for pretty much all of my life. I don't need foot holds or hand holds to climb trees."

Kaskin gave up trying to climb the tree. "Well, as I said, dinner is in an hour. Thuoj's inviting us."

Satreih stood and jumped off of the branch. He gracefully landed on the ground.

Kaskin said, "That tree is impossible to climb."

"I got up there, didn't I?"

"Yeah, you did. C'mon, let's go eat."

✳   ✳   ✳   ✳

An hour later, Chikara, Satreih, Kaskin, and Yia were in the dining hall with Thuoj. There was every sort of food imaginable stretched out on the table. They all ate, though Satreih just nibbled at his food. Even though the dwarfs didn't give him any food while he was in the prison he didn't have much of an appetite.

"So," said Thuoj, "You've already destroyed three moriths."

Satreih answered. "Yeah. We have. How does everyone know what we're doing? Sure, the king and queen of the Hasini clan and Keelu and Queas know, but that's because we've helped them destroy the moriths that were in their lands. We've been trying to keep our quest secret."

"Word has spread."

Chikara lifted her head, and sniffed the air.

Satreih saw this and asked, "Smell something?"

Blood. I also smell the other scents of battle.

Suddenly, someone entered the dining hall.

Thuoj stood and asked him, "Phillip, what is happening?"

Phillip didn't answer him; he just stared at Thuoj with glassy eyes. Chikara immediately knew that something was wrong. Phillip pitched forward. They all saw an arrow sticking out of his back.

Chikara and Satreih rushed to Phillip's side. Satreih pulled out the arrow, leaning him up against Chikara. His wound instantly healed.

Phillip spoke, though he was still in shock. "M-My Lord, Verteq's Wi'oks are attacking. There was no warning. Some of the warriors are trying to fight, but they don't have any armor on."

Thuoj started to head for the exit. "Chikara, Satreih, and Kaskin, you can help fight if you want. I am not making you. Yia, stay in here and watch out for Phillip." Thuoj ran out through the door.

Kaskin asked, "Satreih, do you have you're ophilla on?"

"Yeah, but my weapons are in that room."

"Same here. We should make a quick stop there and then help fight after."

I'll follow you, but along the way, I'll take out some of the Wi'oks as we go.

Chikara, Satreih, and Kaskin all ran out of the room. Outside, there was fire everywhere. The Wi'oks were fleshless skeletons. Their clothes hung off of them like rags. The eye sockets were hollow and empty, but they knew where to attack. There were thousands of them. They were good fighters.

A small child ran up to Chikara, with fear in her eyes. She was one of the children that had been climbing on her earlier. A Wi'ok was chasing her. Chikara breathed golden fire. The Wi'ok fell. The child was fine. She hugged Chikara's leg, whimpering and crying in fear.

Satreih put a hand on the child's shoulder, pointing to the entrance of the dining hall. "Go in there; you will be protected."

The child ran for the dining hall and went inside.

Satreih and Kaskin went back to retrieve their weapons and found a Wi'ok trying to make off with them.

Kaskin cried out, "You! Stop there!" The Wi'ok turned around. It saw Satreih and Kaskin approach.

Kaskin stopped Satreih and walked in front of him, turning sideways, so that he wasn't facing the Wi'ok head on. He circled the Wi'ok, keeping a wary eye on it.

The Wi'ok took out its own sword, holding it ready. Kaskin approached it. The Wi'ok swung the blade. Kaskin ducked and swept his legs, sending the Wi'ok crashing to the floor. They began to wrestle for the Wi'ok's weapon. Kaskin pulled the weapon out of the Wi'oks bony hands, slashing it across the Wi'oks neck. The Wi'ok went limp. Its bones blew away in gray dust. The only sign that it had been there were the clothes that it had been wearing.

Kaskin got up and smiled. He grabbed their weapons, tossing Satreih's fire sword and arrows to him.

Satreih gaped at Kaskin in shock. "You didn't even break a sweat!"

"I've had practice."

They ran outside. Chikara was fighting twenty Wi'oks at once. Her chief weapons were her fire and tail. She saw Satreih and Kaskin exit the building.

They climbed onto her back. Chikara flew towards the concrete wall that sur-rounded Meikosa.

Ladders had been put up along the concrete wall, with Wi'oks climbing on them. Some of the warriors were trying to fight, but most lost their lives. Chikara breathed fire along the opposite wall. The ladders and the Wi'oks burned. But that was not enough to stop them.

Satreih and Kaskin jumped off. They started fighting the Wi'oks on the wall.

Satreih heard something hurl toward him from behind. He ducked aside. A spear flew past.

A Wi'ok was facing him. The Wi'ok grabbed a spear out of a fallen Meikosan warrior, holding it up to Satreih. Satreih turned sideways and approached the Wi'ok. The Wi'ok thrust the spear forward, striking Satreih on his chest. Satreih wasn't hurt. The ophilla under his shirt had protected him.

Satreih sheathed his sword, making the Wi'ok cock his head in surprise. Satreih took out his bow and knocked an arrow. He shot the arrow—and missed. The Wi'ok defensively threw up the spear, making the arrow ricochet off of it.

Satreih heard someone call his name, but he didn't recognize the voice. He turned in the direction of the voice and saw a fallen warrior on the ground. His legs were bleeding. A Wi'ok was sneaking up on him, but it was cautious in case the Meikosan warrior decided to fight to his last breath.

Satreih shot the Wi'ok with an arrow, making it fall. Another warrior picked up his fallen friend, carrying him off to a safe place. Satreih felt a pain on his right wrist. He whirled around, and saw another Wi'ok. It had struck him on the wrist with the staff of its spear, causing Satreih to drop his bow. The Wi'ok struck out again, but Satreih dodged and picked up the bow with his other hand. A sword flashed. The Wi'ok fell. Kaskin stood behind it, holding up his sword.

Kaskin yelled over the sounds of battle, "Maybe you should go back to the dining hall!"

"I still want to fight!"

"You can't fight with your left hand! You'll be safer in the dining hall."

Satreih nodded and ran, dodging Wi'oks along the way.

*   *   *   *

Yia was trying to comfort the small child that had entered the dining hall. The child was worried about her parents, who were fighting.

She looked up as she heard the door open. She expected to see a Wi'ok, but it was Satreih who entered the room. He looked a little annoyed.

Yia asked, "What happened?"

"I broke my right wrist. My dominant hand is my right hand, so I can't fight any more."

Yia pulled out some of the gauze that she had in her pocket and said, "Here, let me see your wrist. I'll heal it."

Satreih sat down next to her, allowing her to heal his injury.

The child looked up at him and asked, "Where's your dragon?"

"She's still fighting. I'm sure she's fine."

Yia finished, and let Satreih take back his hand.

"Thanks."

"No problem."

They all heard the sound of breaking glass. Yia and Satreih stood up. They both looked over to the direction of the sound.

Yia looked to Satreih and said, "Give me your bow."

Satreih obliged, also giving her some of his arrows.

Yia jogged off in the direction of the sound.

The child hid behind Satreih's legs. She asked, "W-What made that sound?" There was a fearful quiver in her voice.

"I don't know. Some Wi'oks, maybe."

After some minutes, Satreih heard Yia call to him. "Satreih, come over here! Hurry!"

Satreih looked to the child and said, "Stay here with Phillip." He ran down the hall, and saw Yia trying to hold the door shut with her body. Satreih's bow was on the floor next to her.

Yia saw Satreih approach and said, "Help me hold the door shut!"

He did and asked, "Where did the sound of breaking glass come from?"

"The Wi'oks knocked down some of the windows further down the hall. I shot them with your arrows. I'm using magic to keep the other Wi'oks from getting in that way."

"You're using magic? You're a witch?"

"Yes. I'm not fully advanced with witchcraft, but I know some spells. Is there any problem with my being a witch?"

"No. Not at all. If you can use magic, then why do you need me to help you hold the door shut?"

"Remember, I'm not fully advanced with witchcraft. If I try to use magic to hold the door and the broken windows shut, I'd probably kill myself."

Satreih heard the sound of the Wi'oks coming in through the windows. The lights went out.

Yia said, "On three, we'll move away from the door."

"What! Are you crazy!?"

"Crazy? Oh, yeah. But I know what I'm doing. One, two, three!"

They both jumped back from the door as it burst open, letting in the Wi'oks and the cold, winter air from outside.

The Wi'oks who came in through the windows came within sight.

Soon Satreih and Yia were surrounded by Wi'oks, with nowhere to go.

Yia held her hands in front of her, forming a red energy ball between them.

Satreih watched with astonishment.

When the red energy ball was big enough, Yia quickly drew her hands away to her sides. The energy ball split apart into a number of long tubes. The beginnings of the tubes formed into a snarling head of some sort. The tubes were flung into the bodies of the Wi'oks. All of them fell. The lights came back on.

Satreih gaped at Yia in stupefied shock. He said, "I thought that you weren't fully advanced with witchcraft."

"I'm not. If I were, I would be able to stop all of the Wi'oks at once, even the ones outside. I guess you're not familiar with witchcraft. If you were, you would know that the spell I just used is amongst the simplest."

"That's a simple spell?"

"Compared to the others, yes. This spell took me a long time to master. It can still be made more powerful." Yia paused. "The barriers for the windows are back up. Help me move that grandfather clock over there to block the door."

They moved the grandfather clock over to the door. As soon as it was in place, Wi'oks hit it. The clock barely moved.

Yia said, "We should go back to the room where Phillip and the child are."

When they arrived, the child asked, "What was that noise?"

Yia answered, "Just some Wi'oks that got in. I took care of them. They won't bother us."

Satreih added excitedly, "Hey, did you know that Yia's a—"

Yia slugged him in the arm.

"Ow! That hurt! What was that for?"

Yia said through clenched teeth, "Don't tell her. I don't want her to freak out."

The child asked innocently, "Yia's a what?"

Yia answered, "Nothing, nothing."

The child went to sleep. Soon the sounds of the battle died away. Chikara and Kaskin entered the dining hall.

Kaskin asked Satreih, "How's your wrist?"

"It's fine." Satreih looked to Yia and asked, "Can I tell them?"

Yia looked to Phillip and the child to make sure that they were still asleep. "Yeah, go ahead."

Satreih said quickly, "Yia's a witch."

Chikara asked, *How'd you find that out?*

"You know those barriers on the windows outside?"

Kaskin said, "I've been wondering what those were."

"Yeah. They're magical barriers."

Kaskin asked Yia, "Do you know Akaidi?"

"Yes, I do. Actually, she was the one who introduced and taught witchcraft to me. Did you run into that annoying vampire by any chance?"

"Yeah. I did. Akaidi came to my rescue and whacked it over the head a couple of times with an old broomstick."

Satreih started sniggering. The image of an old woman beating up a vampire was ridiculous. He got an idea. He stopped sniggering and asked, "If Akaidi lives in Rasiamoramisa, then how'd you get in? The dwarfs hate elves. I know. They threw Chikara and me in prison."

"I can change my appearance."

"Prove it."

Yia smiled and stood up. Her ears grew short and less pointy; her skin became wrinkled. She hunched over a bit, and her hair turned gray. Her eyes were the same. She spoke, and her voice sounded like a tiresome old woman. "This is my personal favorite appearance, though I have many others." She transformed back into her usual self.

Chikara and Satreih stared at her in shock. Kaskin let out a low whistle and said, "Whoa."

What's the difference between wizards and witches, other than the fact that wizards are men and witches are woman?

"Wizards use magic staffs, but witches don't. We use our mind-powers to kill foes. Wizards are more inclined to find things out through research, though witches usually go outside and try to find things out for themselves, without having to look in books. All witches, even very young ones, can change their appearance at will, but wizards have to gain power. I know of only a few wizards who can change their appearance, and they are very powerful."

Kaskin asked, "Do you know the wizard Weuh?"

"Yes. Actually, he and I used to be very good friends before he became evil."

Satreih asked hopefully, "Do you know how his mind works? Does he know that you're not an ally?"

"I know how his mind works, but he doesn't know that I'm not one of his allies anymore. He thinks that I'm on Verteq's side."

"You're not, are you?"

"No, I'm not. I can give him false information about you. He won't suspect until something happens to him that is not to his liking."

THE PROPHESY

King Thuoj came into the room. He looked tired and sad.

Satreih asked, "What was the outcome of the battle?"

"Five hundred of my warriors lost their lives fighting. There is an elf walking around the corpses. He's probably looking for his wife, who was fighting."

Yia offered, "I'll go help the poor elf," and started to head out the door.

Satreih tried to follow, but Yia's voice entered his mind, stopping him. *The elf is Weuh. Stay here. Stay hidden. If he sees you, he will kill you. I'll go talk to him.*

Yia saw Weuh. He was in the middle of the corpses, stepping on them. He had no respect for the dead. Weuh appeared as a Meikosan warrior. Weuh didn't see Yia approach. His back was facing her.

Yia approached Weuh from behind. "Hello, Weuh. Long time no see."

Weuh spun around, surprised. "Yia, don't sneak up on me like that." *So Verteq recently let me out of the prison to recruit Yia? Sly.*

Idiot. I guess old age has taken a toll on him. Otherwise he would have known I was coming. "What are you doing here? The vile Meikosans won the battle."

"Rumors that Satreih is in Meikosa came to my ears."

"Satreih was here. Not anymore. He, the dragon, and the man fled shortly after the battle."

"Why would they flee? They won."

"They know where the fourth morith is. They fled to find it and destroy it. Tell me where the morith is, Weuh. I do not know of its location. If I do, I promise that I will chase after Satreih and stop him. I would kill him, if I could.

You and our Lord would not have to worry about a thing. Trust me. You've trusted me for all these years. There is no reason to stop trusting me now."

Weuh looked around, making sure that no one was listening. He said quietly, "The morith is located in—"

He didn't get a chance to finish his sentence. Verteq appeared out of nowhere, stopping him from divulging the morith's location.

Yia knew that Satreih was watching the event through her eyes. She felt his surprise and fear when he saw Verteq. She made him forget what he saw and forced him out of her mind. She knew that if Verteq sensed his presence he would kill them both.

Yia bowed low to Verteq. "My Lord, please accept me into your ranks. I will be a great ally. I am an old friend of Weuh's."

Verteq sneered, "Are you certain? Once joining, there will be no turning back. You will lose all of your—loved ones," he said, knowing of the eventual infatuation that would spread between Yia and Satreih.

Yia nodded. She and Verteq made eye contact. Yia felt a burning pain. It felt as if all of her nervous system were on fire. It took every amount of will power not to gasp or blink.

Verteq stretched out his hands as fiery rings erupted from them. They wrapped themselves around Yia's body, and she again felt the burning pain. She felt as if she were in battle, as if her blood were draining from her body after a vicious attack. Yia gasped and fell to the ground. The rings, Verteq, and Weuh disappeared. Yia was left alone in the middle of the field in the middle of the corpses, shaking. She knew where the morith was.

$$* \qquad * \qquad * \qquad *$$

Kaskin asked, unbelieving, "What? Weuh's here?"

Satreih answered him. "That's what Yia said. He must have changed his appearance. Otherwise King Thuoj would have captured him."

Yia entered the room. Satreih noticed that she was very pale. She looked like she was about to faint. Satreih picked up his canteen and gave it to her. Yia took the canteen and drank gratefully.

Satreih asked, "What happened?"

Yia shook her head violently. She walked over to the table, and laid her head on her arms. Yia closed her eyes.

*   *   *   *

"My Lord, don't you think that was a little rough? Yia is a distant relative of mine."

Verteq grunted with disbelief. "If she can't deal with pain, then she can't be accepted amongst my ranks. You know that as well as I do." He spared Weuh a sideways glance. "You are very lucky that you aren't directly descended from her line."

Weuh looked at Verteq curiously. "You killed off the rest of her line. Why have you accepted her?"

"Allowing her to live will have its usefulness." *I will not attack them. Not yet. I'll wait for their lust to broaden.*

*   *   *   *

King Thuoj had given Satreih and Kaskin one room, and Yia another. Yia was in her room, sitting on the bed with her head bowed. She heard the sound of the door to Satreih's and Kaskin's room close. She wrote a short note, leaving it on the mantelpiece.

After Yia had waited for a few hours, she quietly stole into Satreih's and Kaskin's room. She made sure that Kaskin was still asleep. He was. She cautiously approached Satreih and whispered softly, "I'm sorry for this, Satreih. I really, truly am. This is the only way I can complete my task. Please forgive me."

Yia put her hand on his shoulder. She was putting sleeping and invisibility spells on him. He would not wake until she removed the spell.

Yia picked up Satreih and placed him underneath the bed, hiding him so that Kaskin would not notice him. She stood up and noticed his sword and map on the bedside table. She took them both as she disappeared.

Yia reappeared in a shack. A tall mountain face rose up behind her. She got the feeling that somebody was watching her. Yia looked up into the rafters. "Go away, Vineras. Don't attack me." Yia sat down on the couch that smelled like mothballs and waited.

Yia heard footsteps coming down the stairs. Yia said, "Hello, Akaidi. It has been a while."

Akaidi approached Yia. "Indeed, indeed it has." She held out her hand.

Yia gave her some vedis. Akaidi counted them. "Mmmm. This is more than usual. You want me to do you a favor?"

"I need you to appear as Satreih and spend some time in Meikosa."

"I've only met Kaskin. I do not know what Satreih looks like."

Yia took a step back from Akaidi. She transformed into Satreih, saying in his voice, "This is what he looks like." She didn't transform back.

"Why are you doing this? Why do you need me? I am an old woman, you know."

"I know. But I'm playing with Verteq's and Weuh's minds. This is the only way I can complete my task and fool them."

"That's a dangerous position that you're in."

"I know. I don't have any other choice. Please do this for me, Akaidi."

Akaidi transformed into Satreih, and shortly afterwards disappeared from sight.

Yia took out a dead animal from one of her cloak pockets and tossed it up into the rafters. "There you go, Vineras. A treat for you."

She disappeared from the shack. Yia reappeared in Meikosa, just in time to see Akaidi enter Satreih's and Kaskin's room. Yia, who still looked like Satreih, walked over to Chikara, who was sleeping just outside the room. She shook her awake. "Hey Chikara. Wake up."

Chikara opened her eyes and yawned. *What do you want me for, Satreih? It's midnight.*

"I've been studying the map. I think I figured out where the fourth morith is."

Chikara was suddenly wide awake. *Where is it?*

"I can't pronounce the name; it might be in werewolf tongue. It's east from here."

Should we wake Kaskin and Yia from their sleep?

"No. Kaskin's hard to wake up, and you saw how upset Yia was last night. We should let her sleep. Besides, we can destroy the morith by ourselves. We don't need their help."

All right, climb on. It's in the east, right?

"Right," said Yia, as she was climbing on Chikara's back.

Chikara made sure that Satreih was fully on, leaping up into the sky.

*   *   *   *

Kaskin woke to find that Satreih was desperately searching for something. Kaskin stretched and asked in a sleepy voice, "What're you looking for?"

Akaidi looked at Kaskin with dread. She truly didn't care about the sword or the map, but she knew that Satreih would. "My sword and map are gone."

"Gone?"

"I placed them on the bedside table right before I went to sleep. They're not there!"

They searched the room for a long time. After a while, Kaskin gave up and sat on the bed. "They're not here. Yia's a witch. Maybe she knows who took them."

Kaskin and Akaidi were facing the door that led to Yia's room. Kaskin knocked. "Yia, it's us. Can we come in?" There was no answer. Kaskin lightly pushed on the door, opening it.

Kaskin and Akaidi went into her room. Yia's bed was nicely made. There were different shaped bottles all around the room. All of them were filled with some type of potion. There was a cauldron near the back of the room.

Kaskin saw a note on the mantelpiece. "Hey, Satreih. Check this out." He handed the note to him.

Satreih and Kaskin,

Mother is sick. Even though she is a witch, she refuses to use magic ever since father passed away. She cannot heal herself, since depression greatly affects those who can use magic. I went home to help her.

Yia

Akaidi knew that the note was false. Both of Yia's parents had died when she was a child. Akaidi herself had raised her.

*   *   *   *

Yia and Chikara were quickly approaching their destination, a forest full of thick trees. Yia knew that no sun got to the forest's floor. She was worried. She had heard about this forest. As its name hinted, it was home to the werewolves.

They had traveled all day. It was already dark. Yia looked up to the moon. It was full. Some clouds were covering it a little. She shivered. The werewolves would be in their beast form, and if she were bitten—she tried not to think about the possibility.

Chikara flew over the forest. *There is no place for me to land. The trees are too thick. But the morith is here. I sense its evil power.*

Yia jumped off of Chikara's back.

Chikara exclaimed, horrified, *Satreih, you fool! Why did you do that?*

Chikara swooped down, trying to catch Yia. Yia gracefully landed on a tree branch, without getting hurt.

Oh.

"I'll go find and destroy the morith. Circle around the forest above." Yia climbed down the tree and disappeared into the forest.

*   *   *   *

Yia knew that Chikara could not see her. She transformed back into herself. The forest was dark. Yia waited for her eyes to adjust. They didn't. Her other senses sharpened. In the distance she could hear snarling, but the snarling was too far away for her to worry.

Yia unsheathed Satreih's sword, making the forest light up in a dim glow. Flames were swirling around the sword. *So. Satreih owns one of the two legendary fire swords.*

Some of the flames leapt from the sword and landed on a bush. A fire grew. Yia watched in awe. The fire grew to a small size, then stopped. She leaned closer to the fire. Inside its depths, she saw two men violently fighting. She could not see their faces. One man was slain. The other man collapsed in exhaustion.

The fire dimmed, then went out. The bush was ashes on the ground. Other than the ashes, there was no sign that it had ever been there. Yia knew that she was just shown a prophesy, but didn't know what to make of it. She memorized the event.

Yia turned her attention back to the forest. The snarling in the distance continued. She held the sword up defensively, and kept looking behind her to make sure that nothing was sneaking up on her. Every little noise sounded ominous. The forest was evil. She could feel it.

She felt something pulse to her right. She turned and headed in that direction. A ringing grew in her ears. Yia walked for a long while. With each step, the ringing grew louder. She knew that she was not far from the morith.

Yia came to a den that was big enough to enter. She felt something pulse from inside. *The morith is in there. This—this is a werewolf's den. I don't have a choice. I must enter.*

Yia raised the sword higher and ventured inside. A werewolf was on the ground, fast asleep. The morith was between its paws. The werewolf caught the scent of a woman. Its eyes opened.

Yia froze. The beast had woken up. Its eyes were a mix of green and yellow. The pupils were slits, like a cat's. They widened when the werewolf saw her. It growled and opened its mouth. The beast had multiple rows of teeth, and it had fangs. A stream of saliva flowed from its mouth, forming a puddle on the floor.

Yia pointed the sword at it. *To get to the morith, I must first kill the beast.*

The werewolf got up and charged. Yia ran out of the way. It smashed itself against the wall of the den, letting out a bellow of pain. Yia slashed at its hindquarters with the blade. The werewolf growled in pain and rolled in the dirt that covered the floor. It got up, swiping at Yia. Its claws raked against her skin, leaving cuts on her chest.

Yia rolled between the werewolf's front legs. She was underneath it. Yia thrust the sword upwards. The sword became stuck in fur and skin.

The werewolf moved aside, with the sword lodged in its stomach. It growled in pain when it felt its pelt burning. It lunged at Yia and bit her on the shoulder, near the neck. Yia gasped, grabbing its pelt. With her powers, she flung the beast off of her. It hit the wall, falling down dead.

Yia was using all of her power to prevent herself from turning into a werewolf. It was difficult. Her heart was beating faster, and the urge to kill a human was strong. She fought it. Yia withdrew the sword from the body of the werewolf. She stabbed the morith with all the force she could muster. It burst into pieces.

Yia remembered that she had promised Verteq that she would fight Satreih. She didn't want to fight him. He was a friend. Yia cut herself up with Satreih's fire sword. The pain was incredible. She sheathed the sword and walked out of the den.

Yia transformed back into Satreih. When she transformed, her injuries went away. She didn't look injured in Satreih's appearance. She could still feel the pain. As soon as Yia turned back into herself, the injuries would return. She climbed the tallest tree she could find. Climbing usually came naturally for her, as it did for most elves. She could easily climb a tree without any foot holds or hand holds. This time she had trouble climbing. After some difficulty and some painful falls, she made it to the top.

She saw Chikara flying and called to her. Yia saw Chikara turn and fly toward her. The urge to kill was stronger than ever. Yia resisted it.

"Time to go. The morith is destroyed."

Chikara nodded, allowing Yia to climb on her back.

*   *   *   **

Akaidi kept checking the sky.

Kaskin walked up behind her and said, "I'm sure Chikara will be back soon. Don't worry about it." He left.

Akaidi still looked like Satreih. She wasn't worried about the dragon, but she was worried about Yia. It was taking her a long time to get back.

Yia's voice echoed in her mind, *Akaidi, I-I was bitten by a werewolf. The urge to kill is strong. It's hard riding on Chikara. The werewolf part of me wants to kill her. We are nearing Meikosa. Hide yourself. Chikara won't like it if she finds out that I deceived her.*

Akaidi hid behind some old boxes and transformed into herself. She felt the ground shudder, and heard Satreih's voice. "Thanks, Chikara. Look, I know that you want to check out those mountains that surround Meikosa. You can do that now, if you like."

Yia watched Chikara fly toward the mountains. The werewolf inside of her pined. Yia turned around and saw Akaidi approaching. She transformed back into herself.

Akaidi was stunned when she saw the numerous cuts on Yia's body. "My word, child. What on earth were you doing?"

"Can you heal these cuts?" Yia pointed to the werewolf cuts on her chest, and the bite on her shoulder that was close to her neck.

"Only those cuts? Why not the others?"

"I need the other wounds later." She ignored Akaidi's skeptical look. "Please, can you heal them quickly? It is hard controlling the werewolf part of me. I have potions in my room that can heal bites."

"Yes, yes. Come with me."

They went to Yia's room. Yia sat on the bed and closed her eyes. The werewolf inside of her wanted to kill Akaidi more than it wanted to kill Chikara. It was cautious over Chikara, since it knew that she would be a hard foe. Akaidi was an elder. Yia knew that werewolves mostly prey on elders and children.

Akaidi looked at all the potions that were in the room. They were all made perfectly, but there were none for werewolf bites. Akaidi asked, "Where do you keep your potion making supplies? There is no potion for werewolf bites. I'm going to make one."

"In the cabinets on the mantelpiece."

Five minutes later, the potion brewing in the caldron was ready. Akaidi took an empty bottle and filled it with the potion that she had just made.

Akaidi stuck a finger into the potion and started to dab it onto the wounds. Yia knew that the potion was working. She felt the werewolf's pain. After the cuts were healed, the longing to kill Akaidi vanished completely.

Yia stood up. "Thank you Akaidi. I feel much better. I'm going to take the invisibility and sleeping spells off of Satreih. You can go back to Rasiamoramisa now."

"You came here at the right time. If you had arrived here any later, you would have transformed into a werewolf every full moon for the remainder of your life." Akaidi disappeared.

*   *   *   *

Yia walked out of her room. She snuck into Satreih's and Kaskin's room. She looked under Satreih's bed. She saw him. Even though he was under an invisibility spell, she was the only person who could see him. Yia pulled him out and placed him on top of the bed. She removed the spells. He rolled over in his sleep. He wouldn't wake until morning. Yia noticed that her blood had fallen on the floor. She cleaned it up with magic and disappeared from the room. Her next move scared her, but she didn't have any other choice.

*   *   *   *

Yia reappeared in Verteq's tower. Verteq saw her appear and hissed, "Well?"

Yia bowed low and did not get up. "My Lord, I apologize with deep regret. I could not stop Satreih from destroying the morith."

Verteq looked at her injuries. He said with mock surprise, "Your injuries have burns around them."

"Yes. Satreih owns the other legendary fire sword."

Yia left Verteq's tower. She knew she had escaped most of Verteq's anger. Even though the first snow had fallen everywhere else in the world, no snow fell on the slopes of Mt. Ogick, the volcano that Mosiania was built on.

*   *   *   *

Yia appeared in her room in Meikosa. The injuries from Satreih's sword were painful. She started to prepare a bath. The tub wasn't anything advanced, just a large boulder that had been hollowed out. The water drained to the outside. Yia found a healing potion that she had recently concocted, pouring it into the water. She started to take out her braids.

*   *   *   *

Satreih woke up. Kaskin was still asleep on the next bed. The morning sun was streaming in through the window. Satreih sat up. He felt like that he had been asleep for way too long. He checked the position of the sun in the sky. Satreih decided to see if Yia were awake. He knew that she usually got up before now.

Chikara saw Satreih leave his room. *Where are you going?*

"To see if Yia's up yet."

Chikara said, *Don't go into her room. If you do, I'm sure she'll kill you.* Chikara meant that as a warning. She could smell the bath water.

"I'll be fine."

Your funeral.

Satreih knocked on the door to Yia's room. "Yia? May I come in?" There was no answer. Satreih opened the door and walked inside. He saw that there were a lot of different kinds of potions in the room. One was empty. He thought as he read the label, *Healing Potion?*

A door on the other side of Yia's bed was closed. Satreih walked over to it. "Yia?"

From inside the room, Yia saw that the doorknob was starting to turn. "If you come in here, Satreih, I'm going to whack you so hard that you won't be able to tell the difference between night and day. You *will* die young." Yia grabbed a towel and wrapped it around her, even though she was still in the tub. She didn't care if it got wet; she could always dry it with magic. Yia also grabbed her dagger.

Satreih opened the door and instantly wished that he hadn't. A dark streak hit his head. Yia was out of the tub. She was holding the wet towel around her with one hand; her dagger in the other.

Yia hissed, "I *told* you that you would die young if you came in."

Satreih turned and ran, with Yia hitting him as hard as she could on the head with the dagger's hilt. She screamed, "Get out! Get out! Get out!"

He ran out of the room. Out of the corner of his eye, he saw that Chikara was shaking with laughter. He also saw a tree ahead of him. Satreih scurried up the tree and clung onto the trunk for dear life, careful not to make eye contact with her.

Kaskin woke to hear Satreih and Yia screaming at each other outside. As he walked out of his room, he saw that Satreih was clinging desperately to a tree; Yia was below him. Kaskin noticed that she wore only a towel and her hair was completely loose, without any braids. He didn't notice how pretty she looked without them. Her dagger was in her free hand.

"Satreih, you *pervert*!"

"I-I didn't know …!"

"I *told* you that you would die young, but you entered anyway!"

Kaskin asked, "What's going on? I'm afraid to ask." *I don't know what to think.*

Yia answered him, but her voice had venom in it. "I was taking a bath. Satreih peeked. Now I must kill him."

"Have fun." Kaskin ignored Satreih's little noise of protest.

Yia threw her dagger, but it missed its mark. Satreih had scurried to the opposite side of the trunk to avoid the projectile.

Yia stormed into her room. Kaskin and Satreih heard the door lock.

Satreih cautiously climbed down the tree. He walked over to Kaskin and shakily said, "Women are *scary*!"

"Did you really peek at her?"

"I didn't know that she was taking a bath! Anyway, the water smelled like healing herbs."

"Healing herbs?"

"Yeah." He growled. "Why did you say 'have fun'?"

Like a teacher educating a student, Kaskin held up his index finger for emphasis. "Satreih, trust me, you now know how scary some women can be when it comes to stuff like this. It's best to stay on their good side."

"Oh, so what, you didn't want to become the next target of Yia's boxing practice?"

"No, I would pass on that."

Yia came back out of her room. She was fully dressed and had her braids back in. She gave Satreih a glare that had his death warrant stretched across her face.

Satreih ducked behind Kaskin. He whispered, "Protect—me—"

Yia walked away.

FAMILY NEVER
COMPLETELY DIES

Chikara, Satreih, and Kaskin left Meikosa. Yia decided to go with them, even though she still had not forgiven Satreih.

After flying for most of the day, they stopped and made a camp on a cold, frozen plain. A lake and mountains were in the distance. There was no wood or moss around to start a fire. Yia cleared some of the frozen snow away using magic, and then lit a fire with no supplies.

Satreih and Kaskin started to spar. Satreih's broken wrist had been completely healed by Chikara, but he sparred with his left hand anyway. He thought it would be best to know how to fight with either hand. Yia put magical seals on both of their swords so they wouldn't hurt each other. She had first debated whether or not to put a seal on Kaskin's sword, but she did anyway, figuring she had given Satreih enough pain to last him a while.

Kaskin swung his sword, striking Satreih on his back. Satreih stumbled, but kept his balance. He tried to attack Kaskin, aiming for his arm.

Kaskin sidestepped. The attack didn't even come close. Kaskin switched hands, bent down, and hit Satreih's leg.

Satreih fell to the ground and sat up. He asked, annoyed, "How did you get to be so good with both hands?"

"I broke my left arm in a battle and learned to use my right."

Yia was watching them spar. She was smiling slightly. Kaskin was a much better fighter than Satreih was. She asked, "Your left arm?"

Kaskin turned to Yia and said, "Yeah. I'm left handed."

Satreih quietly got up from the ground, with his sword in hand. He walked up behind Kaskin and raised his sword. He brought it down, but without looking Kaskin swung his sword to meet Satreih's. The swords clashed. Kaskin hit Satreih on his chest with his sword. Satreih lost his balance and fell to the ground once again.

Kaskin knelt down and put his leg up against Satreih's neck, pinning him. "Never make the first move."

"The first move is okay if your opponent is not paying attention!"

"I was paying attention. I was expecting you to do that."

"How did you know that I was going to attack?"

"I know how your mind works."

Satreih muttered under his breath, "You have eyes on the back of your head, that's what."

Kaskin released Satreih, helping him up. Satreih walked over to Chikara and sat down, leaning up against her. "That's it. I'm done for tonight."

Kaskin walked over and sat down next to him. "So, what's your plan for looking for the seven remaining moriths?"

Yia said softly, "Six."

Satreih looked over to her. "Huh?"

She looked to Kaskin. "Do you remember when I went home to heal my mother?"

"Yeah."

Satreih asked, "You went home? When?"

Yia quickly glanced at him; then looked back to Kaskin. She said in a whisper, "I found a morith close to my home. I destroyed it using my dagger and magic powers."

Kaskin nodded and asked Satreih, "What do you mean, 'when'? You were there when we found Yia's note that said that she had gone home to heal her sick mother."

"I was? I don't remember it at all."

Kaskin shook his head in disbelief.

Yia got up. "Speaking of mother, I'll go see how she's doing."

Satreih said quickly, "Wait. How will you find us? I guarantee we won't be in the same spot when you come back."

"I'm a witch. I'll find out." With a wave and the swish of her cloak, Yia vanished.

I have a feeling that she likes you, Satreih.

Satreih scoffed. "She hates me. That wave was meant for you and Kaskin, not me. Those whacks from her dagger hurt! Care to feel my bruise?"

Believe me. She likes you. Just don't tell her I said that, or else my head will be next on the chopping block. It won't matter that I'm a dragon.

*   *   *   *

Satreih stayed up the rest of the night, keeping watch. Soon the sun rose over the hills in the distance, and Yia still hadn't shown up. Chikara started to stir.

Satreih studied the map. He felt certain that moriths would be near the orange dots on the map. That was his plan. Search all of the locations that contained orange dots. He couldn't think of anything else.

Satreih touched Chikara's side. "I'll go down to the lake."

Chikara yawned. *Do you need me to go with you?*

"No, I'll be fine. You can stay here with Kaskin."

The lake was huge and frozen. It took Satreih a long time to reach it. He took his fire sword from its scabbard and swung it across the ice. The ice on the entire lake melted. Satreih took a step back in surprise. He had no idea that his sword was so powerful.

He bent down and splashed some water on his face. It was cold. To Satreih, it felt like frozen needles were piercing him. He turned and looked back towards his friends. Kaskin was up.

Something wet and slimy wrapped itself around Satreih's waist, throwing him to the ground. His sword flew from his hand. He yelped in surprise, struggling to turn around. Satreih saw that the thing that had wrapped around him was a tentacle that belonged to a giant squid. His sword was out of his reach.

The giant squid started to pull Satreih into the lake. It was already getting hard for him to breathe. The giant squid pulled Satreih under the water. Just as he was pulled under, Satreih saw Chikara look over in his direction.

Satreih kicked at the giant squid. It was getting harder to see. The giant squid pulled him up to its mouth. He looked inside its mouth and saw that it had many layers of teeth. *Great. I'm going to die in the bowels of a big, elf-eating fish.*

The giant squid screeched in pain, causing Satreih to wince. It released him, and Satreih desperately swam for the surface that seemed miles above him. Below him, the giant squid was writhing in pain. It started to sink into the depths of the lake.

Satreih started to black out. He heard a splash and felt strong jaws clamp onto the back of his shirt.

Satreih was lifted up and out of the water. He was gently placed on the ground, near the edge of the lake. He lay there, trying to get his breath back. Satreih heard a familiar voice.

And you said you didn't need me.

Satreih sat up. He was shivering. "I didn't expect that to happen."

Kaskin put a hand on Satreih's shoulder. "Talk about a wake up call. What *was* that?"

"No clue. I've never seen anything like it. Some sort of a big, elf-eating fish. Brr! That water's freezing!"

Kaskin gave Satreih one of the blankets that King Thuoj had given them. Satreih took the blanket gratefully. Chikara was looking at the lake, and didn't draw her gaze away from it for a while.

Satreih asked, "What's wrong? Do you think that a morith's in that lake?"

There is no morith. I would be able to sense its evil power if it were here. I did not kill that thing. It will be back, and it will be angry. We should leave quickly, before it has a chance to come a-nibbling at us again.

Kaskin asked, "What about Yia? She still hasn't shown up yet."

Like she said, she'll find us. I have no doubt that she will.

Tentacles burst out of the water, waving angrily. They attacked, launching themselves at Chikara, Satreih, and Kaskin at an incredible speed. Satreih scooped up his fire sword. Kaskin withdrew his sword and held it up defensively, while he and Satreih backed up against Chikara.

Get on. Hurry. Chikara breathed fire at the oncoming tentacles, but it didn't have any effect. It just made them angrier. She felt that Satreih and Kaskin were on her back and she jumped into the air, flying away from the tentacles. The giant squid leapt out of the water, trying to capture its prey, but its prey was out of its reach. It roared in anger.

✳   ✳   ✳   ✳

Yia appeared on the slope of Mt. Ogick. A Wi'ok looked at her in surprise. It wrapped its arms around her. It spoke, and its voice was slow and whispered death. "You … have no business … in Mosiania. I am taking you to … the Underworld, where you … will be tortured."

A staff with a crystal on the top struck the Wi'ok's head. The Wi'ok instantly let go of Yia and looked to the new arrival.

Weuh said, "She does have business in Mosiania. Leave now, you cretin."

The Wi'ok sulked away.

Yia gave Weuh a sideways glance. "I could have attacked him myself."

"I know you could have. But Verteq would not like it if you attacked one of our own people. Besides, you came at the right time. Verteq wants a meeting with us."

They started walking toward Verteq's tower.

"He does? What for?"

"You'll find out when we get there."

Yia looked around. "Mosiania seems busy. Are you preparing for war?"

"You're very knowledgeable, as always. Yes. We are preparing for war."

"Against who?" Yia thought for a bit. "The Race of Men?"

Weuh smiled. "How did you know?" They started to climb the spiral staircase.

"The man's heart is weak. Anger, hatred, and mistrust are easily bred." Yia took a chance. "What is Verteq's overall plan?"

"If the choice were up to me, I would tell you. But the choice is Verteq's to make. He would kill me if I told you." Yia and Weuh came to the door. Weuh held it open and motioned her inside. Yia gave him a sideways glance as she walked into the room.

Verteq's back was turned to them. Yia looked at him with unblinking eyes. *He seems pleased with himself.* She noticed that Weuh had come up behind her.

Weuh asked, "Is the task complete?"

Verteq laughed softly. Weuh took that as a "yes."

Verteq turned around and looked at Yia.

She immediately felt the burning pain.

Verteq said quietly, with menace, "Why have you come to me at a time like this, when Mosiania is so busy?"

"I had a feeling that you wanted me for something."

Weuh asked, "Isn't there a meeting that Yia might want to hear?"

"There is a meeting, but it is not for her ears."

Yia asked, "Why, my Lord? Do you not trust me?"

Verteq hissed, "I know nothing of your whereabouts when you are not in Mosiania. I do not completely trust you. Do me a favor and leave the room and Mosiania."

"Yes. Of course, my Lord. I would be happy to do anything that would please you."

Yia walked outside Verteq's tower. *I remember Satreih mentioning something about his father being held captive here. If he were, he would be in the cells.*

She saw an unsuspecting pig creature sniffing the ground. Yia walked up to it, ready for anything. "You! I am in a top-rank position. Tell me the location of the cells."

The pig creature looked up. "The cells are underground. Over there," It nodded in the direction where they were situated. Smoke was rising from the area. "But if you were in a top-rank position, you would know where they are."

Yia replied with a ready lie, "So much has been happening. It slipped out of my mind. Now get back to your position and stop slacking off!" She was trying not to laugh at the creature's stupidity.

"Yes, Mistress. Right away. Sorry."

Yia found out that the cells were very depressing. Smoke could be smelled, but she didn't know where the fire was. There was a steel door. *He's in there.* Yia held her hands out, and magic specks formed around the heavy bar.

Rasnir was sitting on the slab of stone, playing with his rock. The steel door screeched and opened. *This is different. When the Spies come in, they have a key and the door doesn't make this noise.* He launched himself off the slab of stone, scurrying over to the wall. He tried to make himself as small as possible.

The door screeched open. A young woman walked into the room. If Rasnir hadn't been so terrified, he would have thought that she was pretty. She asked, "Are you Satreih's father?"

Rasnir didn't speak. Normally he wouldn't be so terrified, but the creatures of Mosiania had changed him. For some reason, this woman was different from the beasts outside. Rasnir croaked out, "Y-Yes. How do you know him?"

Yia walked over to Rasnir. She helped him up. "My name is Yia. I was severely wounded by a Spy. Satreih found my body and took me to Meikosa. They healed me there. I now travel with him. I'm helping him find and destroy the moriths. I am playing with Weuh's and Verteq's minds."

Rasnir stared at her in shock. "You are? T-That's nearly impossible. Does Satreih know that you're here?"

"No. He doesn't. I told him that I'm checking on my sick mother."

"Your mother's sick?"

"No. I no longer have a mother. She died when I was still a child."

*   *   *   *

Kaskin had his sword out and ready. He was crouching behind some rocks; his eyes were locked on his prey. A falcon. He, Chikara, and Satreih had flown to the nearby mountains after being attacked by the giant squid. It was snowing heavily.

Kaskin crept forward to the falcon. *I wish I were better at archery. I should have brought Satreih with me.* The snow crunched underneath him. The falcon squawked and flew off. "Augh!" Kaskin threw his sword at the falcon, but it missed.

*   *   *   *

"Okay. I'm stuck. There are absolutely no fire making supplies, and Yia's not with us." Satreih sat down on a big clump of snow.

Maybe you can use your sword.

"It only works when I'm fighting. It can't light fires by itself, without any fuel."

Have you tried?

"No."

Then how do you know it only works when you're fighting?

Satreih shrugged and laid the sword on the ground. It flared up and didn't go out, despite the heavily falling snow. He said, "Oh. Well, then I guess we can cook whatever Kaskin brings back."

"I didn't bring back anything."

Satreih jumped. "Kaskin! Don't sneak up on me like that! You didn't bring anything back?"

"Nothing. There's hardly any food here. The falcon that I was trying to get flew off."

I'll see if I can find anything. Chikara leapt into the air and sped off.

Satreih and Kaskin both took blankets from the supplies that they had brought with them for their journey. King Thuoj had also given them food, but they were running low and decided to save the rest for when they needed it most.

Kaskin shivered as he drew the blanket close around him, leaving none of his skin unprotected. "Brrrr! I don't like the cold. I'm more used to the heat." He scooted closer to Satreih's fire sword. "Any idea when Yia will be back? She said that she went to just check on her mother, but she's been gone for two days. Maybe she's doing chores."

"I seriously doubt that. I can't picture her doing house chores. Besides, she's a witch. It'd take her a second to do the dishes."

"Yeah, well, she could be doing other chores."

"I still doubt it." Satreih looked to the sky. "Chikara's coming back. Looks like she got something big."

"I don't see anything."

"Elves have keener eyesight than men."

Soon they were all eating. Chikara had brought back a yeti.

Kaskin said between greedy mouthfuls, "Where did you find this? I couldn't find anything." He had never tasted yeti before, but he liked it.

They blend in with their surroundings. Even if you did find one, it'd probably kill you. It took me quite some time to get this one.

∗   ∗   ∗   ∗

Satreih woke from his sleep. It was morning. Chikara and Kaskin were still sleeping. Satreih yawned and stretched. He jumped in surprise. Yia was already making breakfast. Satreih asked, still half-asleep, "What time did you come back?"

"Sometime around midnight."

"Is your mother okay? It took you some time to get back."

"Yes. She's fine. I stayed a couple days because she kept getting fevers." She put two of the eggs that she was cooking on a plate and gave it to Satreih. "We need to go to Sakametio. I've been hearing rumors that something is going to happen there."

"Sakametio? Isn't that where the men live?"

"Yeah."

"Do you think that there's a morith there?"

Yia walked over to Kaskin and placed his eggs underneath his nose. "I don't know. Maybe." *There is no morith in Sakametio. Verteq is preparing to have war there. I will lead Satreih and his friends there, but once the war starts, I'll have to leave.*

After everyone was up and had eaten something, they started traveling, trying to get out of the mountains. Satreih, Kaskin, and Yia were walking on a narrow piece of rock. It was the only way out of the mountains. On one side of them, a mountain face rose high up into the air. On the other side, there was a long drop.

Chikara was flying, since the narrow piece of rock was too small for her. She kept a careful eye on all of them, ready if anyone slipped and fell.

Suddenly, Chikara was blown into the mountain, which started an avalanche. The wind was fiercer and it started to snow harder.

Satreih looked up. The avalanche was heading toward them. He withdrew his fire sword, holding it up. The avalanche touched the tip of the sword. It melted.

Yia said, impressed, "I could have stopped it myself with magic."

Kaskin let out a low whistle.

Satreih replied, "I'm sure you could have, but it was my turn to save the day." He grinned.

Are you guys okay? Sorry about that.

Yia looked up. "We're fine." She looked around her. They were now in the middle of a blizzard. "This storm was sent by Weuh."

Satreih spun his sword and sheathed it. He had to shout, due to the fiercely blowing wind. "How do you know that?"

"I can tell! Weuh is especially skilled at creating storms!"

Satreih looked around. He could faintly make out the outlines of a cave. "Maybe we could use that cave for shelter! I think it's big enough for Chikara!" He pointed to it.

The cave was big, and it stretched off into unknown depths. Satreih asked, "What do you think, Chikara? Is it safe to venture in further?"

Yes. There are sick horses at the end, but they're the only creatures here. They won't harm us. Besides, they'll probably bolt for it when they see me.

"How many are there?"

Three.

It took a while to get to the back of the cave. As Chikara said, there were three horses. They were only skin and bones. They looked up when they heard the newcomers approach, but they were too weak to run. One was jet black with a diamond shape on its forehead, one was all brown, and the other one was brown and white.

The jet black one tried to run, but it crashed to the floor, panting. Yia walked over to it. She grabbed its muzzle and held onto it firmly, but gently. She stroked the horse's muzzle, calming it down.

Satreih used mind-speech to let the other two horses know that they were friends. Their minds weren't as clear as Chikara's, but he got the message across.

Kaskin went over to the brown and white horse and petted it. "Poor horses. I can tell that they were formidable creatures when they were well. I wonder who did this to them."

I do not know. There is a man's scent here, but it's stale. He hasn't been here in a long time. Chikara touched the horses with her flank. They looked better, but they still needed food. *I don't think we can take them with us, once we leave the cave.*

Yia was still stroking the black horse. "Why not? If we don't, they will die here." She took an apple out of her pocket.

The black horse bumped the apple with its head.

Yia scolded, "Not yet." She cut the apple into thirds with her dagger. She gave one piece to the black horse. She tossed the other two pieces to Satreih and Kaskin. They fed the pieces to the other two.

They will hinder us. I don't want to leave them, but we don't have any choice.

"If we take them with us, you won't have to carry us all the time. They might come in handy later. As Kaskin said, these were formidable horses when they were well. It wouldn't be right for them to die here, in this condition." Yia felt the horse nudging against her pocket. She looked to it and said, "No, sorry. I don't have any more."

*   *   *   *

They spent the rest of the night in the cave. Chikara agreed to take the horses. In the morning the blizzard finally stopped. They gave the horses more food. Chikara leaned up against each one. Yia used some of her magic to help heal them. The horses looked better.

Chikara, Satreih, Kaskin, and Yia moved past the last of the mountains. A vast, flat land stretched out in front of them. The land had nothing on it. The horses behind them reared up and whinnied. Kaskin calmed them down. Yia looked out onto the empty land, clenching her jaw in anger.

Satreih walked up behind her. "What?"

"They say that you can see Sakametio from here. I see nothing." *Verteq attacked fast. When I was in Mosiania, they weren't even half done with the preparations!*

Satreih took out his map. "The map says it should be here." He paused. "That horrible thing that you were telling me about the other day. Did it already happen?"

"Looks like it."

Chikara growled, *I smell rivers of blood. I don't think anyone survived.*

*   *   *   *

Soon all of them arrived at what was left of Sakametio. There were the remains of a castle. Small villages were around it, but all of them were destroyed. Bodies were strewn everywhere. Satreih looked up at Chikara. "Who did this? Was it Verteq?"

Yes.

Kaskin walked over to a fallen man. He checked his pulse. Kaskin called, "Hey! He's still alive!"

Satreih hurried over, picked him up, and leaned him against Chikara. The man had silky black hair. Satreih looked at him for a while. "He reminds me of someone."

Kaskin looked out onto the sea of corpses. "Should we start digging graves?"

"Yeah."

*   *   *   *

Usthil slowly opened his eyes. His vision was blurry, but he could make out that he was leaning against something. *I have been moved.* Usthil sniffed the air. He had never smelled this scent before, but there was no mistaking it. He was leaning up against a dragon. Usthil scrambled to his feet, trying to get away, but he fell over. *That's right. I broke my leg in the battle. Get away from me, dragon!*

Satreih, he's awake.

Satreih walked over to the man. "Don't worry. We're friends. We came down from the mountains. What happened here?"

Usthil looked at Satreih, still unsure if he were a friend or not. People claiming to be friends had tricked him many times before, and he had paid dearly for it. "We were attacked by one person."

"Verteq?"

"I couldn't see his face, but I could tell that it was definitely him." Usthil noticed that the other two people were digging graves. *Maybe they are friends.* He fearfully glanced up at Chikara.

"Don't worry. Chikara won't attack you. Dragons have remarkable healing powers. That's why I leaned you up against her."

They talked for a few more minutes. Satreih got up and started to help dig the graves. Usthil thought, *Satreih seems to be around my age. Maybe a little younger.*

He was still leaning against Chikara. He could actually feel his broken leg and his other injuries being healed. Usthil went to sleep.

*   *   *   *

Satreih, Kaskin, and Yia continued to work on the graves. They heard someone approach and looked up. It was a Wi'ok. It attacked. Satreih dodged to the side and tackled the Wi'ok, pinning it to the ground. He held his fire sword up and asked, "Why did Verteq attack?"

The Wi'ok laughed quietly. "He was … planning to attack … but it looks like the … Zorothaxs beat him to it."

"Who are the Zorothaxs? Why would they do this?"

"I do not know … of their … true nature. They have had … a grudge against the men … for generations. They plan to destroy … their entire race. Sakametio … was the first domino … in their path … of destruction. I think they plan … to attack the … Hasinis next."

Kaskin tensed. "When do they plan to attack?"

"You ask me as if … I should know … the answer to that. Why should you care … about their fate? Are you … one of them?" Without waiting for an answer, the Wi'ok threw Satreih off and disappeared.

Satreih was stunned. He didn't know that the Wi'oks could do that. He asked, "Yia, are the Wi'oks associated with witchcraft and wizardry?"

"No, but Verteq did give them the power to disappear like that."

Satreih turned to Kaskin. Kaskin looked at him in the eye and said, "I need to return to my people. I know they are unaware of the upcoming attack."

I can carry you back, if you wish.

Yia said to Chikara, "Satreih needs you more than Kaskin does." She looked at Kaskin. "I can teleport you. It will be much faster than riding on Chikara."

Kaskin nodded.

Satreih said, "Be careful."

"I will. After we defeat the Zorothaxs, I will try to find you. Don't you *dare* go into Mosiania without me. Remember, I promised that I'll help you rescue your father." Kaskin turned to Yia. "I'm ready."

Yia nodded.

Kaskin disappeared.

*   *   *   *

Usthil woke from his sleep. It was morning. All of the graves were finished. Yia and Chikara were sleeping. Satreih was sitting in a burnt tree, keeping watch. Usthil climbed up and joined him.

Satreih heard him coming up. "Hey. You're awake. Feeling better?"

"Yes." Usthil looked around. "Where's Kaskin?"

"Kaskin is the prince of the Hasini clan. A Wi'ok told us that there were plans to attack his clan. He left to help fight."

Usthil nodded. "Last night you said that I reminded you of someone. Have you remembered yet?"

"No ..." Satreih had a vision. "Wait. I have. Who's your father?"

"I never knew him. The woman who raised me was not my mother. She said that my father's name is Rasnir. Apparently he left the village, thinking that I had died."

"Rasnir suffered a very depressing life before you were born."

Usthil demanded, "How could you know that?"

"Usthil, you and I are brothers."

"We're brothers? How ...?"

"Rasnir is my adoptive father. He adopted me soon after my mother was murdered by the Spies. I don't know what happened to my real father."

Usthil asked, "So you know Rasnir? What's he like? I have—a power that normal men shouldn't."

"What's that power?"

"I can smell things like animals do."

Satreih said, "Ahhh. You inherited that from him. He has a strong sense of smell, and he has keen eyesight and hearing."

"Where is he now? Is he still alive?"

"Yes, but he's being held captive in Mosiania. That's why I left the forest that we were staying in; to go rescue him."

"Let me come with you. It would be a nice surprise for him."

"It'll be dangerous. We still need to destroy six more moriths."

"I've faced danger before. I know how to handle it."

Satreih said, "Well, it's okay with me if you come, but you might want to ask Chikara."

"We won't be riding on her all the time. You have horses, right?"

"Yes we do. We found them in the mountains a few days ago."

Usthil looked at the horses thoughtfully. "These horses. I think they're the ones that King Asuv was looking for."

"King Asuv? Is he the king of Sakametio?"

"He was the king. He died in the slaughter."

"Oh. You said he was looking for them?"

"Yes. The horses that you have discovered are the three horse rulers. They don't need saddles to be ridden. They would proudly bear a friend into unknown danger and darkness if the friend wishes. The brown horse is Maasianii, the pinto is Okanee, and the black horse is Hakku."

A FAMOUS KING
FROM THE PAST

Kaskin appeared on the ground right above his Hasini clan. He went underneath and was shocked to find that there were no people. *Have the Zorothaxs already attacked? Or had my clan already gotten wind of the attack and fled?* Kaskin walked around. Everything was burned, and the walls were charred. He searched the entire underground. In one of the lower rooms, Kaskin found a small child. She had burns all over her body. She was crying silently, with her head hidden between her legs.

Kaskin approached the child and kneeled next to her. He asked in a soft voice, "What happened?"

The small child looked up. She instantly recognized him. With a little cry of relief, she flung herself into his chest, but sobbing harder than ever.

Hugging the small child for her comfort, Kaskin softly asked again, "What happened?"

"F-Fire. Everyone ran away to the outside. I was left behind. No one knew where I was. I couldn't get out. I-I don't know where they went."

"If you come with me, I can help you find them. I'm looking for them as well." Kaskin held out his hand to the small child, and asked, "Can you walk?"

She shook her head.

"All right. No worries." Kaskin easily lifted her, planning to carry her back to the clan. "As soon as we find them, I'll get Ebony, one of the doctors, to heal you."

The child said, "T-The desert is big. How will we find them?"

"I know the desert by heart. I know where the clan would go if there's an emergency."

They went outside. Kaskin found out that the child loved to talk. She said, "Hey, the king and queen said that you went away. What for? Why did you come back? Are we in danger? How big is the desert? Have you crossed it? Is the world entirely made up of desert? Why did our clan choose to live underground? Are there—"

Kaskin interrupted. "Slow down so I have a chance to answer. I left to go help some friends after they helped us. I came back because I felt that I've been away too long. We are not in danger, for now. The desert is huge. I have crossed it. The world is not entirely made up of desert. We chose to live underground to get away from the heat and cannibals." *I don't want her to know about the Zorothaxs.*

"Oh. For now? Are we going to be in danger? Who's going to attack us? Can I help fight?"

Kaskin didn't attempt to answer any more; the child still had a stream of questions coming out of her mouth and showed no signs of stopping. Kaskin scanned the desert, looking for the Hasini clan.

He was pulled away from his thoughts when a tiny snowflake caught his eye. Kaskin caught it on his finger. *Verteq's power is growing.*

The child pulled his finger toward her, looking at the snowflake curiously. "What's this? I've never seen this before."

Kaskin was amazed that the never-ending questions came to a stop for the time being. "A snowflake. They're normally not found here, because the desert is too hot."

The child looked at the sky. "Hey! There are more of 'em! Are they dangerous? Will we die a horrible death if they touch us?"

"I touched this one, didn't I? I didn't feel pain at all."

"Maybe that one is a baby and it doesn't know how to hurt us yet." The child continued to ask endless questions about the snowflakes.

Kaskin didn't pay attention. He was lost in his own thoughts.

A group of people appeared in the distance. All but one was looking towards the sky in wonder. Two people were standing a distance away from the group.

Kaskin and the child approached. He said to the two people, "Ah. Jacob and Mithal. Doing a fine job keeping watch, eh?"

Jacob and Mithal jumped. Mithal stammered, "Y-Your Majesty! We didn't see you approach!"

"You're supposed to be keeping watch. I easily snuck up on you two."

Jacob complained, "But we were watching these!" He pointed up to the sky. "What *are* they?"

"Snowflakes. They shouldn't be here. The desert is much too hot for them. They would normally melt before being visible."

Mithal asked, "Then why are they here? Is this Verteq's doing?"

The child asked, "Who's Verteq?"

Kaskin didn't answer her. He said to Mithal, "That's what I think."

A woman ran over and hugged the child, taking her from Kaskin's arms. "You're okay! Thank goodness!" The woman looked up to Kaskin. "Thank you. Did you find her?"

Kaskin nodded. "She was still in the Underground."

"Well, I'm glad she's safe." She muttered, mostly to herself, "I'll have to do something about those burns."

Kaskin offered, "Ebony's always willing, unless she has her hands full."

Without waiting for a reply, Kaskin walked over to his father. He was sitting next to someone who was lying on the ground. She was completely covered in a blanket. Kaskin's father had a worried expression on his face.

Without looking up, he said, "You've returned to us, Kaskin. Why is it snowing here? In the desert? Is Verteq getting more powerful?"

"Yes." Kaskin lowered his voice, so only his father could hear. "Have you heard of the Zorothaxs?"

"Yes. You should know of them, too. They are our allies."

"I wouldn't think so. They attacked Sakametio, or what was left after Verteq went through. There's nothing left of the place."

King Helioff looked up, surprised. "They attacked Sakametio?"

Kaskin nodded. "They're coming for us next."

"Huh. We have been allies with them for generations. They will not attack us."

"I hope you're right. Who are they?"

"Cloaked men and elves. They are powerful. I wonder why they attacked Sakametio."

"Maybe Verteq convinced them to." Kaskin changed the subject. "Who's that?" He nodded to the person on the ground.

"Your mother. She's been ill ever since you left. I've had her covered up in a blanket because of the snow, trying to keep her warm."

A few days passed. Two inches of snow already covered the ground. The nights seemed longer. The moon and stars were never in the sky. There was some talk about heading back into the Underground. Three scouts were sent back to see if the Underground was once again safe to enter.

During his free time, Kaskin introduced the concept of a snowball fight to the children. They were restless, and they welcomed the chance to have some fun. Kaskin made it a point not to have snowball fights with the sand.

The scouts returned a few hours later. The king approached them and asked, "Well? Is it safe to enter?"

"There is still fire raging below."

Kaskin walked over. "There is? When I went underground, there were only traces of fire." He felt something pulse from inside one of the scout's pockets. Kaskin looked at the scout and demanded, "Empty your pockets."

"B-But Y-Your Majesty, there is nothing in them."

"You lie."

"A-All right! I found a ruby gem, and it was hard to retrieve it. I don't want to give it up."

"Are you a dwarf? Give me the gem. It is for your own good."

The scout hesitantly withdrew the gem and placed it on the ground at Kaskin's feet. Kaskin took out his sword and stabbed the morith. It was destroyed instantly. Its pieces shattered everywhere.

The scout complained, "Your Majesty! I went through a lot of trouble to get that!"

That was too easy. What is Verteq planning? "Only a dwarf would think that the gem is precious. Anyone else should have easily realized that the ruby was evil."

The scout sulked away.

✳   ✳   ✳   ✳

Satreih and Usthil were riding on Maasianii and Okanee, racing. Yia had disappeared again, saying that she needed to check on her mother. Hakku was running alongside them. Chikara was flying above them.

Satreih was scanning the land for any sign of a morith. Usthil flew by him and won the race. The finish point was a boulder.

Usthil smiled and asked, "What's wrong? Is Okanee a bit too fast for you?"

"No. I let you win. I was just looking out for any moriths."

Satreih heard Kaskin's voice inside of his mind. *I destroyed a morith.*

You did? When?

Just now. It was too easy. One of the scouts had it. I stabbed the morith once with my sword, and it was destroyed. My sword is not that powerful.

Just once? Maybe Verteq has something else in mind.

Maybe. Just letting you know.

Usthil called over, "Hey! Look at this!" He had climbed off of Okanee and was staring at the ground.

Satreih came over and stood next to him. There was a big hole in the ground that seemed to lead to somewhere. Both Satreih and Usthil felt something pulse from inside.

Usthil pulled out his bow and arrows and jumped inside.

Satreih heard him fall on the ground. It was too dark to see anything inside. Satreih called, "Usthil? Are you okay?"

Usthil's voice echoed from below. "Yeah. I think so. Bend your knees before you hit the ground! It's a big fall."

"I don't know if I'll hit you!"

"You won't. I moved out of the way. Jump!"

You don't have to. Chikara flew inside the hole, since it was big enough for her. Satreih jumped on her back and they flew toward the bottom.

Satreih took out his fire sword and the hole lit up. It was a cave with several tunnels leading in different directions.

Usthil came up behind Satreih. "I think the sword will come in handy. Erm, which way shall we go?"

They felt something pulse from one of the tunnels ahead of them. Satreih said, "That way," and pointed toward the tunnel with his sword.

The tunnel was long. At the end, it opened up into a cavern. On the far side of the room, an old elf was sitting in a chair, hunched over. He was breathing heavily. The morith pulsed within him.

*   *   *   *

Kaskin looked over the desert. He couldn't even tell that it was once a desert. It was now a frozen wasteland. The snow underneath him started to churn. Kaskin withdrew his sword and tried to get off of the churning spot.

Kaskin was thrown high up into the air. He landed heavily. The fall knocked the wind out of him. He heard his warriors shouting to each other to attack something. Kaskin sat up. His sword was out of reach.

In front of Kaskin, there was a huge beast of some sort. It looked like an overgrown phoenix. But unlike the gentle birds from the legends, this one was evil. Its wings shimmered with the broken pieces of the morith. One piece was immensely huge, seemingly housing more evil than the others, if that were possible. The large piece was on its chest.

*   *   *   *

The old elf looked directly at Satreih. "So. You are the next chosen one?"

Satreih nodded. "Who are you? What happened?"

"My name is Meithoko."

Usthil said, "You can't be Meithoko. The story says that he was murdered by brigands."

Meithoko snapped, "Do you believe everything you hear?" He said more quietly, "I escaped from the brigands, seeking refuge in a nearby volcanic spring. Verteq was there, the one that I had killed so long ago. He replaced my heart with one of his moriths, then moved me here. I am unable to move from this spot. The morith is torturing me. Satreih, come here."

Meithoko took something that was hanging around his neck and held it out to Satreih. He said in mind-speech, *The necklace is powerful. As long as it is in your possession, you and your loved ones will live long lives.*

*   *   *   *

Kaskin shouted to his archers, "Aim for the large piece on its chest! Distract it!" The phoenix attacked his men as Kaskin made a mad dash for his sword. He was out in the open. Kaskin scooped up the sword. He threw it towards the large piece, since none of his archers had managed to hit it yet. The phoenix saw it coming, easily batting it out of the way. Kaskin thought, *So. I was right. That is the weak spot.* The phoenix thrust its beak forward, aiming for Kaskin. Kaskin stumbled, trying to get out of the way, but knew he wasn't going to be fast enough.

The spirit of a woman appeared in front of Kaskin, repelling the attack. The phoenix was thrown backwards as the pieces of the morith exploded from its skin. It lay on the ground, panting. The fire that usually was enveloping its body dimmed almost to the point of extinguishing.

Kaskin followed the spirit's lead in walking over to the phoenix. The spirit lightly placed her hands on the phoenix's head, making comforting noises, apparently in its language.

Kaskin cautiously reached forward, touching the phoenix's feathery side. To his surprise, it felt cool to his touch, even after it regained its fire. He and the spirit watched as it shakily flew off.

As the spirit watched the phoenix fade into the distance, she said, "That phoenix is the guardian of the Sakki desert. His name is Thorax. To see Verteq gain control over proud beasts like him, sickens me."

Kaskin nodded, agreeing with her. "Do you know how Verteq gained control over him?" he asked, knowing that the morith alone could not subdue him.

"That I do not know." The spirit paused. "My son needs you more than your clan does. Leave them in my care. Your mother will recover in no time."

*   *   *   *

Meithoko said softly, "Please. Kill me."

Usthil looked at him in disbelief. "Why? We do not kill needlessly."

"The morith is torturing me. My body cannot function properly. I cannot eat, drink, or move any part of my body at will. I would regain composure as a spirit. Verteq may be powerful, but thankfully, he has granted me no further punishment after death."

Is this truly what you want?

Meithoko nodded. "Death would be a relief. Killing me would also destroy the morith that is my heart. It is the only way that you can destroy it, ultimately, the only way to destroy Verteq. The hourglass of my life is empty. Please, I beg you, shatter it completely. I have no need to live life any longer."

Chikara nodded, if somewhat uncertainly. The morith burst from Meithoko's chest. It lay on the floor at their feet, beating like a human heart. It exploded once it realized it was out of its host.

Meithoko looked peaceful, finally at rest.

Usthil gasped, "What—?"

I took his life, like he wanted. Right before he died, he said that he wanted to be laid to rest in Meikosa. His heart is back to normal.

*   *   *   *

Chikara flew out of the hole slowly. Meithoko was on her back. Even though he was relatively light, Chikara could not bear Satreih and Usthil. They had to climb out of the hole themselves.

Chikara saw that Yia was sitting on Hakku. Yia's eyes were wide with wonder. "Is that Meithoko?"

Yes. He wants to be laid to rest in Meikosa.

Even though they were very far away from Meikosa, it only took them a few days to get there. The horses were faster than any other, and did not need to take a rest. Usthil stayed at the place where Sakametio used to be, to rebuild it to its former glory.

Satreih saw that there was a man standing next to the concrete wall. Satreih waved. "Kaskin! What are you doing here? I thought you went back to protect your clan?"

"I did, but I came back. I met your mother. She said that you needed me more than my clan does. She'll protect them."

Satreih and Chikara met with King Thuoj. King Thuoj had Meithoko's body placed inside the hall where other great Meikosan kings rested. There was no funeral service due to Meithoko's request.

VENGEFUL SPIRIT

Kaskin was alone in the library. A dusty book was open on a nearby table. A spider was crawling on it. The title of the page caught his interest. In the lower right hand corner of the page, there was a picture of a necklace. The necklace had a diamond pendant, with two silver dragons spiraling around each other and the diamond.

THE NECKLACE OF EIÉONER

Eiéoner was the strongest of all dragons. He gave a diamond necklace to Meithoko after he defeated Verteq. The necklace had special powers. One of its two silver dragon pendants gives the bearer and his loved ones long life, unless they die in battle. The other dragon gives great health to the bearer and loved ones.

The necklace was said to have vanished after Meithoko was murdered, which caused all of his loved ones to die. This theory was proven to be incorrect. Chikara was seen with a newborn baby after the necklace "vanished." People assumed that she was powerful, so she somehow avoided the

The rest of the words were faded and could not be read. Kaskin tried to make them out, but it was futile. He thought, *So Satreih's mother was a friend of Meithoko's.*

All of the candles that were in the library suddenly went out, and the book shut on its own. Kaskin felt that there was somebody breathing down his neck. He turned around, but nobody was there.

$$* \qquad * \qquad * \qquad *$$

Satreih and Yia were walking around. They noticed that everyone had fear in their eyes. A thick fog was covering the ground and wouldn't go away. A Meiko-san warrior approached.

Satreih asked him as he approached, "What's going on? Why is everyone so tense?"

The warrior walked past Satreih and didn't stop. He whispered, "I don't know. People are claiming that there is a spirit. I don't believe in such things, but still—" He disappeared around a corner.

Satreih looked at Yia. "Is there a spirit?"

"Yes. I can feel its vibrations."

"Okay. I can fight it."

Yia laughed softly. "Do you know anything about fighting spirits?"

"No. But my mother is a spirit, and she was the one who let us out of the prison in Rasiamoramisa."

"Let me rephrase that. Do you know anything about fighting *vengeful* spirits? Besides, your mother is on your side, so she doesn't count."

"Uhh … no. Is there a difference between fighting regular spirits and fighting vengeful ones?"

"Oh yeah. Fighting vengeful spirits is a lot more dangerous, especially if you don't know how to fight them. Let me handle this one."

Satreih asked, "How do you know that this is a vengeful spirit?"

"The fog. There are spirits everywhere. The fog only rises when there's a vengeful spirit around. Also, its vibrations are more evil."

"What happens if the vengeful spirit defeats you?"

"Your soul goes to Hell automatically, even if you've been good all of your life."

"Oh-kaaay. That's kind of creepy." Satreih edged a little closer to Yia.

"Creepy is one of the things that you'll have to worry about the least. Let me handle this one."

"Right, right. But what if it defeats you?"

Yia said confidently, "It won't."

Satreih changed the subject. The thought of there being vengeful spirits around spooked him. "Where's Kaskin?"

"I heard that he was in the library; with his nose stuck in some book."

A voice came from behind them, "Not any more."

Satreih jumped and said, "I thought you liked reading."

"I do. But—some things happened that I can't explain."

Yia asked, "Oh? Things like what?"

"Well, I got the feeling that I really shouldn't be there, the candles suddenly went out with no warning, and the book shut by itself."

Satreih glanced at Yia. "I think he found your spirit."

"Yeah. See you two later." Yia walked off, heading towards the library.

Kaskin looked at Satreih curiously. "There's a spirit?"

"Yup. A vengeful one."

"And Yia thinks that she can kill it?"

Yia's voice echoed in both of their minds. *I'm not going to kill it. I'm going to disintegrate it. You can't kill spirits. They're already dead.* She drew away.

Kaskin said, "That was creepy. How did she know what we were saying? You can only use mind-speech to talk to people, not eavesdrop on their thoughts."

Satreih shrugged. "She is a witch."

Yia was not inside the library, but in the hall where the kings of Meikosa lay resting. She walked over to where Meithoko's body lay. He was encased inside a silver, see-through coffin. His body was slightly glowing. Yia thought, *So Chikara gave him a gift. His body will never decay.*

Yia placed her hand on the coffin. She asked in mind-speech, *Who is the vengeful one? What does he wish?*

Even though he was dead, Meithoko's voice came back to her. *Who are you? Answer me.*

My name is Yia. I am a friend of Satreih's. Who is the vengeful one?

His name is Awitl. He is one of the Zorothaxs. That is all I can tell you. I know no more. Please, let me rest in peace. Meithoko's voice drew away and didn't return.

Yia walked into the library. She definitely got the feeling that she shouldn't be there. The air was musty. It was hard for her to breathe. The fireplace and the candles were out.

Yia said loudly and clearly, "Awitl, I summon you!"

A bluish-whitish figure appeared in one of the leather chairs. His head was bowed. His cloak hung off of him like a rag. Awitl looked at Yia angrily and seethed, "What do you want?"

"To ask you what you want. You should not be here. Your time on this cursed earth is over."

Awitl came close. He hissed, "Why would a human care? Humans do not understand us!"

Without blinking, Yia answered, "I'm not a normal human. Tell me what you want. Everyone in Meikosa senses your presence, even those who do not believe in spirits."

"You say that as if I should care."

"If you don't leave this cursed earth willingly, then I will disintegrate you."

Awitl's eyes grew livid. "You, a mere mortal, dares to threaten me?"

"I do threaten you. Tell me what you want. I will give it to you, if I can. I won't back down, no matter how much you try to scare me."

"I want the destruction of all beings that oppose the Zorothaxs and Verteq."

"Not a chance," Yia growled. "I must disintegrate you."

Awitl laughed. "And how do you plan to disintegrate me, puny human?"

"Do not underestimate me." Yia focused her mind on Awitl, concentrating all of her powers. Awitl shrieked in anger.

His shriek cut right through Yia's heart, which made her suddenly realize how disastrous her game with Verteq and Weuh could end. Awitl burst into light as he disappeared. Yia fell to the ground, unconscious.

*   *   *   *

Kaskin headed toward the library. He wanted to know if Yia had disintegrated the spirit yet. If she had, Kaskin wanted to read or try to decipher more of the book.

He heard a shriek of anger. Kaskin ran toward the sound and opened the door to the library. The fire and candles were lit. He saw that Yia was on the ground, and not moving. Kaskin ran over to her and put his fingers on her neck, searching for a pulse. He breathed a sigh of relief. *Phew. She's only unconscious. But that shriek. That wasn't hers. Maybe it was the spirit.*

*   *   *   *

Yia's eyes opened. She was in the same room where she had woken up after fighting the Spy.

Satreih was sitting in a chair, next to the bed. "Hey. You're awake. Are you all right?" He pressed his canteen into her hands.

Yia gratefully took the canteen and took a sip. "Yeah. I'm fine. How long was I unconscious?" She gave the canteen back.

"Only a couple of hours. Did the spirit attack you?"

"No, he didn't. I just used a spell that was a little complicated for me to disintegrate the spirit."

"Maybe I should keep an eye on you more often."

Yia asked, "Why? Don't you trust me?"

"I mostly do. You hurt yourself a lot." Satreih paused. "And I doubt that you disappear to check on your mother. You're gone for days at a time."

Yia got out of the bed, angry. She glared at Satreih and said coldly, "You have no idea how much pain I have endured for you."

Satreih watched her leave the room. He thought, stunned, *Where did* that *come from?*

Yia didn't know where she was going to go, but she let her feet guide her.

Kaskin saw Yia walking alone. He walked up to her. "You're awake." He noticed that she looked angry, and that she was blatantly ignoring him. "What's—?"

Yia interrupted him. "Please leave me alone. If you're so concerned about what happened go ask Satreih. I won't tell you." She disappeared into the forest.

Kaskin found Satreih. Satreih walked up to him and asked, "Where'd Yia go?"

Kaskin pointed. "Somewhere over there, in the forest. What's going on? Why was she suddenly so angry?"

"Something I said. I told her that I didn't believe that she was disappearing to go check on her mother."

"Did you tell her that immediately after she woke up?"

"We talked for a little bit first, but I pretty much told her that right away. Maybe I should've waited a bit. She replied, 'you have no idea how much pain I have endured for you,' and then left. Any idea what that means?"

"No. Why don't you go talk to her and try to find out where her head is."

A half hour later, Satreih found Yia sitting on the bank of a pond. The soft, dim moonlight reflected off of the water. Yia's back was facing him. Her head was buried in her knees.

Satreih approached and sat down next to her. Yia turned her head away from him. She did not want him to see her tears.

Satreih said softly, "Yia, I'm sorry if you took what I said the wrong way. But I had to tell you how I felt."

"No. It was my fault. I shouldn't have gone off on you like that. The fight with the spirit …" Yia was still trying to stop the flow of tears.

"I'm glad you did. I could tell that you were upset about something, but I didn't know what."

Yia faced Satreih. "And you want me to tell you?"

Satreih nodded. He wiped away her tears with a gentle finger.

Yia said, "I can't. Not completely. I will tell you this: an unbearably heavy burden has been placed on my shoulders. I can't tell you what it is. The one who placed it there will kill me. I cannot be freed from his grasp."

Satreih pulled Yia up onto his lap and held her. He expected her to try to break away, but she didn't. Satreih said, "I will free you from his grasp, and from this burden; no matter how complicated it is."

Far above them, Chikara and Kaskin were watching. Chikara's voice entered Kaskin's mind, *Awwww! They're so cute!*

Kaskin complained, "Who are? I can't see a thing."

Fine. You can watch through my eyes.

Kaskin felt himself being pulled away from his body. He lost control of it. The next second, he was watching Satreih and Yia, but from Chikara's point of view.

Kaskin had no control of his mouth. He asked in mind-speech, *What did you just do?*

I pulled you from your body so you can watch. Look.

Chikara looked at Kaskin's body. It sat there, not moving an inch. Its eyes were glassy, as if Kaskin's body was being hypnotized.

Kaskin said in mind-speech, *Okay. This is creepy. Stop looking at me! I want to see Satreih and Yia.*

As you wish. Chikara turned her head so that they were looking at the two below.

Satreih and Yia stayed like that for a while, his head resting on hers. Satreih looked up, and saw the silhouettes of Chikara and Kaskin. Without taking his eyes off them, he asked, "Hey, Yia?"

"Mmm?" Yia was nearly asleep.

"Do you know any repelling spells?"

Yia looked up at him and said, "I know a couple. Why do you ask?"

"Look at the sky."

Yia looked up, and saw Chikara and Kaskin. "The repelling spells that I know will severely hurt them. But I can teleport them somewhere else without injuring them."

"Okay. Do that."

Uh-oh. Satreih sees us.

We're too high up.

You're forgetting. Elves have much keener eyesight than men do.

Kaskin looked around. They were in the dining hall; he was back in his own body.

What just happened?

"Yia teleported us. I guess she saw us, too, or Satreih told her." He started to walk out the door. Chikara followed him.

Yia kissed Satreih on the cheek. "Thanks. I needed that." She got up and walked away, heading to the room that King Thuoj had given her. Satreih followed her. The room he shared with Kaskin was right next to Yia's.

Outside the two rooms, Chikara and Kaskin were talking. They backed away when they saw Satreih and Yia approach. Yia went into her room without a word. Satreih whacked Chikara and Kaskin lightly on their heads.

As Satreih was about to go inside his room, Kaskin complained, "Hey! What did you hit me for? We were too high up for me to see anything!"

"You saw us somehow." Satreih disappeared into his room.

TEACHINGS FROM A
UNICORN

Chikara, Satreih, Kaskin, and Yia left Meikosa early in the morning. Satreih wanted to find and destroy the remaining four moriths quickly.

The daylight lasted for only a few hours. It got dark again quickly. There were no stars and no moon. Snow was completely covering the ground, even though it was spring. Verteq's power was growing by the second.

They found a place to rest an hour later. They were outside the borders of a forest. All the trees, including the evergreens, were leaf bare and dead.

Satreih was leaning up against Chikara, taking a small nap. Chikara was napping as well. Yia stood, watching the forest. She felt something evil in its heart. A shadow silently moved between the trees. Yia watched it. She slowly bent down and picked up Satreih's bow.

Kaskin saw what she was doing. "What?"

Yia whipped around to face him, and put a finger to her lips. Two vines rushed toward Yia, wrapping themselves around her. Other vines wrapped themselves around Chikara, Satreih, and Kaskin. Chikara and Satreih immediately woke up, struggling to get free. More vines came. Some shut Chikara's mouth so that she couldn't breathe fire. The others took Satreih's, Kaskin's, and Yia's weapons.

The vines lifted them off their feet, moving them into the depths of the forest. After a while, the vines placed them back down, but in a prison that was made from Laxuivies bark.

Satreih muttered under his breath, "Great. I'm in prison again for no good reason."

Kaskin walked up to a wall. He asked in wonder, "What type of bark is this? I've never seen anything like it." He reached out to the wall.

Chikara warned, *I wouldn't touch it if I were you.*

"Why not?"

Satreih answered, "It's Laxuivies bark. It'll make your hands bleed if you touch it." He called to the moving shadow outside the cell. "Who are you? Some type of forest-dwelling dwarf who enjoys putting elves in prison?"

The shadow spoke. "Hah! Dwarfs! That's a good joke. We care nothing for priceless gems."

"Then who are you?"

The shadow moved forward. He was a centaur. "My name is Castelo. I am the king of the centaurs." King Castelo ran his hand along the door to the cell. Although the door was made of Laxuivies bark, his hand didn't bleed.

The door groaned. It sunk underneath the ground.

King Castelo asked, "I believe that these are your possessions?" He held up their weapons. They all nodded.

King Castelo returned the weapons. He turned around and walked away. He said without looking back, "Come with me."

The king of the centaurs led them toward a building that seemed to be made of the forest's trees. It must have been made when the trees were still alive. The buildings were the only things that were green.

Once inside the building Castelo asked, "What brings you to these parts?"

Yia answered, "We felt something evil stir in the heart of this forest."

Castelo snorted. "As it goes for the rest of the earth. This forest is safe, even from Verteq. It has always been safe."

Chikara growled slightly. *Are you blind? All of the trees are dead, snow is covering the ground in spring, and night fell in the morning.*

"I am not blind, young dragon. I know that the earth is crumbling. Besides the trees being dead, the snow, and the early night, nothing evil is in the forest." King Castelo looked irritated.

Satreih asked, "May we stay here for a few days? If there is something evil in the forest—I'm not saying that there is—we can destroy it."

"Yes, you may stay. Rooms will be given to you." King Castelo paused. "Satreih, after you get settled in your room, come back here. A very good friend of mine wants to meet you."

As usual, Satreih and Kaskin shared a room, and Yia had her own. Chikara stayed in the forest, out of sight.

*　　*　　*　　*

Satreih walked back to find King Castelo. The king of the centaurs was gone.

Satreih thought, *What do I do now?* His answer was a feeling that he had to go somewhere. He followed that feeling out of the building and further into the forest. It was a good feeling, one that filled him with hope. Satreih didn't care that he was heading deeper into the forest, even though there was the possibility that a morith was nearby.

Satreih found himself in a clearing when the feeling stopped. He looked into the distance, and saw something hurtling itself towards him with a speed that he couldn't believe. He couldn't see its true form. It was just a blur. The trees around it seemed to come alive for a second, but then returned to their normal dead states after it had passed them.

He bent his legs, preparing to spring out of the way if the thing had any intention of running him over. He realized that he shouldn't have bothered; the thing came to an abrupt stop right in front of him.

Satreih stared in awe and wonder. Before him was a unicorn. All the trees around the clearing sprang to life when the unicorn placed its hooves into the clearing. The unicorn was so white that it made the snow look a very dark shade of gray.

Satreih gasped, "Y-You're the friend that King Castelo wanted me to meet?"

The unicorn spoke with a voice that rang through the forest. "Yes. And you are Satreih, the chosen one?"

Satreih nodded. "Yeah, but I can't say that I'm happy about it. Who chose me? You?"

"I did not choose you." The unicorn nodded at the sword that was strapped to Satreih's side. "The sword did."

"It did?" Satreih asked, dumbfounded. "How?"

"I do not know the details. It is a very powerful sword. It can obliterate an army of ten thousand—no matter the race—in a single swing. That is the extent of its power. Only one person besides Verteq ever mastered it. His name was Satreih. Yes, you were named after him."

Satreih asked, "I was? What happened to him?"

"He fought with Verteq several times. The last battle they shared ended with Satreih's death. Satreih obtained magic from a friend and attacked Verteq's body with it. Verteq reversed the spell, instantly killing Satreih. The sword was broken because its master was lost. It was entrusted to the Hasini clan of the Sakki Dessert."

Satreih asked, "What of Verteq?" He was no longer interested in the unicorn's beauty; the forgotten legend was all that he could focus on.

"Verteq was once a wizard. But having been attacked by magic, his own magical powers were suddenly drained. He didn't know the reason why. He was weakened for centuries. Peace was returned to the earth. Day began to show its lovely face again; all the perpetual snows thawed. Century after century, the earth knew only peace. No wars were ignited. All needs and requirements were easily fulfilled.

"Verteq eventually recovered over centuries. Darkness returned to the earth. Wars were brewed. Mouths could not be fed. Meithoko, amongst others, realized what was happening. He ended the longevity of darkness and winter by killing Verteq."

Satreih asked, "So Meithoko never owned the fire sword?"

"He never did. The only reason he defeated Verteq was because he called upon the powers of ice; the same power that was honed by the mythical Ice Goddess."

Satreih thought, *So when I kill Verteq, if I kill Verteq, I will die a horrible death afterwards?*

The unicorn said, "Yes, you will die a horrible death. Unless you find a way of cleansing the earth of Verteq forever." The unicorn started to walk away. "You do not know the extent of your power. If you fight Verteq in your current condition you will certainly die a horrible death. This is all we will discuss for tonight. Tomorrow night I will teach you the ways of that sword." The unicorn dashed away, but Satreih heard its mind-speech. *A sword is not powerful if it is in hands that do not know how to use it.*

*   *   *   *

Satreih walked into his room, and felt Kaskin's eyes on him. Satreih looked over at him and exclaimed, "Wow! You're still awake! Usually by now you're asleep, judging from the amount of darkness."

"I was waiting for your return. Who was the friend that King Castelo wanted you to meet?"

"A unicorn."

Kaskin let out a low whistle. "Really? There are fewer unicorns than there are dragons."

"Yeah, it was a real unicorn. Beautiful, too. It told me that my fire sword could wipe out an army of ten thousand of any race in a single swing. Did you know that it could do that?"

Kaskin answered, "Yup. It was told as legend to the children of the Hasini clan, but I thought it was just a myth. I think the other children did, too."

*   *   *   *

Satreih waited for the unicorn in the same clearing. A feeling of hope was all around him. He knew that the unicorn was not far away.

A voice came from behind Satreih. "Well, you still need to improve your senses. Even though I make the dead trees come to life, and give everyone around me an intense feeling of hope, I still had no trouble sneaking up on you."

Satreih whirled around, shocked. "I thought you were coming from the same direction as you did last night. Besides, I'm not like my father."

The unicorn was standing right behind him, looking bored. "Rasnir was given an unusual gift for a man." The unicorn changed the subject. "Come at me with the fire sword. I want to see how much you've improved on your own."

"But—"

"No buts. I am immortal. Even with that blade, you cannot kill me. Come at me."

Satreih withdrew his fire sword, raised it, and charged at the unicorn. He attempted to attack with one of the moves that Kaskin had taught him. The unicorn moved to the side with very little effort, stabbing Satreih in the chest with its horn.

Satreih felt like he was falling into oblivion. He woke, and he was lying on the ground. His fire sword was still clutched in his hand. He felt to the place where the unicorn had stabbed him, but there was no wound. Satreih looked to the unicorn in confusion.

The unicorn said, "A good attack, but you left yourself wide open."

"W-What just happened?"

"I killed you. That feeling of falling into oblivion is the same feeling that you'll get if you are killed by a foe."

"Okay. But if you killed me, then why am I still—?" Satreih was still on the ground.

"You died, but since I am immortal, I have the power to trap your soul here if I wish. You are not injured either. I also have the power to wound and kill, but the injury heals itself. Come at me with the sword again. Do not leave yourself out in the open."

Satreih was "killed" three more times before he went back to the room that he shared with Kaskin. He was tired and a little sore.

A REQUEST FROM
THE DWARF KING

King Castelo agreed to keep the horse rulers in a safe place nearby. He told Satreih that horses, centaurs, and men were distant cousins.

Satreih, Kaskin and Yia spent their time learning about the centaur culture. They learned that they called their city Starlitih. Chikara hid deeper in the forest. Only the king had seen her. He had not yet told everyone else that there was a dragon in their midst. When Satreih wasn't busy learning about the centaurs, he spent his time with Chikara.

The time soon came when there was no light at all, even during the "day." Everyone was having difficulty adjusting, especially Kaskin. The centaurs liked the night, but only if there were stars. In Verteq's everlasting night, there were no stars.

*   *   *   *

Satreih, Kaskin, and Yia were walking together, talking. They all noticed that the women and children centaurs seemed to be going somewhere. They all looked a little depressed.

King Castelo approached the three of them. "Yia, I'd like to see you, please." He walked away.

Chikara's voice echoed in all of their minds. *He wanted me, too. I'm already inside his house.*

Yia asked, *What does he want us for?*
No idea.

Inside the building, Chikara and Yia were facing King Castelo. Satreih and Kaskin weren't invited to the meeting.

King Castelo said, "The war against Verteq is fast approaching. The Dwarf King has ordered that all women and children from all races be temporarily placed underneath the mountain of Rasiamoramisa until the war ends. Everyone else will be automatically drafted."

Yia burst out, "This is insanity! If Verteq finds out about this, he'll attack the place where everyone is cowering! The Dwarf King has no right to order people from other races to do his bidding!"

Satreih and Kaskin cannot be drafted. Much larger responsibilities have been placed in their hands. Chikara was just as surprised at this request as Yia was.

King Castelo countered, "All the kings met in Meikosa to discuss the plan. Frankly, we all agreed to the Dwarf King's wishes. How would you feel if your children never felt the warmth of sunshine on their faces, and you could have done something to prevent it?"

Yia growled, "It will only be a matter of time before Verteq attacks the place underneath the mountain. Having all the woman and children kept there will prove to be genocide for all races. Verteq will win the war."

"It was the Dwarf King's idea, not mine. I just agree with him. And I'm asking if the two of you will go. If Verteq does decide to attack, you two will be able to defend everyone else."

Chikara snorted with disdain, *I don't care how powerful we are. Verteq will know that we will be there. He'll attack with numbers.*

King Castelo took a threatening step towards Chikara. "I am not going to argue with you. You have no choice in the matter. You're only allowed to bring five belongings with you." King Castelo started to walk out of the building.

*   *   *   *

Satreih asked, "Yia? What's going on?" He sensed her anger, hoping that none of it was aimed at him.

They were inside Yia's room. Yia was making her caldron and some potions smaller so she could carry them easier. She wouldn't follow the rules. She could teleport her belongings to Akaidi's shack, if need be.

Yia grudgingly answered, "Apparently the Dwarf King has ordered every woman and child from all races to stay underneath Rasiamoramisa for the duration of the war with Verteq. Everyone else will be drafted. The other kings agree with him."

"What!"

Yia growled. "That's what he said. Since I'm a woman, I have to go … and Chikara has to go as well."

Satreih was getting angry at this news. "He can't do that! I need you and Chikara with me!"

"Both Chikara and I want to stay with you. But we have no choice. Chikara's not happy with this new development either."

Satreih argued, "Hey, you're a witch, right? Can't you make yourself and Chikara appear as men?"

"I could, but Castelo knows that I'm a witch. He'll notice if two new men begin to hang around you and Kaskin." Yia's anger was mostly diffused. Talking with Satreih helped. She added, while walking out of her room, "Not many women or children can fight—that's the sad truth. When Verteq does decide to attack, Chikara and I will be right up front to defend them."

Satreih followed Yia to the top of a hill. Chikara was there. The women and children centaurs were still leaving their homes. Yia watched them for a while and said, "They do not know where they are going. Chikara and I will lead them to Rasiamoramisa."

Chikara took her eyes off the centaurs and nudged Satreih's shoulder affectionately with her head. *Try not to worry about us too much. Yia and I are capable of taking care of ourselves.*

Satreih asked, "You'll come back to me after this war is over, right?"

Yia quickly climbed onto Chikara's back. She smiled mischievously. "Bet on it."

With a quick, worried glance towards Satreih, Chikara jumped into the sky and flew off.

As Satreih watched the silhouettes of Chikara and Yia get further and further away, he couldn't tell which emotion was stronger: annoyance, anger, sadness, or fear. He was already afraid for all of his friends, and for himself. He darkly wondered if this split up was all according to Verteq's plan.

Even though he was unsure of the future, Satreih got a feeling of hope that vanquished all other emotions. He didn't understand it at first, but then realized that the unicorn was trying to call him.

Before Chikara and Yia were completely out of sight, Satreih started to head down the hill.

*   *   *   *

Kaskin called for his friends. He hadn't seen all of them for a while. He saw Satreih in the distance. Kaskin jogged up to him and exclaimed, "There you are! Wait! What's going on? Where are Chikara and Yia?"

"They're gone."

Kaskin waited politely for Satreih to explain.

Satreih said, "The Dwarf King has ordered all women and children from all races to move to an underground place in Rasiamoramisa for the duration of the war. Everyone else will be drafted. The other kings agree with him."

Kaskin asked with wide eyes, "So that means Chikara and Yia have to go?"

Satreih nodded. "They've already gone."

Kaskin looked to the ground, thinking. He looked back up and said quietly, "There won't be enough room for everyone."

"My thoughts exactly." The feeling of hope got stronger and more insistent. "I have to go. The unicorn is trying to call me."

Satreih left Kaskin alone with his thoughts.

The unicorn was already in the clearing by the time Satreih arrived. Satreih asked, "Is this split up part of Verteq's plan?"

"No. Your friends will survive the attack when it comes, but Yia's life will be in extreme danger."

There was a long pause. Satreih asked, "Who is going to hurt her?" He thought for a bit. "The person who put the unbearably heavy burden on her shoulders?"

The unicorn nodded.

Satreih demanded, "Who is he?"

The unicorn said, with a touch of amusement, "I would bet that you could figure that one out if you think hard enough."

The answer came to Satreih fast, hitting him like a punch to the head. He asked softly, "Verteq?"

* * * *

Chikara and Yia had reached Rasiamoramisa. The women and children centaurs were not frightened by Chikara. They were too upset to be leaving their home.

Two dwarfs appeared outside of the mountain. One said, "King Lathik orders all of you to go beneath the mountain." The other dwarf whispered something to the dwarf that spoke. They both looked at Chikara suspiciously.

Chikara guessed the reason why they were eyeing her. *I am not a regular dragon. I care nothing for precious gems. You don't have to worry that I might steal any. Is this so-called "King Lathik" the one who ordered all women and children here?*

One dwarf nodded, then quickly ducked behind the other. Chikara looked at them, amused. *Do I frighten you?*

Yia was watching from Chikara's back. She decided to let the dragon have some fun.

One dwarf said, "We have had conflicts with dragons in the past."

I'm not like them. Don't worry; I'm not going to eat you. You guys are humoring me!

Yia chuckled a bit and said to Chikara in mind-speech, *You're having fun tormenting the poor dwarfs, aren't you?* She made sure that only Chikara could hear.

Heh. Heh. Heh. Yeah. Chikara tore her attention away from the dwarfs. She smelled something curious, and saw two orb-like eyes staring back at her through the dead trees. They were like cat's eyes. The eyes disappeared as soon as the thing noticed that Chikara was looking at it.

* * * *

The unicorn nodded.

Satreih asked, "Does Verteq know that Yia has betrayed him yet?"

"Not yet. He'll find out when he sees her defending the women and children."

Satreih thought for a bit. "Who are the Zorothaxs? Are they in league with Verteq?"

The unicorn laughed softly. "The Zorothaxs are a gentle people. They would never side with Verteq."

"But they attacked Sakametio and nearly killed my brother. How could they be *gentle* if …?"

"Do you remember what I told you—that the fire swords have the power to wipe out an entire army of ten thousand with a single swing?"

Satreih nodded.

"That is why now, more than ever, you need to learn to use the special abilities that the sword possesses. Losing Sakametio was a crushing loss to the men, but Sakametio was not their only home."

"They have another home? Where is it?"

"Have you heard of the Ugulaly Ocean?"

Satreih answered, "Rasnir told me a story about it when I was a child. It's just a story to amuse youngsters, right?"

"No. It's real. The Ugulaly Ocean is hidden from sight. It is extremely treacherous for anyone to try to cross it. The other land across it is absolutely swarming with men."

"So I have to save Yia from Verteq, cross this treacherous ocean, and convince the men over there to help fight?"

The unicorn answered, "You do have to save Yia from Verteq, but it is Kaskin who will convince the men to help fight."

"Whoa, just Kaskin? I can't go?"

"No you can't. Chikara and Yia can't go as well. Kaskin would have to go by himself."

Satreih asked, "Why can't we go with him?"

"Elves, dwarfs, dragons, unicorns, and centaurs are presented to the men in the other land as fairy tales. To them, we do not exist."

*   *   *   *

Chikara and Yia were in the room that King Lathik had prepared for everybody. It was already filling up rather quickly.

Chikara growled slightly. *This room may look enormous, but there will not be enough room for everyone.* She looked to Yia.

Yia was standing next to Chikara, with her hand on the dragon's shoulder. Chikara could tell from Yia's expression that she was thinking the same thing.

A half-forgotten scent flowed into Chikara's nostrils. A friendly voice called over. "Hey! Chikara! Long time no see!"

Chikara turned around, which wasn't easy to do because it was so crowded. She grinned. *It has been a long time. How are you, Sakuri?*

Sakuri, the water nymph that Chikara had saved, said, "I'm fine. How've you been?"

I'm okay … I guess. I'm not too happy about the stupid decision that Lathik made. I'd rather be fighting by Satreih's side.

Sakuri nodded with sympathy. "We don't have a choice. How are Satreih and Kaskin?"

They're fine, but they're not too happy about the decision either. Hang on. I want you to meet somebody.

Chikara nudged Yia's shoulder to get her attention. She introduced her to Sakuri.

✳   ✳   ✳   ✳

The unicorn wanted to have sparring practice with Satreih. Satreih obliged. He wanted to know how to use the sword's powers. It was the only way to save Yia from Verteq, and he had promised her that he would. Also, neither Chikara nor Yia were around to fight with him. No matter how many times the unicorn "killed" him, he planned to stay up all night until he learned and mastered a new skill.

Satreih was "killed" five times before he learned a new skill.

The unicorn came at him with its horn lowered. Between him and the unicorn, Satreih saw a very faint wave of heat. He could barely make it out. Nevertheless, he slashed the sword across the wave of heat. Time seemed to stop. A strange voice that Satreih didn't recognize echoed in his mind.

"The fire created acted in two ways. It shielded the user from any oncoming attacks. The fire exploded from the sword, trapping the attacking foes in a fiery vortex. Nothing is left of the foes; not even their ashes."

What the strange voice said proved to be true. A fiery vortex enveloped the unicorn. When the fiery vortex disappeared, there was nothing left of the unicorn. The trees around the forest clearing returned to their normal, dead state.

Satreih stood there, shocked. An extreme feeling of sorrow came over him and threatened to kill him. The sword dropped from Satreih's hand. He fell to the ground. It was getting harder for him to breathe.

Through his agony, Satreih heard a familiar, impossible voice. "What are you weeping for? Get up."

The extreme feeling of sorrow disappeared. Satreih once again felt hope. He noticed that his face was wet with his own tears, which, by now, had frozen. He looked up—and saw the unicorn. Satreih stared at it in confusion.

For the first time, the unicorn complimented him. "Well done! The attack that you just learned is called 'Dermstract.' It will work against many enemies." The trees were once again lush with vegetation.

Satreih was still on the ground. He spoke slowly. "What just happened?"

The unicorn knelt down next to him and said softly, "Not all unicorns were immortal. I was their leader. The men from the other land killed all of the others. Every one of the murderers felt that feeling of extreme sorrow, and died from it. You would have died as well, but since I am immortal, you only felt half of what they felt. As far as I know, you are the only one to survive after 'killing' a unicorn."

"Why didn't you tell me that I would experience this before I 'killed' you?" Satreih realized that the unicorn was speaking softly because it was trying to hide the vengeance that was in its voice.

"Because I knew that you would not want to 'kill' me, and therefore, you would not want to learn the skills required to master the sword. I am the only one who can teach you those skills."

Satreih tried to choose his words carefully. "If the men from the other land killed your kin, then why do you want them to come over to this land to help us fight?"

"It would be a better fate for both lands. Never-ending night and winter poisons our land—never-ending day and summer poisons theirs. Every part of the earth needs to experience both times and seasons. Otherwise, it will be Armageddon for the entire planet."

The unicorn let Satreih think about this new information for a while. It stepped away from him and transformed into an ancient old man. The unicorn's human form was clad only in white. His beard and hair fell all the way to the ground. Its eyes showed kindness and wisdom. The unicorn stood up, offering Satreih his hand.

Satreih took the hand and allowed the unicorn to pull him to his feet. Satreih asked, "What's your name?"

"Makue." The unicorn placed his hand on Satreih's shoulder. "I think that's all we'll do for tonight. You will soon find that once you learn a new skill, you will be overcome with weariness." Makue left the forest clearing as a human. The living trees followed him.

A PLAYFUL CAT

Chikara was looking at a small crevice in the rock wall. She smelled the same curious scent that she had smelled outside. She noticed that the smell had a scent that was close to a cat's, but had a tint of magic to it.

Yia put an invisibility spell on herself so that she could find King Lathik. She wanted to talk to him. An unfamiliar voice entered her head.

You no find him if you keep goin' in that direction.

Yia closed off the rest of her mind to the invader. She could tell that it was some sort of creature. She prepared to inflict some of her mind-powers on it if it asked anything suspicious. *Who are you? What do you want?*

Nothin', the voice replied innocently. *Just tellin' you that you won't reach King Lathik by goin' in that direction.*

Oh? I won't? You're some sort of magical creature aren't you? You should know that I'm under an invisibility spell.

Idiot. People'll see your shadow. Some will smell you, as I do now. There are guards guardin' entrance to king's room. Too many of them for you to kill with dagger or magic.

Yia peered around a corner. True to its word, the creature was right. There were too many guards to fight without raising an alarm. Yia asked it, *How do I get in?*

Easy. See that window?

Yia turned around and saw the "window." She nearly laughed. *You're calling me an idiot? That's not a window. It's a ventilation shaft so the dwarfs can get some fresh air.* It had a cold breeze blowing through it.

Has nasty bats inside it?

Yeah.

You know what I mean. Crawl inside. It'll lead you to king's bedroom.

Yia did as she was told. As she crawled along, the voice talked to her about other things. It also told her which way to go when there was more than one option.

That your pet?

What pet?

Dragon. Has nasty stench to it. Dragons have same smell. Always. Turn left.

Um, no. The dragon belongs to a friend of mine. Yia didn't tell the creature Chikara's name. She still didn't know if she could trust it.

Take right here.

Who are you? What are you?

No tell. Don't know if I trust you. Straight.

Yia came to the end of the ventilation shaft. The cold, frosty wind was cutting through to her bones. She shivered.

You no be so cold if you had fur coat. You take invisibility spell off now. No one can see you. You up too high.

Yia gratefully did as she was told, replacing the invisibility spell with a warming spell. She breathed a sigh of relief.

You see window?

Another ventilation shaft?

No! Window! You look up!

Yia grinned slightly. The creature got annoyed easily.

Yia appeared right next to the window and quickly snuck inside the room beyond.

The creature sang gleefully in her mind, *I knew, I knew, I knew you was witch.*

Yia smiled. *You should have known earlier with the spells that I used on myself.*

This fun! Bye!

Yia shook her head. The little creature amused her. She looked at her surroundings. A cozy fire was burning in the hearth. Yia took off the heating spell. Beautiful gems littered the walls. The bed looked extremely comfy. The entire room looked warm and inviting.

Yia heard running water shut off. The sound of a door opening came to her ears, along with the sound of someone merrily humming a tune. Yia quickly ducked behind a velvet curtain.

King Lathik appeared. He was wearing a silky nightgown. He had a black beard and hair. Yia was amazed. His hair and beard were neatly brushed. The other dwarf's beards and hair were scraggly.

King Lathik approached Yia, not knowing that she was there. He was still humming the tune. Yia realized that she had left the window open. She silently cursed.

*   *   *   *

Kaskin listened to what Satreih had to say with wide eyes. Once Satreih finished, Kaskin said, "So I have to find the Ugulaly Ocean, cross it while braving its dangers, and get the men on the other side to help fight?"

"That pretty much sums it up." Satreih said quietly, "I understand if you don't want to go. I could always get someone else." Satreih had already told him that he himself couldn't go because he was an elf.

Kaskin smiled, laughing, "Of course I want to go!"

Satreih laughed. He was half expecting the answer.

The smile fell off Kaskin's face as he recognized reality. He asked softly, "How do I build a ship when all the trees are dead? And I don't even know *how* to build a ship. That complicates things."

"I could probably get Makue to help."

"Who's Makue?"

"The unicorn."

Kaskin stared at Satreih in shock. "It told you its name? The unicorn just gave you some extent of power over it."

"I know. Anyway, he makes the dead trees that are around him come to life. Maybe tomorrow we could get him to help."

*   *   *   *

Still, even if this was the result of her own stupidity, Yia took it as an opportunity. She appeared silently in front of the door while King Lathik shut the window. He was still humming, but suddenly stopped when he spotted Yia.

He turned three shades of red, out of anger and embarrassment. He opened his mouth, getting ready to shout for his guards. The woman jabbed a finger at him, making him unable to speak, let alone shout.

King Lathik got his point across by using mind-speech. *How in the bloody hell did you get in here, you cretin? You scoundrel! You wretch! Take this speech impairment off me, now! Wait, you're an elf! Y-o-u ...!*

Yia simply sat on his bed, waiting for him to finish, knowing that he'd tire himself out eventually. Of course, her sitting on his bed just made King Lathik angrier. She watched him. His face was turning interesting colors as he used all of the horrible mind-speech.

Yia finally said, when he was out of energy, "I just want to talk with you. You were the one who had me sent here. I'd much rather be fighting alongside my friends." Yia was not going to lose her temper. "Why did you make this request? It is genocide for all races. I don't think you see that."

King Lathik growled at her. He knew she was not going to leave unless she got an explanation.

*   *   *   *

Satreih led Kaskin to the clearing where he had met Makue. To his surprise, a marvelous ship had already been built and was waiting for them. Satreih and Kaskin stared in shock. Makue, in his original form, appeared on the ship's deck.

Makue grinned. "Didn't think I'd help unless you asked, eh? It's not every day you see a ship this size that could be sailed by one man."

Satreih asked, dumbfounded; "Only one man can sail it? That's impossible."

"If the ship's made by a unicorn, it isn't. But other men could lend a helping hand as well."

*   *   *   *

Chikara was uncomfortable. There were too many people, and still more were flooding into the room. Their reaction was almost always the same when they spotted her. Fear.

Chikara sniffed the air. Yia was coming back, but she had somehow gotten hurt.

A second later, some dwarfs appeared and rudely shoved Yia into the room. She stumbled, but managed to keep her balance. Her head was bleeding. The dwarfs shouted angrily at her, then slammed the door to the room. They were out of earshot.

Yia walked up to Chikara and leaned her head against her. The wound instantly healed.

What happened?

With her head still on Chikara, Yia answered, "I snuck into the king's room, and put a speech-impairment spell on him so he couldn't scream to his guards. Unfortunately, he was so enraged that the spell shattered."

So in other words you didn't get any information?

Yia growled, "None at all. Lathik is going to keep a close eye on me, too, from now on."

An unfamiliar voice called, *Spell not powerful enough?*

Chikara growled in surprise and shot a threatening glare to the crevice in the wall. The mind-speech was coming from there.

Relax, dragon. I no wound you and your friend.

A strange creature emerged from the space. It walked erect on its back legs, but its legs were bent at an odd angle. It was small, maybe two feet high. Its fur was black and looked like it had been washed thoroughly. Its face was definitely cat-like, complete with whiskers. The eyes glinted with mischief and playfulness. The creature's tail was long and wrapped around its feet.

No one else in the room paid any attention to it.

What exactly are you?

Yia smiled and answered, "He's a werecat. They have a friendship with witches. He helped me find a secret way into the king's bedroom."

The werecat hissed under its breath, *Stupid, stupid, stupid king. Sent too many people into home.*

Does the king know you're here?

The werecat looked down at the floor. *King no knows I'm here.* The werecat gasped and looked at Chikara. *Have friends? Kaskin and Satreih?*

The werecat got a very close view of Chikara's fangs. It shrank back, shivering, but stayed where it was.

Chikara growled. *This is putting you very close to the edge of knowing too much.*

Kaskin about to go on dangerous journey. Crossing Ugulaly Ocean. Already has ship.

Chikara's only answer was another growl.

Yia scolded, "Chikara, stop it. Werecats can tell what's happening to their friends even if they are far away. This one doesn't know Satreih or Kaskin, but he has subjected himself to me."

Chikara's answer was a growl, but she drew back.

Yia asked, "Kaskin's crossing the Ugulaly Ocean?"

Yup. Just Kaskin. Already has ship.

"What about Satreih? Where is he?"

Hmmm. He's tricky to find. The werecat was silent for a while. *He still with centaurs. He no want people finding out where he is. Hard for me to get at him.*

Yia asked with surprise, "He's still with the centaurs? He and Kaskin rarely stray from each other."

No. Kaskin crossing ocean. Satreih with centaurs. You witch. You perform Scrying Rituals?

"Yes, I can. But I need to perform the ritual in a private place. This is far from private."

Suddenly, everybody in the room disappeared except for Chikara, Yia, and the werecat.

What just happened? The people are still here. I smell them.

Yes, yes, people still here. We *still here. But people no see us.*

Yia smiled. She already knew of the werecat's powers. When her mother was alive, she had told her stories about the werecats. Chikara was still skeptical, but Yia took out her caldron and made it grow until it was its normal size. She was not worried about the caldron being too big. The werecat made enough room for it.

Yia took a vial from a coat pocket. She emptied its contents into the caldron. The liquid turned clear. The werecat jumped up onto her shoulder and stayed there, watching. With the tip of a finger, she touched the clear liquid and announced in a clear voice, "Kaskin."

*   *   *   *

The ship was marvelous. It responded perfectly to any adjustment. It was easy to control, even though it was the first time Kaskin had ever been on a ship. It seemed to Kaskin that he was only half-steering it. The ship knew where it needed to go. It performed most of the jobs itself.

Kaskin would have enjoyed himself, if he could see anything. The fog was too thick. The wind howled softly. The ship completely took over.

Kaskin sat down on the deck. He still felt that weird sensation that he had felt when he first boarded the ship. As soon as he had stepped on the deck for the first time, Satreih and Makue disappeared. So did the forest. Kaskin was shocked to see that he somehow was already on the Ugulaly Ocean, but he figured that

Makue had orchestrated the surprising turn of events. Therefore, that meant that everything was completely normal. That happened almost an hour ago.

Suddenly, the wind stopped. Everything was deathly quiet. The sails sagged, and the ship slowed to a stop. The weird sensation went away, but it was replaced with a foreboding one, along with a tingling that snaked its way up Kaskin's spine. He did his best to ignore it. After a while, the tingling went away, but the foreboding sensation was still there.

Kaskin stood up. All of his senses were alert. Nothing happened. He went below the deck and pulled a lever. He heard the sound of the ship's oars being lowered into the ocean.

The ship once again started moving.

*   *   *   *

Yia frowned at the now empty caldron. "That's weird. Why would they split up at a time like this?" She had checked both Satreih's and Kaskin's locations. "And why on earth is Kaskin trying to cross the Ugulaly Ocean on that spirit ship of his?"

Is not spirit ship. Ship built by unicorn.

"Whatever. The actions of men are hard to understand, especially the actions of the younger ones."

Chikara and the werecat both agreed, though the werecat added, *The human ones.*

Yia was half thinking to herself, half talking to her friends. "But why would they ...?" She let the question hang in the air.

Chikara mind-spoke, *They must have had a good reason.*

*   *   *   *

Kaskin had spent days on the ship, fighting beasts the entire time.

Kaskin thrust his sword into a particularly nasty sea serpent. It fell back into the water, with foam spurting from its mouth. Some of the foam splashed onto Kaskin's hand. He cried out in pain. He quickly wiped it off with his sleeve. A big, red, nasty gash was left there.

After a while, the heavy fog lifted. The beasts stopped attacking. The wind picked up once again. Kaskin looked up at the sky and gasped. He saw a full moon and stars. In the distance he could see that the sky was beginning to grow lighter.

Kaskin laughed with amazement and relief. It had been so long since he had seen light. He stopped laughing, but a smile stretched seemingly from ear to ear. He knew that he was within the boundaries of the other land.

Still smiling broadly, Kaskin treated himself to something that anyone in his homeland couldn't. He climbed up the mast of the ship and watched the sunrise.

THE DISTANT SOUND
OF WAR

Once again, Satreih was sparring with Makue, intensely determined to learn another skill. Makue had told him that the strange voice he had heard after he learned the first skill was the voice of the fire sword. It will talk when the user learns a new skill, but never again speak once all the skills have been learned.

Whenever Satreih saw a faint wave of heat between him and Makue, he never cut it. He knew that it would "kill" the unicorn, and that would mean he would have to experience the feeling of extreme sorrow for no reason.

Makue tried to stab Satreih with his horn. Satreih blocked the attack with his sword, and sidestepped.

Makue snorted in disgust. "Counter a block with a strike. That is when your opponent is most vulnerable."

Satreih did as he was told when Makue tried to attack again. He struck Makue's flank, and the unicorn bled. Makue didn't seem to notice.

Satreih asked, "How many hidden skills are there?"

"Three. One you have already learned. It is amazing that you learned it so quickly at such a young age." Makue tried to stab Satreih again, but to no avail. "Your skills are improving. When we first sparred, you were on the ground more often than not."

Satreih countered the attack, but his aim was off. "Gimme a break. I started off with archery!"

"Knowing both archery and swordsmanship is better than just knowing one of the sports."

Satreih didn't have an answer to that. He just kept sparring. Satreih smiled. He could faintly make out a heat wave. It curved around him, and it was also between him and Makue. It was much fainter than Dermstract was.

Satreih thought, *That's weird. Oh well. Let's try it.* He sliced the blade across the two heat waves, making sure to do the one around his body first.

"Heat whirlwinds were created. Little devils themselves, they tore up the ground where they passed. Anything caught inside them is doomed to die. As usual, no remnants are left behind."

Makue was not harmed. He had looked into Satreih's eyes and immediately knew what he was thinking before he unleashed the hidden skill. With amazing agility, Makue dodged the ten heat whirlwinds.

Satreih smiled, proud of himself. The smile fell off his face when Makue said, "That attack isn't going to do anything against speedy opponents."

"C'mon! I've unlocked the second hidden move!"

"That wasn't a hidden move."

"Yeah it was! The sword spoke to me!" *The thought of a sword talking to someone is pretty ridiculous.*

I think so, too.

Whoa, Kaskin?

That's me.

Satreih said, *You know, I'm kind of sparring with Makue right now.*

You were.

Even though they were using mind-speech, Satreih could tell that Kaskin was pretty happy about something. *What are you so happy about?*

I just saw the sunrise.

What! Lucky! I guess you're in the other land's boundaries, right?

Yeah. I had to fight many of Verteq's beasts, though. One sea serpent had a particularly nasty attitude. He managed to hurt me a bit, too, but not much. Have you been talking to Yia and Chikara using mind-speech?

No, but I felt a tingling sensation along my spine that felt a bit like Yia's magic.

That's weird. I felt the same thing.

Satreih asked, *So did my swimming lessons come in handy yet?*

Not yet. They probably will soon, though.

The conversation ended. Kaskin knew that Satreih had to concentrate on his sparring lessons. Even though seeing the sunrise put Kaskin in high spirits, he knew it was a bad thing. People could only see the sun rise or set at the boundary line. Over here, it would be day and summer all the time. Still, Kaskin looked forward to the heat.

Two days later, Kaskin pulled up to a dock. He was excited. As he tied the ship up to the dock, an old man looked at him with surprise. "Boy, where's your crew? 'Tis impossible to sail a ship without one."

Kaskin replied, "The ship doesn't need a crew; one man can easily get the job done."

The old man looked at the ship. "Doesn't even have a name? 'Tis bad luck to sail a ship with no name."

"I didn't have any time to make a name."

The old man shook his head in bewilderment and walked away.

Kaskin ran after him. He caught up and asked, "Who rules this land?"

"Are you from the other land?"

"Yes, I am. I've been sent to tell the king here some urgent news." *Not the complete truth, but definitely not a lie.*

The old man pointed. "The king's down that way. In the city of Lupine Hills."

"Thank you, sir." Kaskin started walking quickly in that direction.

Kaskin thought, *Satreih and Makue were right. This place is absolutely swarming with men.* A couple of hours later Kaskin arrived at a palace. Guards were standing in front of it. Kaskin guessed that the biggest one was in charge of the group.

Kaskin boldly walked up to the leader and said, "I have been sent here by King Asuv to tell your king urgent news." *They might know of King Asuv, considering the fact that he was the king of the race of men.*

The leader lied gruffly, "I haven't heard the name of that king." He said more sternly, "Things have been happening here recently, and someone has to pay!" He nodded to two other big guys, who grabbed Kaskin's arms, preventing him from escaping.

Kaskin was surprised. "What do you mean 'pay'? I didn't do anything! I was sent here to give your king some urgent news."

Kaskin's words were drowned out by the other guards who were chanting, "Pay, pay, pay, pay!" They were egging the leader on.

The leader said to the others, "C'mon friends. Let's show this stranger what he gets for lying."

Kaskin protested, "I'm not lying!"

One man took one hand off Kaskin and grabbed his sword. He threw it to the floor, while he and his buddy dragged Kaskin off. The leader followed with a grin on his face.

They brought Kaskin to a shack. Right before they forced a bag over his head, Kaskin got a quick glimpse of a spiky whip hanging on a wall.

The two men tore off Kaskin's shirt. He continued to try to break free, but it was futile.

Itimei walked out of the palace where she lived with her father, in an attempt to find the child who wanted archery lessons. The first thing that she noticed was that the guards were gone, and an unfamiliar sword lay on the steps. Picking up the sword, she thought, *Stupid guards. You should know by now to stay at your pos—*

Itimei heard a scream of pain that interrupted her thoughts coming from the guards' shack. *What, the guards moved to torture some poor person with that whip of theirs?*

She approached the shack, and all but three guards were outside of it shouting, "Pay! Pay! Pay! Pay!" They fought each other for the window, knocking each other out of the way so they could have a better view. The screams continued each time the whip struck the person.

Itimei shot arrows just above each of their heads to get their attention. The guards, seeing her, bolted.

She stormed into the shack and growled, "Enough!"

The leader dropped the whip. The two guards holding the stranger let him fall to the ground. The stranger moaned when he hit the floor. The guards were smart. They ran out of the shack before Itimei could get to them.

Itimei knelt down next to the stranger and pulled his head onto her lap, running her hand through his wavy, brown hair. "I will take care of you." She knew that he didn't hear her. He was already unconscious.

Kaskin slowly became aware of his surroundings. He was lying on a comfy bed, much like his bed at home before the fire destroyed everything. He didn't open his eyes; he wanted to hear a conversation that two other people in the room were having.

"… Father, the guards were torturing the poor man with that whip of theirs."

Kaskin somewhat recognized the voice, but couldn't remember where he had heard it.

"And they have been punished for it. Do you know this man?"

"No. I'm guessing from the way he's dressed, he must be of royal blood from a distant land."

"Do you know if he said anything before the guards attacked him?"

"He said something about wanting to deliver you some urgent news. That's what the guards said. I do not know what it is. I'm sure he'll tell you when he wakes."

"Well, in any case, he's under your care. If some distant land wants help, I doubt that I'll be able to give it, since we are suffering ourselves."

Kaskin wanted to hear more, but the conversation ended. He heard footsteps walking away.

About ten minutes later, Kaskin opened his eyes. His sword was on the bed-side table. Sitting in a chair next to the bed was a woman. She was a brunette, and had pretty blue eyes. She was skinny, and looked like she could fight well when she put her mind to it.

She said, "Ah. You're awake. My name's Itimei. The guards who committed that crime against you have been punished." Itimei pushed a canteen into Kaskin's hands.

Kaskin took it gratefully and drank from it. He asked, "What do they use that whip for, other than torturing people?"

"They're only supposed to use it as a weapon of war, and for a sport they play." She looked at Kaskin's hand curiously. "What did you do to your hand? That cut is not from the whip."

Kaskin smiled and answered, "You wouldn't believe me if I told you." *That's the wound from the sea serpent.*

"Who are you? Am I right for guessing that you're of royal blood?"

"You are. My name is Kaskin. I'm the prince of a clan that lives in a desert of the other land."

"What is happening? Something over there is affecting this land."

"I know. You have eternal day and summer. We have eternal night and winter. We are at war with someone named Verteq, who has made the normal weather and seasons unbalanced. I've come here to ask for help. A lot of men have already been killed; their home and king destroyed."

Itimei stood up and said, "Come with me. I'll take you to my father, the king."

A few minutes later, Kaskin and Itimei were walking across the castle's court-yard. The sun beat down relentlessly.

Wiping some sweat off her brow, Itimei said, "Doesn't this heat bother you?"

"Not at all. I love it. Like I said, I'm from the desert."

"How would an entire clan survive in the desert, if there's no water available?"

"We trade with people outside the desert. This heat is nothing compared to what I'm used to. The clan escaped to underground tunnels to avoid the heat. But since Verteq has gotten powerful, it has started to snow in the desert."

Itimei stared at him in shock. "How could one person be so powerful?"

Kaskin leaned closer to her and whispered in her ear, "He's a wizard. I'm *not* joking."

"This Verteq is a wizard?"

"Well, he was. His magical powers were disintegrated. I think he has regained some of them." Kaskin looked at her squarely in the eye and said, "All those tales about elves, dwarfs, and dragons, you'd better start believing in them now."

Itimei asked, "They're real?"

"I don't know about the stories, but the creatures are definitely real. I know. My best friend is an elf. The only reason he didn't come with me was because he knew, in this land, elves don't exist."

King Stephenson was talking to his trusted advisor. Out of the corner of his eye, he saw his daughter and the stranger approach. He excused his trusted advisor, telling him to go get his work finished.

As soon as Kaskin and Itimei were a couple of arm's lengths away from the king, Kaskin bowed respectfully.

Itimei looked at her father and said determinedly, "Father, we need to send some men to help in the war."

"What war?"

Kaskin explained quickly. He left out the part of mythical creatures being real. The king would probably think that he was crazy. Kaskin could tell that his daughter had more of an imagination than her father.

The king nodded often, and asked when Kaskin finished explaining, "What type of men would you need?" He was a little hesitant.

"Men who could fight without thinking, and could act only on instincts. Men who are loyal, and they need to expect every possibility at all times."

"I'll grant you five thousand men, and the ships that you need. Though I must ask you this: return the men to me after the war, even the ones who do not survive. They should be buried in their native land, not left forgotten on some distant battlefield."

Kaskin nodded. "Of course, Your Majesty."

Itimei said, "Father, I'll go as well."

"It's too dangerous. You're staying here."

Itimei argued, "These men have no idea who Kaskin is, or if they should trust him. All they know is that you're trusting their lives to a foreigner. If I go with them, they will be a little more at ease."

King Stephenson looked at his daughter for a long time. He said with a sigh, "All right, you can go."

Itimei smiled. "I'll get the ships ready. You already have one, don't you Kaskin?"

Kaskin nodded. "You can't miss it."

Itimei walked off toward the dock.

When she was out of earshot, King Stephenson looked directly at Kaskin and said, "Don't let anything happen to her. I cherish her deeply. She's my only child; my only heir."

Kaskin nodded, then bowed again. After one last thank you, he ran off after Itimei.

✳   ✳   ✳   ✳

Satreih was sleeping peacefully. To him, it didn't matter when he got sleep; it was impossible to tell the time. He slept with the sword clutched tightly in his fist. He wouldn't take any chances if anyone tried to steal it.

Satreih felt a hand on his shoulder. He was startled out of his sleep, immediately drawing the blade out of its scabbard.

A familiar voice said, "Don't use the sword on me, Satreih. I am not your enemy."

"How would I know that you're not an enemy?" Satreih sliced the blade through the air. It lit the room up, revealing a hooded figure. Satreih recognized him.

Satreih gasped in shock, "King Thuoj! What're you doing here?"

"Verteq is about to attack the village near the Strait of Shinaih. He's sending his whole army, and he's going with them. The village trades supplies with all races, especially weapons of war. If Verteq succeeds in destroying the village, it will be much harder to stop him."

"So you want me to fight with your people because I'm of the same race?"

King Thuoj nodded. "He plans to attack in about two weeks."

"Let me stay here with the centaurs for a while. There is a morith somewhere in this forest. I can ask Yia with mind-speech if she could teleport me to Meikosa after I destroy the morith."

King Thuoj nodded and walked out of the room.

*   *   *   *

Yia absentmindedly stroked Razij, the werecat. He was sleeping peacefully on her lap, purring softly. Either he was having a good dream, or he was still semi-awake and felt the pets. He had told her his name shortly after Yia performed the Scrying Ritual.

Both Yia and Chikara were bored. Occasionally, they talked to some people, but most everyone was still too scared to talk.

A large booming sound echoed from outside the mountain of Rasiamoramisa. People screamed.

Razij instantly woke from his nap. *What was that?*

Chikara growled. *Verteq. He's attacking. I smell his foul scent. This is odd—he's alone. He has no one to protect him.*

"Why did he come alone? He knows that he'll have to deal with the dwarfs … and us." *Does he know that I betrayed him?*

You ask me as if I should know how his evil mind works.

Razij glanced up at Yia curiously. *I smell him. Bleah! Nasty, nasty, nasty scent! Worse than dragons! Much, much worse!*

Chikara growled slightly at the comment that dragons have nasty scents, but let it go. In the distance, she saw the light of fire heading toward the group. She jumped up and flew toward it, taking the brunt of the attack. Chikara growled in pain, but she had saved the lives of everyone else.

Razij jumped up onto Yia's shoulder, growling in fear. His ears were flattened to his head. He wasn't very brave, but always stayed with his friends whenever they needed help, whether he liked it or not.

Suddenly, Verteq appeared right in front of Yia. Yia took a step back as she put her hand on her dagger. She didn't show any fear in her eyes, even though it was tearing at her heart and mind.

Razij shrank back a little, but then jumped up and bit Verteq on his shoulder. If he was given a second choice, he would have run, but he knew that Yia needed help. Biting Verteq's shoulder was the wrong thing to do. Razij immediately released him and fell to the floor.

Fire! Fire! Hot! Mouth burning!

The next instant, Verteq and Yia were gone.

*   *   *   *

Kaskin and Itimei were waiting on the dock for the five thousand men that King Stephenson had promised. They came soon. They were all dressed warmly as the king had asked, but looked completely uncomfortable at the moment. Kaskin introduced himself, and assured them that they could trust him.

All the ships were prepared, including the one that Kaskin sailed. Two days later, they crossed the border of the two lands. The men rejoiced when they saw the sunset.

An unfamiliar voice entered Kaskin's mind. It sounded scared. *Yia gone. Taken by Verteq.*

What! Who are you?

Razij. Me werecat. New friend of Yia's and Chikara's. Yia taken by Verteq. Chikara's tellin' Satreih.

Kaskin didn't like the idea of this so-called werecat knowing so much about them. *Why would Verteq take her?*

I no know. I try to stop. I bite Verteq on shoulder. Verteq hot, like fire. Mouth burned. Before Verteq attacked, Yia thought, 'Does he know I betrayed him?'. I no tell Chikara yet. Will soon. No idea why Yia think that.

How do you know she thought that?

Me mind-read. Uhh, I go. Chikara want to talk. Rather not be served on dragon's dinner table.

Itimei walked up behind Kaskin. "What is it? You look troubled."

"One of my friends was taken by Verteq. But I don't know if that's true. The voice could have been lying, but it sounded scared."

Itimei asked, confused, "What voice?" She already thought that he was crazy.

The people in the other land probably can't mind-speak. "We have something called mind-speech; it's a bit like telepathy. It allows us to talk to people with our minds, even if they are far away."

"O-kaay. How?" Itimei was still confused. She heard Kaskin say in her mind, *Hi Itimei.* Itimei jumped, surprised. "Whoa! H-How …?"

Kaskin laughed. "I don't know how it works. It's difficult to explain. But once you learn it, you'll understand the concept."

*   *   *   *

Rasnir watched with surprise, crouching in his corner. The Spies had brought Yia into the cell. They were chaining her up to the wall. Rasnir didn't say anything. If he indicated that he knew her, that would certainly mean her death.

The Spies left. After a few minutes, Rasnir stood up and asked, "What happened?"

"God dammit, Verteq found out that I had betrayed him somehow."

Rasnir could feel her anger. He swallowed and asked, "Why are you so angry? Sure, being captured sucks, but it seems to me that you have another reason."

"He stole my magical powers and dagger. There's no way we can escape." Yia shook the chains violently in an attempt to free herself, but they didn't break.

A half hour later, a Spy came in and gave a moldy piece of bread and a small cup of fresh water to Rasnir. It left the cell as quickly as it came. It didn't give anything to Yia.

Rasnir held up the cup and the moldy piece of bread. "Want any? We can split it. They only come in here once a day."

Yia refused by sharply jerking her head. Rasnir could still feel her anger.

During several days of captivity Yia didn't eat or drink anything. She didn't talk much, either.

One day, after the Spy had come in to deliver the food and fresh water, Rasnir stood up. "You know what, I'll force you to eat and drink this. This is all they give us. If you keep going like this, you'll die of thirst and starvation."

Yia looked up and threatened, "You ... wouldn't ... dare."

"Oh yes I would." Rasnir tried very hard to get her to eat and drink; and it wasn't easy. She kept leaning away, smacking him in the face with the chains a couple of times.

After about twenty minutes, Rasnir finally managed to pin her against the wall with his body, shoving the moldy bread and water down her throat. He slightly smiled in satisfaction as he sat down on the slab of stone that was his bed. "Heh. I win. You're very stubborn, aren't you?" For the first time in a long while, Rasnir was having a little bit of fun.

Yia just stared at him with angry eyes.

*   *   *   *

After meeting with King Thuoj, Satreih searched the forest for the morith with Makue. Chikara had told him what had happened to Yia, and he was worried. Chikara also briefly mentioned the werecat that was hanging around Yia.

They rounded a corner, and saw the morith. Makue ran forward before Satreih could do anything, piercing the morith with his horn. Even though it was an evil thing, when Makue stabbed the morith it was purified into light. All the forest came to life, but the snow and night remained.

Satreih protested, "Hey, I thought you were going to let me destroy it. But, I didn't expect this to happen." He looked around at the forest.

Makue laid down, tired. The morith had sucked a lot of strength out of him. "That morith could only be destroyed by a unicorn. It stole much of my strength. If you were to stab it with the sword, you would have instantly perished. It would have turned the power of your sword against you, added with a little of its own power. And, if you had attacked, the forest would not have revitalized itself."

"I am wearing my ophilla."

"That doesn't matter. Even with it, you would have perished instantly." Makue paused. "I'll send you to Meikosa to aid King Thuoj and his people."

The next second, Satreih was right outside of the concrete wall that guarded Meikosa. He was on Maasianii. Hakku and Okanee were next to him.

BATTLE FOR THE
STRAIT OF SHINAIH

Chikara growled at Razij. Razij was getting used to her growls. He no longer shrank back.

You're really getting on my nerves; you know that, kitty cat? I have no idea how Yia puts up with you.

I no do nothin' this time! I try to help! You no stop Verteq from taking Yia!

Once again, Chikara growled. *I was too far away because I saved everyone from the fire that Verteq made. Everyone here except me would have been sent to their graves.*

Why not you?

I'm almost immune to fire, unlike your scrawny body.

Fine. You no like me? I go with Satreih. Or Kaskin.

Oh, you'd better not. Chikara growled.

You no stop me. Razij vanished.

*   *   *   *

"Prince Kaskin?"

"Yes?" With a hand still on the helm, Kaskin looked behind him. One of the five thousand men was next to him, holding something in his hand.

The man asked with a raised eyebrow, "What is this?"

The something in his hand twisted around as it bit his hand. *Let me go!* the thing growled. The man's wrist was beginning to turn a light shade of purple; the thing had its long tail strongly wrapped around it.

The man didn't react to the pain. He just stared at what he had curiously, and raised it up to his face so he could get a better view. He told it, "You look like some sort of cat."

Kaskin asked, "Where'd you find him?"

"He was in my bunk. He bit me when I moved in my sleep, because I accidentally squashed him. What *is* he?"

Kaskin bent down until he was at eyelevel with Razij. "You're Razij, right?"

Right. Tell big idiot to let me down.

The man said, "I'm not a 'big idiot'." He looked to Kaskin and said, "Okay, I know the thing's name. But I still don't know what he is."

Kaskin stood back up. "Put him down."

The man dropped Razij, who landed gracefully on his feet. He jumped up onto Kaskin's shoulder. He hissed at the man, with his ears flattened against his head.

Kaskin said, "He's a werecat. I don't know anything about them." He looked to Razij and asked, "Do you need something?"

No. Chikara no like me. I stay with you?

"Well, okay. But I don't think you can swim that well, can you?"

No. You no swim well either. No blame me.

The man asked, "Is that true?"

Kaskin nodded. "I'm not the strongest swimmer."

The man changed the subject and asked, "How far away are we from your—" He was interrupted by screams of fear and surprise.

Kaskin drew his sword. He ran toward the screams. Most of the men were crowded on one side of the ship, staring in shock. A sea serpent was attacking one of the other ships.

Kaskin threw his sword at the sea serpent. His aim was perfect. It hit the attacking sea serpent in the back of its throat. The sword went all the way through its mouth, and landed on the deck of the other ship. The sea serpent fell back into the water, with foam spitting from its mouth. Kaskin called over, "Don't let the foam touch you!"

The men avoided the foam, but they looked with fear at the spot where the sea serpent had fallen.

Kaskin said to the men on his ship, "Remember when the king and I told you that you needed to be ready for anything?"

The men nodded in shock.

Kaskin said, "I meant it." He called over to the other ship. "Can I have my sword back?"

The commodore said, "There's a reef between us! Can't you wait 'till we get back to your land?"

"No! More sea serpents will be attacking all the way! Throw it!"

"I don't want to hit anyone by mistake!"

"You won't! Throw it!"

The commodore threw the sword. It headed straight for Kaskin. Razij ducked behind Kaskin's back. Kaskin expertly plucked the sword out of the air.

Almost two weeks later, Kaskin and the men were back at the forest where the centaurs lived. When he first saw it, Kaskin took a step back in surprise.

Itimei asked, "What is it?" She was having a fun time playing with Razij, who was running around on her shoulders. Itimei's job was to catch him.

"All these trees—they were dead." Kaskin asked the men to stay where they were, then started to walk into the forest. Itimei followed.

Kaskin was shocked to find that there was no one there.

Kaskin walked up to the room that he and Satreih had shared. "Hey! Satreih! I'm back!" There was no answer. Kaskin went inside.

A tired voice came from behind them. "Satreih is not here. I teleported him to Meikosa."

Kaskin turned around and asked, "Why would he have any need to go to Meikosa?" He heard Itimei gasp.

Makue sat down on his haunches. It took him a while to answer.

Itimei cautiously approached him. "Are you ill?"

"No. Just tired." Makue looked at Kaskin and said, "All the kings know that there is going to be a battle near the Strait of Shinaih. They are going there themselves, with their people, to fight. King Thuoj asked Satreih if he would fight with his elves."

*   *   *   *

Satreih was in the formation with all of the Meikosans. He was near the back. The Meikosans were on horseback. The dwarfs were to the right of the Meikosans, on the ground; the centaurs were to the left. The kings were ahead of everyone, each standing in front of his race.

In the distance, Satreih saw Verteq's army approach.

He nudged Maasianii with his legs. Maasianii moved forward without complaint, his head and tail held high. Shocked whispers rose up all around him.

Satreih didn't pay any attention to them. He rode in front of everyone; including the kings.

That made King Lathik incredibly angry. "Insolent pup! Get back to your position!"

Satreih paid no attention to him.

King Lathik shouted, "Get back to your position!" He turned to King Thuoj. "He's one of yours, isn't he, Thuoj? Tell him to get back to his position!"

King Thuoj calmly answered, "He wears my colors because he is of the same race, but he is not one of my people. Calm yourself, Lathik. He has a reason to be where he is."

"I don't care if he has a reason! Tell him—"

Satreih rounded on King Lathik. "Do you think that I would be stupid enough to be up here if I didn't have a reason?"

"Yes. Get—"

Satreih interrupted him. "I'm up here because I'm the chosen one. I'm the only person who even has a chance to kill Verteq."

King Lathik grumbled something under his breath about "elves don't respect me," but didn't reply to Satreih's comment.

Satreih turned back to face Verteq's army.

When Verteq's army was just out of range of the archers, Verteq held up his arm. They stopped, but Verteq kept moving until he pulled the reins on his black steed. He was right in front of Satreih. They faced each other for a long while, waiting for the other to make the first move.

Fear was like an unmerciful beast that was tearing at Satreih's heart and soul relentlessly, but none of it showed in his eyes.

Satreih saw Verteq draw a sword identical to his, and he drew his out of its scabbard. Satreih parried the attack, but that was exactly what Verteq wanted. Verteq immediately blocked the counterattack, locking the blades with sheer force.

Verteq hissed softly, "So you're the 'chosen one,' the one who will try to kill me. That, I'm afraid, will *not* happen. I shall take your life long before you have a chance to take mine."

Satreih and Verteq began to spar. Satreih was barely keeping up. He had the feeling that Verteq was toying with him. Verteq's army rushed past them.

Satreih tried to unleash the heat whirlwinds.

Verteq laughed. "You fool! I was the one who originally made the swords. You cannot harm me."

Weuh appeared by his master's side. He changed the direction of the wind, making it stronger. He pushed the heat whirlwinds back.

Maasianii took over, dodging the whirlwinds. The colors of Meikosa were burned, revealing Satreih's golden ophilla underneath. Satreih turned around. *No! Did Weuh just turn my attack on my allies?*

Verteq took his advantage and cut Satreih on his leg with the sword. Satreih cried out and tried to counterattack, but Verteq easily deflected it. Verteq taunted, "Didn't Kaskin teach you to never take your eyes off of your opponent?"

Verteq watched with surprise. A huge, winged object plummeted down from the sky, deflecting the attack from the people of the land. It flew towards them.

Satreih launched himself off of Maasianii, letting the horse fight on its own.

Chikara felt Satreih's weight land on her. She growled. *Verteq, do you know the reason why I was able to sneak up on you so easily?*

Verteq didn't answer; he just tried to attack.

Chikara maneuvered herself and Satreih out of the way. *There is no moon; no stars for you to see me coming. You only think that you are hurting the people of this land. You are wrong. You hurt yourself as well. You are obsessed with your power; and you abuse it. It will only be a matter of time before Kaskin returns with the men from the other land. When that happens, the men will rise above you to avenge their fallen brothers of Sakametio.*

The battle was long and tiring. Verteq and his army seemed to always have the upper hand. Shinaih Village was in flames. The kings were shouting to their people to retreat, but Verteq's army cornered them, rendering them immobile.

*   *   *   *

Rasnir scurried over to his corner when he heard the steel door open. A Spy burst in. It struck Yia on the side of her head, making her unwillingly fall unconscious. Rasnir jumped up. He intended to save her.

The Spy smacked Rasnir across his face. Rasnir fell. There was so much force behind the hit. Blood began to spurt from his nose.

The Spy disappeared with Yia's body.

*   *   *   *

When Satreih's strength was spent, Verteq screeched something incomprehensible to a Spy, apparently saying something to it in its own language.

The Spy vanished, and then reappeared quickly with Yia. Yia was unconscious. The Spy held her up like a doll.

Satreih and Chikara made moves to free her from the Spy's grasp. The Spy violently struck Chikara with the flat of its sword, breaking her wing. Chikara roared with pain. The Spy scurried up a high pile of stones so that he was out of Satreih's reach.

Satreih tried to climb the pile of rocks. Verteq struck him hard against his head with his scabbard. Satreih fell, barely conscious.

Looking down on Satreih as if he were some lowly bug, Verteq hissed, "You love her, don't you? I guess I'll send her with you, so that she can keep you company in your grave." Verteq nodded to the Spy.

The Spy wrapped his hands around Yia's neck. It shrieked with pain and surprise. It turned, and saw that there was an arrow sticking out of its back. The next arrow was aimed at Verteq. It hit its mark. It stuck out of Verteq's shoulder.

Satreih was fighting to stay conscious. He saw the two arrows hit their marks. He looked past Verteq and the Spy, toward the water. There were ships. Standing on the mast of the nearest ship was a woman with brown hair. She held a bow in her hand, and was reaching for another arrow. Satreih smiled. Standing behind her was Kaskin, with his sword out and ready. That was all Satreih saw before he fell into blackness.

RIDDLE CHALLENGES

The first person Satreih saw was the woman who had shot the Spy and Verteq with the arrows.

"So you're Satreih? Kaskin's best friend?"

Satreih nodded and sat up. "Who are you?"

Itimei noticed Satreih's long ears, but didn't say anything about it. "My name is Itimei. My father is King Stephenson, the king from the other land."

Satreih looked at the little black cat thing on her shoulder curiously.

Itimei got up. "I'll let Kaskin know that you're awake. Razij, stay with him, will you?"

Razij jumped down and landed on Satreih's lap. Satreih looked at it with a raised eyebrow, but then quickly turned his attention to his surroundings. He was in a building that he didn't recognize.

Satreih called out with mind-speech, *Chikara, I'm up.*

A few seconds later, Satreih heard back. *You are? Good. Are you all right? That was a nasty blow that Verteq's scabbard delivered. Good thing it wasn't his sword.*

How's your wing?

That weird girl Itimei did her best to heal it. It feels a little better, though I could tell that she knows nothing about dragons.

A vision of the Spy trying to choke Yia came into Satreih's mind. *What happened to Yia? Is she okay?*

She's still unconscious. Poor thing. She's only skin and bones. She's alive, but something smells different about her. And your father's scent is on her, too.

"Hey! Satreih! Long time no see!"

Satreih jumped. He was so intent on his conversation with Chikara that he hadn't noticed that Kaskin had entered the building.

Satreih grinned. "Looks like you managed to convince the men from the other land to help fight."

"Yup. They kind of freaked out when they first saw a sea serpent. They had only known of them as myth. Are you all right?"

"I'm fine." Satreih watched the strange creature that was on his lap jump onto Kaskin's head. Satreih asked Kaskin, using mind-speech, *What is that?*

Didn't Chikara mention an annoying werecat to you?

Now that I think about it—

Razij interrupted Satreih as he said to Kaskin, *Me mind read, remember? Mind-speech no help.*

Satreih's curiosity spiked a little higher. "He can mind read?"

Kaskin sighed. "Apparently."

Yia was lying in a bed, still unconscious. Satreih was watching her, worried. Chikara was right; she was only skin and bones. He thought about what Verteq had said to him right before he was shot with an arrow.

Satreih shuddered. He hadn't known that he had fallen in love so easily with Yia. That didn't bother him. What bothered him was that Verteq knew so much more about his feelings than he did.

I no worry about that too much if I were you.

Satreih looked up. Razij the werecat was sitting on the windowsill, cleaning his paw. He looked content, and worried.

Satreih answered, "You know, you shouldn't be poking around in people's minds. Some might attack you for doing so."

I small. I hide in places where they too big. Besides, I no choice. Mind reading just happens. I hear everybody's thoughts, all the time.

"Why do you think that I shouldn't worry about this?"

Verteq powerful. The knowledge of him knowing more about you than you know about you ... that'll drive you mad. Perish idea.

Satreih hid a small smile by yawning. The way Razij had phrased that was slightly amusing to him. "Do you know what's going to happen to her?" He nodded his head toward Yia.

No. Only thing I know is she's very weak. Verteq stole magic powers.

Satreih blinked in surprise. He contacted Chikara through mind-speech. *Is this why Yia smelled different to you? The lack of her magical powers?*

Chikara inhaled, taking in all scents around her. *Yes. I couldn't figure out what the difference was. Just smelling magic on her was so normal.*

Satreih heard a soft moan coming from the bed. He turned his attention to Yia and asked, "Are you all right?" He pressed his canteen of water into her hands.

Yia nodded. She took a sip from the canteen and swished the water around in her mouth. She felt Razij land by her feet. He was purring happily.

Yia smiled slightly and said, "Your father is almost as stubborn as I am when he sets his mind to something."

Satreih laughed. Despite the fact that he was worrying not that long ago, he was already in good spirits. "I know. How'd you find that out?"

"I wouldn't eat or drink anything inside the cell." Yia shuddered. "Revolting place."

Satreih stayed away from the subject of her stolen magic. Yia would have to bring that up, not him. Satreih asked, "So, Father tried to shove food and water down your throat?"

Yia nodded.

"Who won?"

She scowled. "He did, but it took him nearly twenty minutes. Every time."

"And you wouldn't eat or drink anything be—"

Razij quickly jumped up and whacked Satreih on the head with his paw. Razij spoke so that only Satreih could hear, *Taking witches' magic makes them extremely angry. They no eat or drink for a long time. No ask me why. Stay away from subject. Stay on her good side.* He said that very quickly.

Yia looked down. "Satreih, I'm sorry."

"What for?"

Yia hesitated. "Remember back in Meikosa when you felt that you had slept for too long?"

Satreih nodded. "How did you know that?" *Where is she going with this?*

"I had to put you under a sleeping spell in order to deceive Verteq and to destroy the morith. My mother isn't sick. She died when I was still a young child. I don't remember what happened to her. I just used her as an excuse so I could see what Verteq was up to. That's how I knew that Sakametio was about to be attacked."

Satreih thought about this for a little bit. Placing his hands under her chin, he raised her head to look at her directly in the eye. He said softly, "I'm just glad you told me."

After talking for a while longer, Yia fell asleep. She felt bad for Rasnir. They barely got any sleep in the cell. When they did sleep, they always had nightmares, always seemingly running from some cruel fate.

Satreih went outside. He felt something jump onto his shoulder. "What's wrong, Razij?"

I too happy Yia's back. I'd wake her up by purring too loud.

Satreih sniggered a little. True to his word, Razij was still purring loudly, as if he couldn't stop.

Satreih made his way to the horse stables. Once inside, he saw that the stalls were very well kept. Some of the horses looked up curiously when they smelled Razij.

Maasianii, Okanee, and Hakku were in neighboring stalls. Satreih thought, *King Thuoj must've moved Okanee and Hakku here. They weren't with me during the battle.*

Satreih entered Maasianii's stall. Maasianii looked rather content. The few wounds that he acquired during battle didn't seem to be much of a nuisance. The horse's ears and tail perked up expectantly when he saw Satreih. His nostrils flared. He wasn't used to a werecat's smell.

Satreih started grooming Maasianii, lightly scratching him in all of his good spots. Satreih did his best to clean the few wounds.

Chikara's voice entered Satreih's mind.

Satreih, I may know of a way to restore Yia's magic. Satreih didn't answer, but Chikara knew that she had his complete attention. She continued, *Verteq stole her magic and separated it into two shards. However, Verteq teleported the two magic shards to the other land. He now knows that men are absolutely swarming in vast numbers over there. If Yia's magic somehow gets into their hands …*

Chikara didn't finish her sentence. Satreih finished it for her.… *it would be a really bad thing and Verteq would have the upper hand, right?*

Right.

Razij joined the conversation. *Men in other land no know of magic. Magic will be used for wrong purposes.* Razij stopped purring and hissed. *I no like this. Yia no has magic. It be hard to retrieve.*

Wow. Razij, you may be annoying, but you do have some intelligence between your ears. That was completely unexpected.

Razij growled. *Watch tongue, dragon.*

Does Kaskin already know about this?

Yes he does.

Everyone was getting ready to leave. Chikara, Satreih, Yia, and Razij were twenty miles from the village.

Razij looked to all of them and asked, *You sure you want to go to other land? I make all of you blend in. I make all of you look like regular men and women.*

Everyone nodded.

Razij asked, *Yia, do me favor?*

Yia nodded. She was still unhappy. "I'll do my best, but since I don't have my magic, I might not be able to."

No, no. Later, once you get magic back. I make everyone blend in. I no can transform everyone back to normal form. You transform everyone back after we get you magic and return here?

Yia nodded. "Sure."

Satreih felt his ears shrink to a normal man's size. He looked over at Chikara, and his mouth hung open in stupefied shock.

Chikara looked like a regular woman.

The only hint of her true form was her eyes. Her eyes looked normal, but had the consistency of a beast within them. She had golden hair that fell to just above her waist. She wore a red, silky dress.

Chikara folded her arms. "Great, why do I have to wear a dress? It will get in the way of fighting! I *abhor* being a regular woman. I can't breathe fire or fly! Where did my fangs and claws go? What happened to my tail? Razij, you ... are going ... to die!"

Chikara made an angry move to snatch Razij. But Razij was just a black cat. He ran between Chikara's legs and jumped up onto Yia's shoulder, meowing pitifully. Chikara fell. She wasn't used to walking, or running, on two legs.

Satreih bent down, offering her a hand. He was grinning.

Chikara looked at Satreih's hand curiously and asked, "What do I do with this?"

Satreih replied, still grinning, "Take it, of course. I'll help you up."

Taking his hand, Chikara growled, "You think this is funny, don't you?"

"No." Satreih lied quickly. The smile fell from his face.

Now back on her feet, Chikara scoffed. "Lucky you. You only have to deal with smaller ears. I have to deal with a whole new body!" She shot Razij an evil look.

An annoyed voice called over. "Hey, Kaskin."

Kaskin raised an eyebrow. The voice sounded familiar, somehow. He turned around. His mouth fell open in shock. Chikara, Satreih, Yia, and Razij were approaching. They all looked different. Satreih and Yia just had smaller ears. Razij was a normal cat. Chikara was a regular woman.

Kaskin asked, completely stunned, "Whoa, w-what happened?"

Satreih had an arm wrapped around Chikara, supporting her a little. He answered, "We're going with you to the other land. Razij transformed us so we could blend in."

Kaskin couldn't take his eyes off of Chikara and didn't answer.

Chikara broke away from Satreih's grip. She stumbled a bit but managed to keep her balance. She growled. "I'm not used to this body."

Itimei walked out of a nearby building, carrying a box full of supplies. "Hey, Kaskin, where do you want me to put—" She didn't finish her sentence. She asked in utter bewilderment, "Chikara? Is—is that *you?*"

"Unfortunately. I hate being in this body. If you want to know what happened, ask the werecat. Though he probably won't say anything."

The trip to the other land was uneventful, aside from the attacking sea serpents. Chikara was getting used to her new body, and had already made a kill before she saw the sunrise. Her chosen weapon was a dagger. She didn't like the sword or the bow. For her, they were too unwieldy. With something small, she could attack more efficiently. Still, always tugging at the back of her mind, was the thought that her claws would do much better.

Yia had replaced her old dagger. She liked the new one better. It had sharper edges.

Once they were back in the other land, the men left to find their families. The only major injury was a broken leg. Verteq's army hadn't recovered because the last minute arrivals overwhelmed them.

Itimei and Kaskin started to lead the way to the palace.

Chikara came up from behind and placed her hands on Satreih's shoulders. She said softly into his ear, "There are two moriths in this new land."

"Moriths? How do you know?"

"I can feel their power. They are in this land, but they're far away. The horse rulers are still on the ship, right?"

Satreih nodded. "We can use them to get to the moriths after we speak to the king."

Kaskin eyed the guards on the steps of the palace warily. They were the same ones that he ran into on his first trip here. His back was still red from the lashes of the spiky whip.

The leader spotted Kaskin. "Well lookee here! You wanna challenge us again? You'll lose."

Kaskin placed a hand on his sword and didn't say anything. He heard Itimei's voice enter his mind. She was getting pretty good at mind-speech. *Don't. Let me take care of this.*

Itimei said, "Let us pass."

The leader scoffed. "Sorry, princess. You've been gone so long, and you missed a small war. I don't think we can trust you." He drew the spiky whip out of a big pocket.

Kaskin withdrew his sword.

Chikara stepped between them. "If you harm him, I will personally tear you apart." She already knew what had happened to Kaskin. Itimei had told her.

The leader said, "Oh ho! A threat? We know what to do with that, don't we boys?"

Chikara found that she was surrounded by men.

Itimei said, "Chikara, don't kill them."

"I won't."

One of the men thrust his spear at her. Chikara parried the attack with her dagger. There was much force behind the dagger. The man dropped the spear. Chikara quickly scooped it up, and began to use the blunt end to attack.

Within twenty seconds, she had all the men on the ground, moaning, including the leader with the whip.

Satreih chuckled and clapped. "Having fun, Chikara? I thought you didn't like the spear."

Chikara was grinning evilly. She nodded. "Just because I don't like the spear, doesn't mean that I'm not—" She didn't finish her sentence. On the palace she saw several men. They all had fire arrows knocked and aimed in her direction.

The men let their arrows fly. Almost all hit their mark.

As she fell, she heard Satreih cry out her name. But he sounded very far away.

King Stephenson and Itimei were doing their best to heal this strange woman. Satreih held Chikara up in a sitting position. There were some arrows sticking out of her back as well. He felt horrible.

King Stephenson said, "I am amazed. Most women would die instantly. Yet this one still lives. The fire from the arrows did not seem to do any damage."

Chikara said softly without opening her eyes, "It is the dress. With it, I am immune to fire." She wouldn't risk revealing her true form.

She made everyone jump. Satreih gasped, "Chikara? You're awake?"

Chikara opened her eyes. She grinned. She tried to act insulted. "What's wrong, Satreih? I thought you knew me better than that!" She didn't flinch whenever an arrow was pulled out.

"Well, you were shot with a bunch of arrows."

Using mind-speech, Chikara said, *C'mon! I'm a dragon! Do you honestly think that I would let some lowly men kill me?*

Chikara yanked an arrow out of her back. "Good. That one was annoying." She surveyed the room. "Where are Kaskin and Yia?"

Itimei answered, "They went back to the ship to retrieve the horses. Razij went with them." She knew that the concept of a "horse ruler" would sound a little suspicious to her father.

"Why did Razij go? Maybe because he knows that he'll feel my wrath sometime sooner or later?"

King Stephenson's trusted advisor walked into the room. His eyes displayed the fear that he was feeling. There was a dark stain on his chest.

King Stephenson stood up and asked sternly, "What's happening, Gregory?"

Gregory answered, trying to keep his voice from cracking. "A—dragon is attacking." Having a creature from myth attack wasn't part of his perfect picture.

Chikara sniffed, trying to catch the dragon's scent. She couldn't. *I'm gonna kill that cat.* Chikara asked, interested, "A dragon, hmm? Maybe I can talk to him."

Gregory shook his head. "I don't think so. Don't dragons attack women for jewelry? That's what the myths say. Besides, you were just pierced with arrows. You would be easy prey for him."

Satreih said softly, "Chikara would have a much better chance talking to him than any of us would."

King Stephenson scoffed, "A dragon? Ha, you are all fools if you believe that they are real." His mind instantly changed when he heard a ferocious roar. The curtains beside the window burned.

Chikara stood up. All of the arrows were pulled out. "I'll go talk to him." She walked over to the window and looked up. She growled. "I need to get to the top of the palace, but I'm not a good climber."

Satreih smiled. "I can help you there."

Chikara said, "Oh yeah, that's right. You spent most of your life in the forest. But how would you get me up to the roof?"

Satreih walked over and opened the window. "No problem. Just climb onto my back."

Satreih easily muscled his way up the palace's side. He used little cracks in the palace for handholds. Chikara had her legs wrapped around his waist.

He paused. The other dragon was directly behind them. His enormous wing-beats pinned Satreih to the wall.

The dragon was a musty red color. Like Chikara, he had eagle-like talons and several rows of teeth. He looked at Chikara, his head cocking from side to side. She looked like an annoying human, but had the scent of a powerful dragoness. He screeched something incomprehensible.

Satreih winced. The screech was painfully loud. He couldn't cover his ears with his hands or they would fall.

Chikara screeched something back.

Satreih asked Chikara with mind-speech, *Translation, please?*

He said his name is Auburn. He's confused about my looks and scent. I think he knows that I'm a dragoness.

Auburn screeched something. Chikara replied in the same language.

Chikara translated, *His land is being infested by dark magic.*

Satreih asked, *Dark magic?*

Auburn and Chikara screeched at each other.

Chikara said to Satreih, *I asked him what it smelled like. He replied, 'A witch's magic: smells of herbs.'* She added excitedly, *That's exactly what Yia's magic smells like!*

Satreih asked, confused, *But he said it was dark magic, and Yia's magic isn't dark.*

Verteq stole it from her, remember? He probably did something to it to make it evil.

Auburn screeched something. He didn't wait for a reply and flew off.

Satreih started to climb back down the building. "What was all that screeching for? I thought dragons could use a form of mind-speech."

"He can't. He's one of the Fwathili types."

"Huh?"

Chikara answered, "The Fwathili can only speak by screeching. Oh, during the last screech, he asked if we could get rid of the magic."

"Okay. But I thought that the only other dragons lived in Seven Waterfalls."

Chikara gave a simple answer. "That was our land. It's different over here. But he is the last dragon in this land. He lives in a mountainous region far from this city. It would be a week's ride, even with the horse rulers." Chikara grinned. "Did you see how big his claws were? Did you see how sharp his teeth were? He had you pinned to the side of the building with only his wingbeats!"

It was Satreih's turn to grin. He spared Chikara a knowing look. "You have an eye on him, don't you?" His answer was a quick whack to his head. *I guess I'm right.*

*   *   *   *

Everyone had been riding for a few days, mostly in silence. Chikara rode on Maasianii, behind Satreih. Razij was on Yia's shoulder.

Kaskin yawned. "All right, I'm bored. Who wants to challenge me in a riddle contest?"

Chikara said quickly, "I'm in."

Satreih laughed. A dragon's love for riddles was widely known. They would never say no to a challenge.

Kaskin asked, "Challenger goes first, right?"

Chikara answered, "That's the traditional way. See if you can crack this one."

> "Only one color, but not one size,
>
> Stuck at the bottom, yet easily flies,
>
> Present in sun, but not in rain,
>
> Doing no harm, and feeling no pain."

Kaskin thought for a bit, then laughed. "C'mon, Chikara! I thought you were better than this! It's not more difficult than last time! This one is easy: a shadow."

His answer was a disappointed look on Chikara's face.

Satreih shook his head in bewilderment. "How did you know that? I'm terrible at riddles."

Kaskin answered, "Practice helps. I had riddle contests often with my mother when I was younger." He said to Chikara, "This one is yours." *Poor Chikara. Dragons normally aren't associated with men. This should stump her for a while.*

> "A man has to cross a river,
>
> with him are a fox, a chicken, and corn.
>
> He could only take one at a time.
>
> If he leaves them alone,
>
> The fox will eat the chicken,

The chicken will eat the corn.
What should he do?"

Yia grinned. "He should find a bigger boat!"

Satreih laughed. "That's my answer."

Chikara gave them sour looks. "If you two wanted to join, you should have said so at the beginning!" She thought for a bit. "Should he find a bigger boat?"

Kaskin smiled. "He could, but that's not the answer I'm looking for. I'm looking for the logical explanation."

Chikara growled.

Yia said, "I know."

Chikara said, "Don't you *dare* say the answer. This one is mine!"

Chikara couldn't figure out the answer in the next couple of hours.

Kaskin smiled and said, "I'll give you a freebee. Yia can say the answer, but you won't lose."

Chikara growled softly, but nodded.

Kaskin asked, "What's the answer?"

Yia asked, "The one with the man trying to cross the river with the fox, chicken, and corn, right?"

Kaskin nodded.

"He should bring the chicken over first; then go back and get the fox. He should bring the chicken back with him and take the corn. If he left the corn with the fox, he could go back and get the chicken."

Chikara slapped herself on her forehead. "Why didn't I think of that? My turn?"

Kaskin nodded.

"My posterior is adorned with feathers.
I have a rather long neck and quite a pointy nose.
I am able to fly, yet I have no wings.
What am I?"

Kaskin grinned. "You should know this one, Satreih!"

Satreih shook his head. "I told you, I'm pitiful at riddles."

Kaskin said the answer. "An arrow."

Chikara growled.

Kaskin said, "My turn."

"They have not flesh, nor feathers, nor scale, nor bone.

Yet they have fingers and thumbs of their own.

What are they?"

Chikara smiled. "Gloves. Take this:"

"It is cold and it is hot,

It is white and it is dark,

It is stone and it is wax,

Its true nature is of flesh,

And its color is red."

Kaskin shook his head. He couldn't come up with the answer for this one easily.

Yia was a different matter. She said excitedly, "I know this one!"

Chikara looked at her. "Ssh!"

Still, after a few hours, Kaskin couldn't spit the answer out. He was disappointed with himself. He said, "All right, you—"

Yia interrupted him. "Hey, Kaskin. You gave Chikara a freebee. Shouldn't she give you one?"

Chikara growled. "Fine." She thought she had him.

Yia smiled and said, "The answer is the human heart. This was old Master Merlin's riddle. I guess all the dragons know it now."

Kaskin said, "Of course you would know that one. He was a wizard and you're a witch." He looked to Chikara. "This one is for you."

They challenged each other with riddles for the rest of the trip. They were even for the most part, until Chikara finally won the match. It came close, with the riddles getting more and more complicated. Yia joined in occasionally, offering hints.

Satreih didn't really pay any attention to the riddle contest. He was more concerned about the land around them. In the distance, he could see a mountain range.

Satreih asked, "Chikara? Did Auburn say which mountain he lived in?"

"No. I guess he must have thought that I still had my nose." Chikara used mind-speech to Maasianii, telling the horse to move next to Hakku.

Satreih didn't fight the horse. Chikara was soon nose to nose with Razij. Razij meowed in alarm and dashed to Yia's other shoulder.

Chikara said coldly, "Kitty, *you're* the only one here with a nose. *You're* going to lead us to Auburn."

Razij mewled and pointed his head to Hakku, Maasianii, and Okanee.

Yia said, "I think he's trying to say, 'they have noses, too!'" She said softly, "To tell you the truth, I think the horses have been leading us."

A shadow flew above the mountains. Satreih saw it and said, "Something tells me that Auburn will come to us."

As soon as he could be heard, Auburn screeched something. Everyone but Chikara covered their ears.

Auburn moved closer to Chikara, Satreih, and Maasianii. Maasianii's legs collapsed underneath him from the wingbeats. Satreih was pressed into the horse's back. Auburn carefully took Chikara and placed her on his back.

Satreih tried to stop him.

Chikara said in mind-speech, *He's not going to hurt me. He'll lead us to his lair.*

Soon they were in Auburn's lair. His lair was a typical dragon's lair; it was filled with priceless treasures. Even though Chikara wasn't interested in such things, she did admit that he had a nice collection.

Screeching to Chikara, Auburn asked, *So he's the chosen-one?*

Chikara was hesitant. *Yes. What do you know about him?*

He's the only one who might be able to bring Verteq to ruins. If he does manage to kill him, he will never die. I'm not talking about the necklace. When Verteq finds him a few centuries after the battle, he will place a morith into Satreih's system. That is what happened to Meithoko, no? That fate is much worse than Hell itself.

Feh! How do you know this? Besides, I'll be there to protect Satreih from that fate! Chikara didn't like Auburn as much.

Your being there will make no difference. Verteq will find a way. If allowed time, the necklace's spell will wear off. Its gift is that of long life; not an eternal one. Satreih will die happily. But, if the morith is placed into him, it will keep him here on this cursed earth for eternity. The pain will be unbearable. You will not be able to do anything about it. There is nothing anybody can do about it, not even the next chosen-one. Verteq will have what he has desired for so long.

Chikara growled. *Makue said that there was a way to rid the earth of Verteq for eternity.*

There is. I have possession of it.

THE TRUE POWER OF
THE FIRE SWORD

Chikara stared at Auburn in open-mouthed shock.

Satreih looked at Chikara and asked, "What did he say?" Chikara didn't seem to hear him. He waved a hand in front of her face. Chikara blinked.

Satreih asked again, "Chikara? Your mouth is hanging open. What did he say?"

Chikara ignored him and screeched to Auburn, *You—you have the key to completely rid the earth of Verteq?*

Yes. It is this. Auburn flew up to the ceiling. He was soon out of sight. Auburn came back, gently holding a rock-looking item in his jaws.

Feh! You had me all worked up. For this? It's just a rock!

Auburn flew back up to the ceiling.

He came back, and contentedly laid on his precious pile of gems. *To your eyes, it appears as a rock. But I know differently. That is its dormant state. Look at Satreih's fire sword.*

Grudgingly, Chikara did as she was told. Chikara turned to Satreih and asked, "Can I see your sword?"

Satreih asked with a raised eyebrow, "Why?" He knew something was happening. He caught a quick glimpse of the rock in Auburn's jaws. He knew it was valuable, because Auburn was treating it cautiously.

Satreih unsheathed his sword. He was shocked to find that the swirling fire in the hilt was gone. He shot a quick, questioning glance to Auburn.

Chikara stood up to her full height, suddenly angry. She growled, *What happened to the sword!? Is it the rock thing's doing?*

The 'rock thing' is the Uasiev. Verteq knows that it is my possession. There was savage humor and malice in Auburn's voice. *He's frightened like a rabbit. So frightened that he had to purge the fire from Satreih's sword—and his.*

Why? Why would he purge the fire from both swords? Is he not weakening himself as well as Satreih?

Auburn was grinning evilly. *He is weakening himself. The swords are like brothers. If you purge the fire from one sword, the same will happen to the other. He gave himself a great advantage, and that came at a great sacrifice. The fire will return to Satreih's blade if I give you the Uasiev.*

Then give it to us!

Auburn said in an obnoxious screech, *I will gladly give it to you*—after *you rid my land of the evil magic.*

Chikara growled at him. *We need that magic, and it is not evil. Verteq knows that the Uasiev is in your possession. He knows that the fire will return to Satreih's blade if you give us the Uasiev. Why would he purge the fire from the swords if he knows we're here?*

Out of the corner of her eye, Chikara saw a spear that was heading directly for her. She dodged it and turned around to face her opponent.

All of them were surrounded by Wi'oks, and Verteq's other minions.

Some Wi'oks rode pig-like creatures. Their fur was jet-black, and it was dripping with blood. Their eyes were lifeless pits. Their tusks and fangs were adorned with spikes. They had hooves with claws.

Regular elves and men were scattered throughout the Wi'oks and the pig-creatures. Their flesh hung off of them, revealing their bones. They had no blood to bleed. Their eyes were rolled back into their heads. They were prisoners and victims of war. Verteq was using their corpses as puppets.

No one moved for the longest time. Satreih thought, *Wow. The battle hasn't even started and we've already lost. My sword doesn't have its power; Yia doesn't have her magic; Chikara is a regular woman; and we're outnumbered ten thousand to five. Six if I count Razij.*

Yia attacked the leader of the Wi'oks. She sensed some magic emitting from his lifeless body. Yia recognized the magic. It was hers. The Wi'ok leader gave her a toothless grin.

Yia's dagger stopped inches from its mark, right between his eyes. Yia couldn't move her body. He was using her own magic to paralyze her! She said to him in mind-speech, *You ... bastard ...*

The Wi'ok leader spared her another toothless grin. He spoke in English, but his voice hinted of death. "Bastard … I may be."

An invisible, painful force pushed against Yia. She cried out, and was thrown into Satreih. He happened to be right behind her.

Satreih's head slammed the ground. It knocked the wind out of him.

Yia helped him up. She said in mind-speech, *The Wi'ok leader has my magic. He used it against me.*

Satreih replied, *So distract him and I'll shoot him with an arrow!*

The Wi'ok leader approached them and said to Yia, "You … have no idea … how far the tiniest … bit of your magic … can go. It has … already … helped me out … some." He nodded to a few of the men and elves.

Yia growled. *Great. My magic has already been used for the wrong purposes. Does this mean that I would be held responsible for the murders after I retrieve it?*

The Wi'ok leader backed off into the ranks of his people. "I trust … that my comrades … will have fun … making you scream." He looked to Auburn. "Thanks … for the Uasiev. Master … shall find a … good use … for it." The leader waved his hand. That was a signal for his people to attack.

The fight didn't last long. Auburn didn't stand a chance; before he could attack, Verteq's minions entirely surrounded him.

Satreih watched his friends fall, one by one, out of the corners of his eyes. He was the only one left fighting. His ophilla had protected him against most attacks. Still, Satreih was already exhausted and out of breath. Fighting against this many people was hard work. He wished that the fire sword were working.

Verteq's minions stopped attacking and backed off.

Satreih thought, *What's going on?*

The Wi'ok leader stepped forward. "I want … to fight."

Between gasps, Satreih said, "Yeah? What, you decide to fight me now, when I'm weak? That shows cowardice."

The Wi'ok leader flipped the Uasiev up into the air, playing with it as if it were a toy. "You … want this … don't you? I doubt … that you … can take it from … me." He placed it into a pocket. "Attack … me."

"If you think that I'm foolish enough to make the first move, you must be a fool."

The Wi'ok leader gave a soft, knowing laugh. "Than … I shall attack … you."

He charged at Satreih with a scythe raised high. Magical energy was forming around the weapon.

Satreih dodged the attack. He deftly jumped around the Wi'ok leader. Satreih had the sword aimed at his exposed back. All of a sudden, he felt pain in his legs. One of the elves had jabbed him with a spear, drawing blood.

Satreih fell to the ground, not ready for the surprise attack. The sword flew out of his hand. Satreih smiled. The sword struck the pocket that held the Uasiev. He saw the Uasiev being sucked into the sword.

The Wi'ok leader stumbled in surprise. His clothes were burning away.

The sword, now back to normal, clattered to the floor. Satreih quickly grabbed it, and gasped. *The sword has much more power than before! I can feel it!*

The fire sword grew excruciatingly hot to Satreih's touch.

Satreih had a vision. He knew what was going to happen. He could hardly believe it. He brought the sword down and slammed it on the floor, exactly as his vision told him.

"My true power can only be brought forth with dire need, and only when the Uasiev is firmly implanted in my hilt."

Satreih fell to his knees, stunned. The sword clattered to the floor, at his side. Verteq's minions were just burned away by an incredible fire. No ashes remained. But Yia's magic, like an angry storm cloud, was hovering in the air.

Satreih looked down. Burned into his hand was a symbol that represented fire. It was cool now, but he could still feel the pain.

Kaskin sat up and shook his head, trying to rid himself of his headache. He saw Satreih.

Satreih seemed to be in a state of shock.

Kaskin smiled and asked, "You just used the sword's true power, didn't you?"

Satreih stuttered, "Y-Yeah, I-I th—" He didn't finish his sentence.

Kaskin raised an eyebrow when he saw his friend fall over. The sound of Satreih's soft snoring came to his ears. *That's right, Makue did say that Satreih would be exhausted after he learned a new skill.*

Yia woke. She surveyed the room with narrowed eyes. She noticed Kaskin was already up. She asked, "What happened to Verteq's army?"

Kaskin smiled. "Satreih used the true power of his sword. He killed them all in a single swing."

Yia let out a low whistle. "Impressive. Where's Satreih?"

Kaskin nodded his head in Satreih's direction. "He's going to be comatose for a while."

A thought occurred to Yia's mind. "I suppose the Wi'ok leader was burned to bits?"

Kaskin nodded. "Yeah, I assume so. Why'd you ask?"

Yia walked over to her magic and reclaimed it as her own once more. "I wanted to kill the creep."

*   *   *   *

Rasnir woke from his nap, shivering. As usual, he was running from a horrible fate in his nightmare.

At that moment, he had a strange thought. *I'm still alive. I-I've been kept in these gruesome conditions a little over a year and a half, I think. They've only been giving me a small piece of moldy bread and a small cup of fresh water once a day. Any normal man would have perished by now. I didn't get an infection when the Spy broke my nose. The injury was exposed. What's going on? Why am I thinking about this now?*

He heard voices outside the door. Rasnir put his ear to the door, listening. Two of the Spies were outside. Even though they were speaking English, their voices always had malice in them, no matter what kind of mood they were in.

"Hah hah. What do you have there?"

"A prisoner from the most recent battle."

Rasnir heard something thud on the floor, and an angry hiss.

"Huh! A prisoner? It's a cat!"

"True, true. But one of our men took it from its mistress' side during the confusion of the battle." The Spy paused. "Satreih just used the sword's true power. We lost some ten thousand."

If the other Spy were angry or upset by the news, he didn't show it. "What do we do with the cat? It's just an animal."

"We put it with the animal-*man*. That's what Master told us to do."

The other complained, "I don't like the animal-man having all these visitors. First Weuh, then the witch, and now the cat."

"I say the same. But these are Master's orders."

The door opened. Rasnir scurried to the other side of the room and cowered in his corner. A cat was thrown into the room. The door slammed shut.

When he heard the Spies' footsteps die away, Rasnir cautiously approached the cat. He sniffed it. The cat hissed, but Rasnir ignored it. *This cat has so many scents on it that I can barely get its own. The smells of battle, but also Satreih's and Yia's scents!*

*   *   *   *

Satreih stretched and yawned.

Yia was the first to notice that he was awake. "Hey sleepy head. You were comatose for about a week."

Satreih asked, "Really?" Even though he was still half-asleep, he caught the worry in her voice. "What're you worried about?"

"I can't find Razij. He's been missing since the battle."

Chikara grunted. "Huh. Maybe one of Verteq's people got the nuisance. Good riddance."

Yia gave her an angry look.

Satreih shook his head. "Impossible. I killed them all in a single swing." He brought his hand up to his face. The fire symbol still interested him.

Chikara offered, "Auburn says that the fire symbol is the symbol of the sword. You are bound to it. No one can take it from you now."

"So meaning if I try to get rid of the sword for whatever reason after the war it won't let me?"

Chikara shrugged. "Maybe. But why would you want to get rid of it anyway?"

Satreih spoke slowly, trying to put his thoughts into words. "I don't know if I like the extent of its power or not."

Kaskin was listening to the conversation. He chirped in, "If it weren't for its power a week ago, we'd all be dead."

"Still, I don't like killing that many. C'mon! I'm only seventeen! With the sword, I'm just as bad as Verteq!"

Auburn looked at Satreih and screeched something.

Chikara translated, "He says that you would be just as bad as Verteq if you *abuse* the power. Look at the sword."

Satreih did as he was told. The Uasiev didn't look like a rock any longer. It was a small dragon, lazily floating in the flames. It looked peaceful and content.

Satreih glanced at Auburn curiously. He screeched something in reply.

Chikara translated, "The Uasiev is a rock when it is outside of the sword, since it would look suspicious if it were a dragon. The sword's power increases when it is implanted in the hilt; which is why you were able to draw out its true power. Oh, by the way, he wants to see your map."

"The map? Why?"

"He can show you where the moriths are in this land."

Satreih said softly, "The map only shows our land."

Auburn screeched.

Chikara said, "That won't be a problem."

Satreih took out the map and handed it over.

Auburn placed a paw on it. The map rippled. It changed to match the features of this land. Auburn pierced the map with a claw, making two glowing spots appear on it. They were right next to each other.

Kaskin leaned over, looking at the map curiously. "I thought there were four moriths left?"

Auburn screeched.

Chikara's face turned pale. "There are two in this land. The third one is in Hell, literally. The fourth one is in Mosiania."

Satreih grumbled, "Great. One's in Hell. How the heck are we going to get to it without dying? Maybe we could find a vengeful spirit and lose on purpose?"

Yia scoffed. "No good. Losing in a match against a vengeful spirit would be the same as dying. There would be no way we could get back. Only one of us would have to go. Any more than that would be too risky. Damn. Verteq hid the morith in a good spot." She looked at Auburn and asked, "Do you know any way to get to it?"

Auburn screeched.

Chikara translated, "He can't help us there. We should worry about the two in this land first." Chikara was half talking to her friends, half thinking aloud. "There was always something guarding the moriths in the past: attacking cannibals, a foolish water nymph and a wizard, a ferocious, powerful dragon, werewolves, and a phoenix. The one that the unicorn destroyed was strangely guardian-free, but I think that's because it was in Makue's forest." She looked to Yia. "Something tells me that your magic is guarding these two, which is why they're in the same location."

Yia swore angrily. "Well, I guess that's better than having unsuspecting men find it, but still …"

Kaskin shuddered as he thought of something unpleasant. "Wait. What if a man *did* find it, and Verteq is letting him use the magic to protect his moriths?"

They all fell silent, alone with his or her own thoughts.

WHEN THINGS GO
WRONG

Chikara, Satreih, Kaskin, and Yia left Auburn's lair. Yia still worried about Razij, but Satreih reassured her that the werecat would turn up eventually.

Much to Yia's dismay, her magic and the moriths were in a large village, much like the village of Lupine Hills.

There was nothing to do during the ride to the village. Chikara and Kaskin passed their time by testing the other's wits at riddle challenges. This time, Kaskin won.

After the last difficult riddle, Chikara wrapped her arms around Satreih. "C'mon, Satreih. Why don't you join in? It's fun!"

"I told you. I'm pathetic at solving riddles."

Chikara started to play with his hair. She purred, "You would enjoy it."

Satreih was trying to keep a straight face. He was being pretty successful. "Are you flirting with me, Chikara?"

"No!" Chikara jumped back further on Maasianii.

Satreih glanced back. "You're blushing." He wasn't lying.

His answer was a quick, painful whack to his head.

Chikara said slowly with venom, "Kaskin, if you don't shut up, I am going to kill you."

Satreih turned around, curious. Kaskin's eyes were closed. He was shaking with laughter. His hands were pressed up against his mouth.

Kaskin removed his hands and said between laughs, "It was your fault for being obvious!"

Maasianii was right next to Okanee. Chikara was getting ready to inflict some serious pain on Kaskin.

Much to Kaskin's gratitude, Okanee bolted forward.

Chikara's attack missed.

After running for a short distance, Okanee turned around to face the others, pawing the ground with her hooves in a taunting manner. Kaskin stroked her neck. "G-Good girl." He could still feel Chikara's death glare.

As they were about to enter the village, Chikara looked back at the mountains. She said sadly, "I really wish I had my wings right now. The mountains look like they'd be a good flying spot."

Satreih said, "Well, as soon as Yia reclaims all of her magic, you can have them back."

They dismounted and left the horses on the outskirts of the village.

Chikara suddenly whirled around in alarm. She felt a pair of eyes staring at her from the crates next to the road. She saw no one. But the feeling that someone was watching her was still there. Chikara placed a hand on the hilt of her dagger just in case.

Kaskin asked, "What is it?" He stood on Satreih's other side. Kaskin knew that Chikara was still in a bad mood from earlier.

"Nothing. I just thought I was being watched." Chikara caught a glimpse of something shuffling between the crates.

Kaskin offered, "Probably just a homeless person. I wouldn't worry about him."

Chikara's vision was obscured when a group of people moved in front of the crates, waiting in line for a shop that was about to open. A bloodhound was with one of the people in the line. The dog caught her scent. The dog looked up at her curiously. He howled and started to tug at the leash.

Satreih led his friends away from the line, and the dog. He said to Chikara, "Why don't you try to stay away from the animals. You still smell like a dragoness, right?"

Chikara nodded. Behind her, she heard the sounds of the dog's master restraining his pet. He wasn't very successful. She heard someone cry a warning. "Oye! Dog loose!"

Satreih turned around and saw the bloodhound running toward them. He stepped out in front of his friends. *Great. We haven't been here for five minutes yet and we've already made a disturbance!*

Chikara pushed Satreih aside. She bent down to the dog's level and growled threateningly. He stopped in his tracks, shivering. His tail snaked in between his legs. The bloodhound turned around and ran, whining in fear.

Yia used some of her magic to listen in on some people's thoughts.

... is one of Mr. Baley's dogs, right? But I thought ...

Who is that woman?

Weren't those types of dogs supposed to be the most courageous? They wouldn't back down from any person.

The growl emitted from that woman's chest was beast-like!

Mommy! Help me! I'm scared!

People who saw what happened started to close in on Chikara, Satreih, Kaskin, and Yia.

Yia shook her head to rid herself of the voices. She said somewhat nervously, "Doggone. Maybe we should leave."

Kaskin answered with a touch of sarcasm, "Good idea. Any idea how? We can't move if you haven't noticed."

Chikara and Satreih both nodded in agreement.

"I've noticed." Yia glanced around, looking for something to make another disturbance with her magic.

Yia had an idea. She saw the crates that Chikara seemed interested in. They were stacked relatively high. Yia narrowed her eyes, focusing her powers on the crates.

The villagers turned around, shocked. The crates behind them had toppled over. The villagers took a couple of steps back in surprise. Behind the crates was the mayor's son, who had been missing for a month. They turned around. Maybe his disappearance had something to do with the strange woman who scared away Mr. Baley's dog?

They never found out; for the strange woman and her friends were gone.

*   *   *   *

Satreih and his companions never stopped running until they reached the village's fountain. The fountain was a long distance away from where they had entered.

Satreih panted, "That was cutting it way too close. I hate to think what would've happened if they found out about our true forms."

Yia said between gasps, "Then don't think about it. But this village raises a question."

"Oh yeah?" Kaskin gasped. "What is that?"

Yia used her hands for emphasis. "How in the world are we going to find two puny moriths in a place this huge?"

Chikara corrected her. "Two questions. That one, and who the heck was behind those crates?"

The others shrugged. Satreih offered, "Maybe we could ask the villagers."

Chikara laughed and lowered her voice. "Yeah. How about this? 'Hi. We really want to know who was behind the crates. Oh, and have you seen any evil ruby gems lurking about? If you don't tell me I'll tear you into mincemeat. I'm a dragon. That's why the dog went ballistic.'"

Kaskin laughed. "Well, you can't say that!"

"Obviously not."

Yia looked to her right. "There's an inn. We can stay here for a couple of days and search the city until we find the moriths."

A wheezy voice came from behind them. "You lookin' for moriths?"

Chikara whirled around, surprised. "You're the man who was hiding behind the crates!" she barked, but not as menacingly as when she had growled at the dog. The man had short red hair and lots of freckles. His eyes had an insane gleam. He was covered in dirt and cobwebs. "I wouldn't stick your nose into other people's business if I were you."

"I know, I know, Miss Fearsome Dragoness."

Chikara growled more fiercely. She withdrew her dagger. "You heard that bit, huh? You won't be telling anyone that." She put her dagger close to his neck.

Satreih said forcefully, "Put it away, Chikara."

Chikara didn't listen.

The man stared at the dagger with no fear showing in his eyes. "Killing me would be a very bad idea. Your friend seems to have the right idea. Listen to him."

Chikara growled.

Satreih said more forcefully, "Chikara! *Now.*"

Chikara reluctantly sheathed her dagger.

The man looked at Satreih. "She seems to listen to you. She's your pet?"

Chikara slapped the man, leaving a nasty-looking mark that instantly began to turn black and blue. "I am *not* a pet. You're lucky that I don't have my claws."

Chikara blinked in surprise. With difficulty, she managed to turn her head in Yia's direction. "Let me go," was all she said.

The man looked to Yia. "So the magic belongs to you, eh?"

Yia said without emotion, "You know that I'm a witch. Just like Chikara, I don't want you to tell anyone."

Kaskin said, "Hey … um …" He glanced around at the villagers. They were starting to push in, curious.

The man pointed to Chikara. He said in a loud voice, "This woman is a dragon!" He pointed to Satreih and Yia. "And they, they are elves! She's a witch!"

Yia released Chikara from the restraining spell. Chikara whipped out her weapon.

The villagers came at them with nets.

Satreih laughed nervously. "You don't really believe him, do you? Elves, witches, and dragons exist only in fairy tales." *Maybe I can try that trick.*

The villagers kept coming. Most were scared by Chikara. One brave man tried to throw a net over her. The net caught fire. The villager shouted in surprise and dropped the net.

Satreih came up behind him and said, "You won't be catching any fish, no matter how big they are." His fire sword was out. Without even waving it, the net had caught fire.

Satreih heard the sound of arrows being released. He quickly slashed the blade across the area between him and the arrows. A wall of flame erupted as if out of nowhere, protecting him and his friends.

They all turned and ran. Kaskin said, "I knew giving the sword to you was a good move!"

Satreih answered, "Yeah. Hey, Yia, I've seen you transform into different people. Can you transform us and yourself using the small bit of magic that you have?"

Yia panted, "That won't work. They'll still know that it's us!"

"Okay." An idea came to Satreih. "Could you transform us into animals? Like cats, or dogs—"

Chikara asked hopefully, "Or dragons?"

Despite the fact that he was running hard, Satreih laughed.

Yia said, "Sorry, no dragons. I don't know if I could transform everyone into animals. I've never tried transforming other people! It'll be dangerous."

Kaskin panted, "More dangerous than this?" He glanced back toward the villagers. They had somehow gotten past the wall of flame.

Satreih dropped to the ground on all fours and growled in pain. He could feel himself transforming. He felt his bones shifting to fit the bones of whatever animal he was transforming into. Mercifully, the pain stopped. Satreih heard a familiar voice.

"Oh good! I have four legs again! Awww, my claws aren't nearly as big as they used to be!"

Satreih turned in the direction of the voice. He drew his lips up in a grin. "Hey kitty cat. You're Razij's relative now!"

"Shut up Furface." Chikara hissed.

Satreih asked with amusement, "I'm Furface? Look at yourse—"

Yia said impatiently, "This isn't the time to stop, remember?" She glanced back at the villagers, who were coming closer.

Kaskin spotted a nice, plump mouse. He crouched down, getting closer to it on light paws.

The mouse glanced up at Kaskin. She squeaked indignantly, "Hey! Don't eat me! You're a man, right? I don't taste good to men."

Kaskin took a step back in surprise. He wasn't used to mice speaking to him. Still, he grumbled a bit. Kaskin dropped down closer to the ground, approaching the mouse. The mouse didn't move.

Yia stepped between them. "Kaskin! Ignore the cat's brain! We need to run!"

Kaskin looked back at the villagers, somewhat confused, with his whiskers and fur twitching in the slight breeze.

The mouse squeaked, "You're trying to get away? I know of a place where you can hide." She looked at Chikara nervously. "Though I never smelled something like you before."

Chikara growled, "Never mind about your nose! Bring us to the hiding place!"

"Right. This way. Follow me." The mouse scurried into a mouse hole.

Satreih complained, "We can't fit in there!"

The mouse's voice came back through the hole, but she didn't show herself. "Use your eyes, Furface. There's a window right above the hole, and that's plenty big enough for you!"

Satreih grumbled, "Great. Am I going to be known as 'Furface' now?" Nevertheless, he jumped through the window, breaking the glass. His friends were right behind him. A wave of arrows flew after them, just as Yia's tail disappeared into the gloom.

MICE IN DISTRESS

The mouse stopped, waiting for the cats to catch up. "Wait here. We mice are having a family reunion, from all over the nearby villages. There are thousands of us! Most of us don't take kindly to cats." She looked at the deep-orange cat with the tiger markings. He was cut up from the glass. "Sorry about that. I didn't know that the men had repaired the window. Right," she squeaked, "I'll be back."

The mouse disappeared into another room, via a hole in the wall.

Satreih sat down, slightly annoyed. He looked around the room. They were in a big warehouse filled with various tools. It was obvious that men hadn't been here in a while. The sunlight was leaking in through some gaps in the roof. Dust and cobwebs were everywhere.

Yia said, "The mouse was right. This place absolutely reeks of mouse scent."

Satreih asked, "Why did it hurt when I transformed?"

Chikara and Kaskin looked at Yia, both expecting the answer.

Yia jumped up onto a machine. She rolled on her back and began grooming herself, in a very cat-like manner. Some of the sunlight streamed onto the machine. Yia closed her eyes, content. The sunlight was making her drowsy, but she shook it off. "Because you guys aren't used to the cat's brain yet. Most of the time you have to fight it, but sometimes it comes in handy."

Yia rolled over onto her back and looked at Kaskin. "Remember when all you wanted to do was eat the mouse?"

Kaskin nodded, dumbfounded. His mind was coming back, and he rejected the idea that he was a cat. He didn't like the fact that Yia was purring.

Yia said, "You have the cat's brain, but you still have your human tastes. That's part of the reason why I stopped you from eating it."

After a while, the mouse hadn't come back.

Satreih said, still annoyed, "Where did the mouse take off to?" He hissed softly. "She went and found her relations, and started to hang out with them. I bet that she forgot that there were four hungry cats on her turf."

He watched the hole for a while, looking for any signs of the mouse's return. Satreih sighed. The cat's mind was telling him to take a nap in the sunshine. *Well,* he thought, *taking a nap would pass the time. Everyone else is already asleep.*

Satreih jumped onto the machine, next to Yia. He rested his head on her shoulder. Without opening her eyes, Yia wrapped her tail around his.

*   *   *   *

"C'mon, Furface, wake up!" The mouse started to tug on Satreih's fur and whiskers to get his attention.

Satreih grunted as a reply and yawned. "My name's not 'Furface.' It's Satreih. Come to think of it, you haven't introduced yourself, have you? Assuming that mice even have names."

"Of course we have names!" said the mouse, insulted. "Mine's Rosettela, if you really have to know. Besides, your tortoiseshell friend called you 'Furface,' so how was I to know whether that was your name or not?"

"All right, all right. Just don't get your tail into a knot." Satreih gently nudged Yia with his head in an effort to wake her.

Rosettela asked, "Speaking of your tortoiseshell friend, what in the world is she? I'd give up all my cheese to find out. I've never smelled a scent like hers before."

Chikara had woken up from her nap and approached Rosettela from behind. "I'm a dragon." She asked dismissively, "So what do the other mice have to say about us?"

Rosettela jumped. "Honestly! Did you really have to sneak up on me like that?" She jumped down from the machine and waited next to the hole. "Eldertail wants to meet with all of you, Furface in particular." Rosettela darted through the hole without another word.

"Hey!" Kaskin called after her. "How about waiting for us?"

Yia said, "Don't worry. She'll be easy to find." She jumped down from the machine. Chikara and Satreih were right behind her.

"Oh?" asked Kaskin, skeptical. "How do you figure that?"

"Do you know how to follow scent trails?"

Kaskin replied truthfully, "Well, no, not really."

Chikara sniffed Satreih's fur, searching for the mouse's scent on him. Rosettela couldn't get away from her now. "I swear. You men only use your noses for sneezing." She walked to the hole and felt the ground underneath it. "The ground is soft here. We could easily dig our way through to the other side. Follow me."

Eldertail's fur was cream colored, and his whiskers were bent with age. He was blind, but his sense of smell and hearing were sharper than any other mouse's.

Eldertail looked to the strangers with sightless eyes when they entered his room. "Rosettela?" he called. "You said we have cats visiting. I do not smell cats. A man is here, but I don't recognize the other scents."

Satreih looked to where the old mouse had his sightless gaze. Rosettela was balancing on one of the ropes that were close to the ceiling.

Rosettela said respectfully, "They just look like cats. The charcoal-like scent that you smell is a dragon, and the other smells are ... are ..." She had never smelled elves before.

"We're elves," Satreih finished.

Eldertail faced him. "What would two elves, a dragon, and a man want with me? Introduce yourselves."

Satreih said, "My name is Satreih. The other elf is Yia, the dragon is Chikara, and the man is Kaskin. The men around here found out about our true forms. They chased us, and Yia transformed us into cats. Yia is a witch. Then we met Rosettela and she led us here." He took a chance. "Do you know about the moriths?"

Eldertail thought for a while. "I do not know what a 'moriths' is. But I can tell you this: I felt evil within the warehouse's walls. An evil that even made me shiver, and whenever I slept I always had horrible nightmares. But that evil is not here now. It seems like it got up on feet and simply walked away."

Satreih asked confused, "It walked away?"

Eldertail nodded. "My extended family was just here for a reunion. They're from every part of this land. They say they have felt the evil as well once every month. But the amount of its power waxes and wanes like the moon. It was here this past month. I barely felt it, even with my 'sixth sense' as you would call it." Eldertail sighed. "The evil gets its power from the moon, though I do not know how. I'm told that the moon never shows its lovely face in this land anymore."

Rosettela called down from above, "Too right! I've never seen the moon in my short lifespan. It sounds wonderful." Her front paws were filled with cheese. She used her back paws and teeth to navigate back down the rope.

$$*\qquad*\qquad*\qquad*$$

Chikara, Satreih, Kaskin, and Yia were back in the room with the broken window. All of them were in their Race of Men forms.

Satreih was on his stomach, staring at his map. "This is weird. The glowing spots that Auburn marked have moved and are glowing more brightly. Eldertail said that the morith's power waxes and wanes with the moon. But there is no moon in *any* land. The sun is always shining here, and it's always new moon in our land."

Yia said, "If Verteq didn't exist, it would be a full moon tonight."

Satreih looked at her over his shoulder and asked, "How do you know that?"

"Magic helps." She said softly, "If we were near the moriths, we would sense their presence. But we wouldn't be able to do anything about it."

"Oh?" Satreih asked inquiringly. "Why not?"

Chikara yawned. "Because we would need the moon in order to see them. If we can't see them, we can't utterly destroy them. They would be impossible to destroy on the night of a new moon."

Yia added softly, "Their powers increase on new moon."

Kaskin said jokingly, "So what we have to do is get on the tallest mountain and convince the Heavens to show the moon again."

Satreih sniggered. "And after we're done with that, we could ask the Heavens to open the Gateway to Hell so one of us could nab the other morith that's down there."

Kaskin laughed. The ideas sounded so farfetched.

"Actually," Yia said, "You guys aren't all that far off."

The sniggering stopped. Kaskin looked at Yia with his mouth wide open and with a raised eyebrow.

Satreih looked at Yia with wide eyes. "Are you saying that that's possible?"

Yia nodded and spoke, "If only we had a moonstone."

Kaskin grinned. He said to Satreih, "I think Father gave you one."

Satreih dug into one of his many pockets. He pulled out the moonstone. "How did you remember that I had this?"

"I have a good memory."

Yia leaned over and took the moonstone from Satreih.

Satreih asked, "What do you need the moonstone for?"

"The highest mountain is impossible to reach."

"Yeah? So?"

Yia smiled. "But the stone, with a little bit of magic, can get us there. But we can only send one person."

Satreih asked, "Why?"

Yia scowled. "When someone smashes the moonstone on the magical rock, the moon will appear in both lands. But after that, that person will be immediately sent to Hell. The only chance to get back is to ask the favor of a spirit that's down there. A spirit that was sent there by accident, and would have no grudge whatsoever against the living. Dammit. This is way too risky."

Yia looked at the floor, her jaws clenched. She never liked to admit defeat.

Kaskin asked softly, "So when the moon is shining, the other three of us would go morith hunting?"

Yia nodded.

Satreih said in a small voice, "I'll go." He hoped that he sounded braver than he felt.

Yia looked at him. "You have no idea what to expect," she said, her voice starting to crack. "You could very, very easily lose yourself."

"I'll have the sword with me. Isn't Hell supposed to be filled with fire?"

Kaskin said, "If you don't want to go, one of us could take the sword from you. You would still have your bow and arrows for weapons."

Satreih laughed softly. "I think you forgot about this." He showed Kaskin the fire symbol that had been burnt into his hand. "No one can take the sword from me. I don't think it matters if the person is a friend or not."

Satreih stood up. He looked to Yia and asked, "May I have the moonstone, please?"

Yia walked up to him and pulled him into a tight hug.

Satreih hugged her back. He was shocked. Normally Yia wasn't the affectionate type.

After holding him for a few minutes, Yia looked at him directly in the eye and said, "Whatever you do, don't you *dare* lose yourself. Or else I will kill you."

Satreih grinned. "That was an empty threat. Technically, if I lose myself, I'll die, right?"

Still holding his gaze, Yia said, "You know what I mean." She let go.

Satreih got hugs from both Chikara and Kaskin.

Satreih asked, "So how do I get there again?"

Yia asked, "You sure you're ready for this?"

"No. But I'm the only one who can go."

"I'll teleport you to the site with the magical rock."

Satreih and the moonstone disappeared in a flash of light.

TIME TO GO MORITH HUNTING

Instantly, the sunlight that was streaming in through the ceiling changed to moonlight.

"Wow," said Kaskin. "That was fast. Wasn't he just here a second ago?" He waved his hand in the empty place where Satreih had been standing.

Yia said, "Time has no meaning in the Heavens." She walked over to the map that had been left on the floor. The spot where the moriths now were was glowing intensely. "Oh, no," she breathed.

"What?" asked Kaskin.

"Itimei and King Stephenson are in danger."

Rosettela stuck her small, furry head out of the hole. Her nose was twitching. She saw the moonlight and started squeaking excitedly.

Kaskin gave Yia a confused glance and asked, "What's she squeaking about? I can't understand her in this form."

"Probably something about the moonlight. Hang on." Yia transformed them all into cats again.

Rosettela was squeaking very fast. "What is this? It's like the sun, b-b-but ... I ... it's cold! I—"

Yia gently pressed her paw up against her mouth. "It's the moon."

"T-Th-The moon? Ruh-really?"

Yia said patiently, "Yes, really."

"I-I-I'm gonna see!" She darted out of the warehouse.

"Well," said Kaskin, "That was different."

Yia said, "She's never seen the moon before, so give her a little slack. I'm going to find her."

Outside the warehouse, Rosettela was staring up at the full moon in awe. She was so enthralled by it that she didn't hear Yia approach.

Yia said, "Pretty, isn't it?"

"Y-Yes, very." Rosettela's squeaking slowed down now that the shock wore off. She reluctantly tore her gaze off the moon and asked, "W-Where'd Furface go? I thought he hung out with you. Did you guys get into a fight or somesuch?"

Yia didn't answer right away. "We didn't get in a fight. It's hard to explain where he went. Besides, you would never believe me."

"My relations think I'm crazy. I am. I'll believe you."

"No, you won't."

"Yes, I will! Tell me!"

Yia thought for a bit. She had the strange sensation of longing. "I will tell you this: Satreih is the reason why the moon is shining."

"Furface made the moon come out!" There was utter bewilderment in Rosettela's voice.

Yia nodded.

"W-Wow. Um, why were those spots glowing on that map?"

"You know the evil that you felt in the warehouse on certain nights?"

"Yeah?"

"The glowing spots show where the evil is."

"They were glowing near Lupine Hills, right?"

Yia nodded.

"My aunt's cousin's brother, Pathe, lives there. He's still here. He plans to leave soon, and maybe you can go with him. He doesn't fear cats." Rosettela jumped down off of the ledge that they were on. "I'll go find him." She disappeared into the warehouse.

Yia stayed on the ledge for a while, wondering how Satreih was doing.

*   *   *   *

"So," Chikara asked, "How long do you think it'll be until their first kiss?"

"Whose first kiss?" Kaskin asked, confused.

"Satreih's and Yia's, smart one! It's obvious that they like each other."

"Do you really want to talk about this? I thought you were jealous."

"Jealous?! Me?"

Kaskin grinned. "Yeah, you. You were the one flirting with Satreih on the way to the village."

Chikara hissed.

Kaskin scooted away from her, just in case. He started licking his paw somewhat nervously. "Um, I don't know. What would you guess?"

Chikara was just about to answer as Yia came back in.

"What are you guys talking about?" asked Yia, suspicious.

Kaskin stammered, "N-Nothing."

Yia gave him a look. She didn't believe him.

Chikara saved Kaskin by changing the subject. "What does the mouse want? She looked at us like she wanted to say something, but thought better of it."

"I don't know. Anyway, she's getting a relative that lives in Lupine Hills. He'll tell us where the moriths are."

Rosettela and another mouse came out of the hole. The other mouse looked almost identical to Rosettela, except that he wore miniature spectacles.

The other mouse sniffed curiously. "You all don't smell like cats."

Chikara answered, "We're not."

"Where's the fourth of you? He hasn't been gone for long. I know that much."

Rosettela said excitedly, "He's the reason why the moon is out!"

"Really? How could one person do something so huge?"

Yia said, "He's special." She changed the subject. "Do you know where the evil in Lupine Hills is?"

Pathe scratched his ear nervously. "'Course I do. It's in the same spot every time. I'll tell you where it is, but I'm not leaving the warehouse until it goes away from my home." He shuddered.

"Where is it?" demanded Kaskin.

Pathe scratched his ear nervously again and started to play with his tail. "It's in the palace's basement. A few of my buddies live there. I hope they left. It's getting stronger every time it comes."

*   *   *   *

Within an hour, Chikara, Kaskin, and Yia were flying towards Lupine Hills on Auburn's back. The horses were running beneath them, easily keeping up.

Auburn had been right outside the warehouse when they left. Everyone else in the village was asleep. They had no clue that the moon was out.

Auburn landed on the ground heavily. He screeched something as they got off. As soon as they were off, he flew back to his mountain.

Kaskin asked, "Translation please, Chikara?"

"He said that he can't take us any further. The morith is draining all of his power and making him sick."

Yia said, "You look a little green yourself."

"I don't really feel the best," Chikara admitted. "I think the two moriths drain all dragons' power. But since I'm a 'woman' I don't feel it as much as poor Auburn did."

Yia asked, concerned, "Do you want to stay here?"

"Stay here! No! No way! Satreih's fighting spirits, and if I stay here, you two would be the only ones destroying the moriths. I'm coming!" She started to lead the way into Lupine Hills.

Yia cautiously opened the door to the palace. Some green fumes billowed out. Yia jumped back in surprise and pushed Chikara and Kaskin out of the way.

Kaskin asked, "What *was* that?"

"Toxic vapors. They force people back into their true forms. Those who are already in their true forms are left unconscious and barely breathing."

Kaskin growled and made a move to go into the palace.

Yia grabbed him by the back of his shirt. She closed her eyes, focusing her powers. The next instant, Chikara, Kaskin, and Yia were protected by a blocking spell.

Inside the palace, the air had a musty scent to it. The lights were out. Unconscious bodies were strewn on the floor.

Chikara looked around. She asked Yia, "Is there anything you can do for them?"

Yia shook her head sadly. "It's taking everything I have to maintain these shields. If I try to use any more magic, I'll pass out."

A voice said from behind them, "Well, well, well! So the villagers didn't catch you?"

Chikara, Kaskin, and Yia whipped around. The man who spoke was the same man that had revealed their true forms to the villagers.

Chikara growled and withdrew her dagger. "You have nerves to be messing with me again, especially after what happened last time."

Chikara struck out with her dagger. A small, black force field developed around the man. Chikara cried out and was thrown against the wall, hard. She got up. A cut had appeared between her eyes; the same spot that she was aiming for on the man.

The man laughed softly. "The force field repels any attacks and turns them back on the attacker."

Kaskin came up behind him, with his sword in his hand. "Who are you?"

The man turned around to face him. "My name is Myxini. My father, the mayor of that disgraceful village, had a lot of power. He was feared. I was abducted by people who wanted to get even with him. I was pulled along behind the abductors, enclosed in a prison wagon. The wagon stopped. Outside I heard screams of pain and terror. The wagon's door was opened. Verteq was standing outside, drenched in his victims' blood. He gave me some magic and asked me to protect his possessions. I agreed whole-heartedly."

Chikara was only half listening to him. She contacted Yia through mind-speech. *The toxic vapors. How are they absorbed?*

Only through the skin. Why?

Get rid of the shield and let the toxic vapors transform me back into my true form. What!

I have scales. They'll protect me.

Yia said softly, *Kaskin and I don't have scales. We would both fall unconscious.*

I'll heal you two.

Yia let Kaskin know through mind-speech. Kaskin nodded ever so slightly, trying not to let Myxini know what was happening.

Chikara roared furiously. She began to tear at Myxini's force field with her claws; hammering it with all her strength. She ignored the sudden sickness that waved over her. It was the same sickness that had tormented Auburn.

Myxini turned around to face her and laughed. "You fool! The force field cannot be destroyed!"

Wrong!

Much to Myxini's great surprise, the force field shattered into little pieces and fell around him.

Chikara breathed golden fire. Myxini didn't have any hope of dodging. The moriths he had been protecting were instantly destroyed when he shrieked with pain.

The toxic vapors vanished when the dragon fire touched them. The lights came on as if the toxic vapors had been smothering them the whole time.

Chikara leaned Kaskin and Yia up against herself. Both of them were still unconscious, even though the toxic vapors had disappeared.

Chikara nuzzled them affectionately with her snout. *C'mon, you two. Wake up.*

Kaskin and Yia stirred and woke.

Yia walked over to the other portion of her magic and reclaimed it. She saw that the other people in the room were starting to wake up. Yia turned to Chikara and said, "Maybe I should transform you back."

A surprised shout came from behind them.

"Too late," Kaskin muttered.

Once again they were surrounded by guards. Fear and uncertainty showed in the guards' eyes.

A familiar voice called, "I wouldn't attack them if I were you."

One of the guards, apparently the leader of the group, turned and said, "P-Princess, this is a dragon."

"I know that. I've seen her fight. Even though you have numbers, you wouldn't stand a chance."

Chikara said to the frightened guard, *I would listen to her if I were you.* She hurried after Itimei, who had just motioned for all of them to follow.

*   *   *   *

King Stephenson stood, facing the floor-to-ceiling window, watching the moon. He still felt somewhat sick. He didn't know why. He heard people enter the room. Still watching the moon, King Stephenson asked, "Are you the people responsible for this?" He gestured toward the moon.

In a way, yes. But Satreih is the real reason why the moon is out.

King Stephenson whirled around in surprise. The voice sounded so familiar, and yet ...

Don't worry. I'm not going to eat you.

... so beast-like. King Stephenson took a step back.

Itimei looked up at Chikara and asked curiously, "Speaking of Satreih, where is he?"

Yia looked at the ground.

Chikara answered, *That's hard to explain. There's no way you would believe me.*

Kaskin told King Stephenson what had just happened with Myxini.

After listening, King Stephenson looked at Chikara. "I have nowhere for you to stay. The guards are frightened by you."

Kaskin gave Chikara a sideways look. "Maybe you could stay with Auburn. I don't think he would mind some company."

Chikara nodded. She flew through the window, which was plenty big enough for her. She called back, *I'll fly now, under the cover of the night sky. Most everyone is still asleep.*

THE GATEWAY TO HELL

Satreih took in his surroundings. The full moon hung in the sky like a pleasant, glowing orb. The mountains towered over him; he felt small and insignificant because of their sheer size. Millions of light pink flowers were in bloom, even though a layer of snow was on the ground. There was a humongous lake. Its water was completely still and clear. Satreih could barely see an interestingly shaped rock on the opposite bank. There was no way around the lake. He had to swim.

Satreih had the moonstone in his hand. He hastily shoved it into his pocket. He didn't care about the lake's temperature. Satreih was surprised to find that the water was relatively warm, even though it was snowing. His breaststrokes barely made a disturbance in the calm water. Once he was in the middle of the lake, Satreih stopped swimming and looked down. Even with his keen eyes, he couldn't see all the way to the bottom.

Satreih made it to the other side, slightly panting. He stood. To his amazement, he found that he was already completely dry. Satreih walked over to the interestingly shaped rock, raised the moonstone above it, and hesitated. Fear came into his mind. He hesitated for a little while longer, but he smashed the moonstone on the rock, shattering it.

The moon disappeared, leaving the mountain valley that Satreih was in completely dark. Satreih didn't know what had hit him. He was lying on the ground.

Smoke and fire immediately filled his lungs. The pain was unbearable. Satreih grasped his sword, making some of the pain vanish. But most of it was still there.

*   *   *   *

Airon cursed Verteq bitterly under his breath. He shook the chains that bound him for the hundredth time, in a futile attempt to break free. He would so love to fight Verteq one-on-one, to avenge his family.

I'd probably lose. The thought made Airon even more furious.

Airon looked up in shock. *A new arrival. Wait—he's not dead?* Airon looked at him closer. His eyes grew wide. *What is* he *doing here!? He is too young to endure this type of pain!*

"Hey. If you let me loose, I'll help you destroy the morith and get you out of this torturous pit."

Satreih looked to his right, shocked. Most of the poor souls here were in so much pain that they couldn't even talk. The elf who had spoken was bound to a rock face, with red-hot wires cutting into his flesh. He had brown eyes and black hair that was almost the same length as Satreih's. He and Satreih had the exact same body type.

Satreih cut the chains that bound him. The chains instantly gave way once the fire sword touched them.

The elf fell heavily, but managed to get back up on his feet with a little help. He rubbed his wrists, in a pointless attempt to get the blood circulating. "Thanks."

Satreih nodded. "Who bound you up like that?"

Airon gave Satreih a sideways look. "You can't guess?"

"Verteq?"

"Yup."

Satreih asked, "What did you do to get him to bind you up like that?"

Airon hesitated. "Who's your mother? Tell me."

Satreih answered, "Her name's Chikara."

Airon closed his eyes as if the thought hurt him. "Then I was right. You shouldn't be here."

"I don't have a choice. Why do you—"

Airon interrupted him. "You don't understand! Chikara was my wife. And you ... you're my only son."

Satreih stared at him for a while. "What's your name?"

"Airon."

Satreih asked softly, "What happened to our family?"

"Verteq hunted us down, one by one. He knew that you would be the chosen one before you were even born. He sent me here as a warning to you." He added, "That's the nice way of putting it."

Satreih grimaced. He had known that he would have to fight Verteq in the end, and he wasn't exactly looking forward to it. But now his mind changed. He wanted to fight Verteq as soon as possible.

Airon said, "Our family wasn't the only one that Verteq killed off."

Satreih said softly, "I know. My friend, Yia, is the only one left in her line. She didn't know what happened to her family, but she was guessing that Verteq did something to them. She recently told me."

Airon nodded. "She's right." He asked slyly, "Is she your girlfriend?"

Satreih turned a little red in embarrassment. "You could say that."

"Hmm!" exclaimed Airon approvingly. "Good choice!"

"Huh?"

"Our family and hers were great friends. We always got along well and were friends with every member of her family. Whenever there was a celebration the other family was always invited, and they would do everything in their power to attend." Airon grinned. "Her family made the best fireworks."

Satreih liked the idea that Yia's family and his got along so well. He asked darkly, "What did Verteq do to them?"

"He stole all of their magic powers. Witches and wizards can't survive for long without magic. Our family tried to help them, but there was nothing we could do. I wouldn't tell her that if you want her to stay behind when you leave for Mosiania."

"Stubbornness is inherited, I take it?"

Airon nodded vigorously. "Verteq is a false wizard. False wizards can only hold so much magic. If they try to hold any more magic than their abilities permit, that will kill them."

Satreih pointed out, "Verteq stole Yia's magic and split it into shards. She survived."

"Then she still had a little bit of her magic left."

"I thought Verteq took all of it."

Airon thought for a bit. "Does she have a werecat with her?"

"Yeah. His name's Razij."

"That's why. He was sustaining her. Werecats have a bit of magic of their own. He was letting her use some, even though he didn't know it. Razij is one of the last werecats left."

Satreih asked, "Why? Did Verteq kill them off before he attacked Yia's family?"

Airon nodded sadly.

Satreih got a sick feeling in his stomach. "Razij isn't with us." He added in a softer voice, "I think Verteq has him."

"Then you must get him back, if he hasn't already been killed. If Yia is attacked again and loses her magic, she won't be around for long without his assistance. I guarantee it."

Satreih was so engrossed in the conversation that he hadn't noticed that his father had led him to a barred, iron door. Evil miasma poured through the cracks.

Satreih said, "Let me guess. The morith is in there?"

Airon nodded. "Only a fire sword can break through that door."

"I won't have a problem." Satreih whipped the fire sword out of its scabbard and slammed it against the iron door. The door instantly vanished. The miasma gushed out of the opening.

Some of the miasma touched Satreih's flesh. "Aaahhh!" Satreih held the sword up to protect himself against it. He looked at his arm. Part of it had melted. "Oww, that hurt." He looked at his father. "Did any of it touch you?"

"No. I won't be able to go in there with you. It vaporizes spirits. One poor soul touched it. I'll bet you anything he's in a more painful place than this."

Satreih asked with a touch of sarcasm, "How can any place be more torturous than Hell?"

Airon replied, "If Verteq wills it, it can happen." He added sternly, "Come back after you've destroyed the morith. I am the only way that you can get back to the other world. I don't want to see my only son perish in a place like this."

Satreih nodded. He walked into the miasma, holding the sword up for protection.

*   *   *   *

Hmm! Yia's got magic back!

Rasnir grinned at Razij. "I knew you weren't a normal cat." He had just watched Razij transform into his true form. "Forgive me for asking. What are you?"

Werecat. People ask me that all time.

Rasnir asked, "When you first came here, I smelled Satreih's scent on you. Where is he now? Do you know?"

Last time I with him—in other land.

"He's in the other land? He made it that far?" Rasnir asked, shocked.

Has three other friends with him. Yia, Kaskin, Chikara.

"Chikara?" *His mother's with him?*

Annoying dragon.

"A dragon, you say?"

Yup. I no like her much. She no like me much. Razij sniffed the air and hissed. His fur was standing on end.

"What?"

Sniff. You smell something evil?

"This place has always smelled evil."

No! More evil than before!

Rasnir sniffed the air and wished he hadn't. He held his hand up against his nose, trying to block out some of the disgusting smell. "You're right. Do you know why?"

Morith has been moved closer to us. Verteq angry, very angry. Ninth morith about to be destroyed.

"What! How do you know that?"

Werecats like me have bit of magic. We know things. Razij's eyes grew wide in shock. He started to bang his head against the wall.

"Hey! Stop it!" Rasnir grabbed Razij's head in both hands to prevent the were-cat from hurting itself.

Satreih no is in other land. He in dangerous place. Very dangerous. He no knows about time limit for living beings!

Rasnir looked at Razij curiously, waiting for him to explain.

*   *   *   *

Satreih's eyes were watering. Even with the sword, he could barely see. The miasma was so thick. Breathing was harder, and started to hurt. There was a ringing in his ears. It got more intense with each step he took.

In the distance, Satreih could just make out the morith. He threw the sword and struck it. The morith and the sword were enveloped in flame. The flame fanned out, going through the miasma and Satreih. Satreih gasped as he fell to the ground.

After a while, he looked up. The morith had vanished. The sword was lying on its side. The miasma was evaporating through the ceiling, the ground, and the walls. A dark magic paralyzed Satreih. He couldn't get up.

Outside the hole, Airon watched in wonder. *I guess he destroyed the morith. There's no trace of the miasma!* He waited for a while, and still Satreih did not come out. *Wait—maybe the miasma does something to people who are still alive?* Airon cursed himself for being such a lousy father as he ran into the hole.

Airon found Satreih. He was unconscious. Airon pulled him into a hug. Satreih and the sword disappeared.

Airon stood up. *He's in his world now. I'm sure of it.*

KASKIN'S LAST
BATTLE

There was an unexpected flash of light. Everyone in the room jumped in surprise.

"Satreih!" Yia ran to his side, gently pulling his head onto her lap. She placed her hands on his forehead and heart, trying to heal him with magic.

Kaskin and King Stephenson came over. King Stephenson looked at Satreih with wide eyes.

Kaskin asked softly, "Is there anything I can do to help?"

"I-I don't … yeah. There is. I know she's probably with Auburn now, but contact Chikara with mind-speech. My magic won't be enough to help him."

✳   ✳   ✳   ✳

Hah! Bet you can't do that, Auburn!

Don't get too cocky!

Chikara had just raked the side of an unused mountain with her claws, sending dozens of boulders crashing into the valley below. All the boulders smashed into pieces so small that even the smallest of dwarfs could easily pick them up. She roared with pleasure.

Kaskin's voice entered Chikara's head, *Chikara!*

Kaskin? What's going on? She had picked out the touch of panic in his voice.

Satreih's back. He's in bad shape. He's covered with burns, and some of his flesh has melted. Yia's trying to heal him with magic, but it isn't really helping.

Right. I'm coming.

Auburn screeched, *The sun's back up now. You'll be seen.*

Chikara growled. *I don't care.*

Kaskin mind-spoke again. *Hey. Yia's saying that she can transform you to your woman form. Oh. Maasianii should be there.*

Chikara looked around. Sure enough, she saw Maasianii trotting towards her.

Chikara flew above the horse. She instantly dropped from the sky. She landed gracefully on Maasianii. He immediately started galloping out of the mountains.

Auburn wished Chikara good luck and flew back to his lair.

✶   ✶   ✶   ✶

The first thing Satreih saw was Yia. She looked worried.

Satreih sat up and managed to irritate some burns. "How long was I unconscious?"

"A couple days. It probably would have been longer if Chikara hadn't helped. Kaskin and King Stephenson are humoring her with some cows. She hasn't eaten in a while. I made her go." Yia slapped her hand against her forehead. "God. I'm such an idiot."

"Why do you say that?"

"I just spoke to Razij with mind-speech. He told me you were unconscious because there is a time limit for living beings in Hell. You came extremely close to going over that limit." She added in a softer voice, "I figured it must have been something like that."

"Don't worry about it. Besides, who can keep track of time in a place like that?" Satreih changed the subject. "Where's Razij?"

"With your father."

Satreih gave her a curious look.

Yia added, "With Rasnir. Why did you look at me like that?"

"That's who sent me back. My blood-related father."

Yia observed, "Something about you has changed. What?"

Satreih said softly, "I knew I was going to be the one to kill Verteq. I didn't want the responsibility. My father told me what happened to my family. Verteq hunted them down and killed them all." *And yours, but I'm not telling you that yet.* He said in a loud and clear voice, "I want to kill that beast now more than ever."

Yia asked with a touch of amusement in her voice, "And do you know how you're going to do that?"

"Um, not really." *I'll figure out that little bit soon.*

Chikara and Kaskin entered the room.

Satreih looked up to Chikara and said, "I thought the guards were afraid of you."

Actually, most of the ones on shift now are the men that Kaskin brought over. They absolutely love dragons. I'm glad you're awake.

Kaskin added, "I am as well." He grinned at Chikara. "They all had to feed you, didn't they?"

Chikara nodded vigorously.

Satreih laughed. "So you have a full belly now, don't you?"

Completely. I couldn't eat a rat even if I wanted to! Chikara rolled onto her back, very content. *I couldn't entirely heal those burns. They were too severe. Sorry.*

"No problem. Are you guys ready to go back to our land soon?"

I'm too full. We would fall into the Ugulaly Ocean. Some of the sea serpents and other creatures are nasty!

Kaskin grinned. "I'd agree with you there."

One of the men who had fed Chikara came into the room. "Are you getting ready to leave? Already?"

Satreih nodded. "Yes. Tell King Stephenson that the next time he sees us there will be normal seasons."

There was wonder in the man's eyes. He left to deliver the king his message.

Kaskin looked at Satreih with a raised eyebrow. He said, "I thought Chikara was the cocky one."

Satreih sometimes gets cocky "when he's mad."

Yia transformed Chikara in mid-sentence. She planned to transform her back when they were next to the ocean, and hidden from man's view.

*   *   *   *

It took a while to cross the Ugulaly Ocean, but not as long as it would have if they had gone by ship.

Satreih took advantage of the time to think up a plan. *Meithoko used the powers of the Ice Goddess. But I heard she's hard to reach and nearly impossible to find. Ha! I've been to Hell and back. That was supposedly impossible. Still, I also heard that she erected barriers that repelled anyone with a fire capability. And when Meithoko fought with Verteq, Verteq didn't have his magical powers.*

Hmm. Magic powers. The Satreih before me borrowed magic from a friend. He used the magic on Verteq, causing the beast to lose his wizardry powers. But Satreih was instantly killed when Verteq reversed the magic. How do I know that won't hap-

pen to me if I use that method? If he does end up killing me, I won't be able to have a future with Yia.

An idea came into Satreih's head. It wasn't a pleasant one. He turned around and asked, "Yia?"

Yia looked up. She was concentrating on forming a complicated spell between her hands. "What?"

"Can false wizards recognize a different person's magic?"

Yia nodded. She concentrated on the spell again.

Satreih turned around, clenching his teeth. *Damn! If I borrow Yia's magic, Verteq will recognize it. He'll kill me with it and would later kill her. I don't want that to happen to her!* He sighed. *Maybe attacking him all-out with no strategy would be the best …*

Satreih used mind-speech with Chikara. *What do you think would be the best way to attack Verteq?*

I honestly don't know. The legends don't really seem to help much. But I know what Kaskin's answer would be if you were to ask him.

What?

If there's nothing to guide you, attack using only your instincts. Thoughts would only cloud your mind. Chikara added, *That's the one major difference between you two. You try to find the logical way even if it is the wrong choice; Kaskin goes only by his instincts. Most of the time, his instincts are accurate.*

Satreih looked down, thinking. He knew she was right.

Chikara said to him, *I wouldn't worry about it too much. You will know what to do when the time comes.*

Satreih nodded. He looked to the ground. They were just passing over Rasiamoramisa. *Can you stop near Meikosa?*

Sure.

Chikara landed in the same spot as she did after she and her friends had escaped from their first visit to Rasiamoramisa.

They made a small camp. Yia caught swallows for Satreih, Kaskin, and herself using magic.

Satreih didn't say anything during the meal. He was too deep in thought. The others noticed this; he was also quiet during most of the trip. They let him be.

One by one, Chikara, Kaskin, and Yia fell asleep. Satreih stayed up.

After a long while, Satreih shook Yia awake. "Come with me, please."

Yia shook off her drowsiness and followed him.

Satreih led her to a beautiful chasm and sat down on its rim. Yia stood behind him, with her hands on his shoulders.

After some time, Yia asked, "Are you about to tell me what's been on your mind?"

"Part of it." He hesitated.

"It has been so long. I can hardly believe that we're probably going to be in Mosiania tomorrow." Yia added softly, "If there is such thing as 'tomorrow' any more. It all seems like one endless night."

"But you're not coming."

"Of course I'm coming! What do you mean I'm not?" Yia had to force down most of her anger.

"No. You're not." Even though he was nearing his eighteenth birthday, Satreih sounded like a tired, old elf. Yia's reaction was exactly what he expected from her.

"Why? You think I'm not good enough?"

"Of course I do," was Satreih's quick answer.

Yia started walking back towards the camp, enraged. "Huh. You need all the help you can get. Going into Mosiania by yourself is suicide! Fine! If you bring the others, how're you going to smuggle yourself, a man, and a dragon into thousands upon thousands of Verteq's minions?" Deciding to throw in some sarcasm, Yia added, "Maybe ask Weuh for an invisibility spell? If you die, you're dead. Your father won't be able to send you back!"

Satreih started, "Yia ..."

"Don't bother. I don't care! If you just—"

Satreih interrupted her tirade. "Stop!" He stood up and pulled her into a kiss. Yia tried to fight and still wanted to, but gave up. She felt a little guilty for going off on him like that, without listening to what he had to say first.

They stayed like that for a few minutes, kissing. For a split second, through the bliss, an unpleasant thought appeared in Satreih's head. This could be the first and last time he would kiss her.

Satreih was hugging her tightly. "Listen to me. The reason I don't want you to come is because I love you. I don't want you to get hurt."

Yia said, "All right. If you wish for me to stay in Meikosa, then I'll stay behind. But you have to promise me something."

"What?"

Yia looked at him, directly in the eye. "Come back, and don't you *dare* do anything reckless. Or else. Promise me that."

"I promise." Satreih couldn't resist. "Or else what?"

"Or else I'll kill you."

"What if Verteq beats you to it?"

"Then I'll kill your spirit."

Satreih grinned, amused. "I thought you couldn't kill spirits."

"Arrgh!" Yia slammed her head against his chest. "You know what I mean." She let go of him and started towards Meikosa, resisting the urge to ask him if he would walk with her. "See you later."

"'Bye." Satreih watched her go. Soon after, he headed back to the camp.

Kaskin asked, "Where's Yia?"

"On her way to Meikosa. I wanted her to stay behind."

"Do you love her?" Chikara hit Kaskin hard on the shoulder with her snout. "Hey! That hurt!"

It was supposed to.

Kaskin shot her an evil look. "You were the one who asked how long it would be before their first kiss."

Shut up Kaskin.

Satreih asked, "What? Fine. If you really want to know, that's already happened."

Hah! I was guessing two weeks! I was right!

"Cheater. You didn't even say what your guess was before! You could have guessed five days!"

If you remember correctly, Yia entered the room just as I was about to answer.

Kaskin countered, "But you didn't say anything after she left."

Satreih shook his head. He was both amused and annoyed. "Are you guys ready to go yet?" He allowed a touch of annoyance to creep into his voice.

Whenever you are.

Kaskin nodded in agreement.

Satreih climbed onto Chikara's back. "When was this little conversation?"

"Right after you were teleported to Hell."

Chikara and Kaskin continued to bicker.

*   *   *   *

The length of the flight surprised Chikara. It had only taken a couple of hours to reach Mosiania. *So how do you want me to kill the guard? Fire? Fangs? Claws?* She hesitated, *Mind-powers?*

Satreih said, "We don't want to kill him just yet. We'll raise an alarm. We won't even be able to set foot inside the place."

Kaskin offered, "I can knock him out quickly. He won't know what hit him."

"Same thing. I'll bet you that some of his buddies are lurking nearby. They will see what happens. He'll be harder to knock out than Verteq's other minions."

They were high above the gates of Mosiania. The guard that just happened to be in the way was a Spy.

Satreih asked Chikara, "Can you fly above the gates?"

I can't. Verteq erected a repelling barrier. It is way too strong for me to break through. The scent of magical herbs flowed through Chikara's nostrils. *I won't need to. Even though she's not here now, Yia is helping us.*

"What!?" Satreih asked, horrified.

The Spy started to drift away from the gates, obviously compelled to check for intruders coming from another direction.

Hmm. I see. Yia set up a diversion spell. The barrier has been destroyed as well.

Satreih exclaimed, dismayed, "But Verteq could recognize her magic!"

Satreih! Morith in cave! Guarded by Weuh!

Thanks, Razij. Can you and Rasnir wait a little while longer?

Yes.

"Chikara, there is a cave somewhere in Mosiania. The morith is in the cave, and it's being guarded by the old wizard. Razij just told me."

Chikara was passing over the gates. *I see it. But I also see the cells where the were-cat and Rasnir are being held. I'll drop you and Kaskin off near the cave. While you're taking care of the morith, I'll go rescue the two captives.*

"We'll be seen! It will be harder trying to get back to each other."

Kaskin gave Satreih a sideways look. "You try to rely on your brain too much."

Only our shadows might be seen. Yia also put all of us under an invisibility spell. Chikara landed next to the cave's entrance. Satreih held Kaskin back. Miasma poured out of the dark, gaping hole. The miasma thinned and vanished.

I guess it helps to have magic. Chikara kept an eye on a group of Wi'oks and pig creatures that were close by. Some of the pig creatures' heads swiveled around in surprise. *Go.* Chikara pushed Satreih and Kaskin toward the cave. *They smell our scents. But they're dumb brutes. They don't see us. That will confuse them for a while. I'll be back—with Rasnir and Razij.*

Weuh looked up, eyeing the corner of the cave suspiciously. "Do you think that I do not see you?" Weuh performed a powerful counter spell, revealing

Satreih and Kaskin. He didn't know that Satreih was already behind him, silently making his way toward the barrier that protected the morith.

Kaskin replied coldly, "How did you know that I was here? There is not enough light in this room for you to see my shadow."

"Wizards and false wizards alike can recognize other magic. Where are the other three?"

Kaskin withdrew his sword. "They aren't in Mosiania. I came by myself."

An irritating ring filled Weuh's mind. He was used to the morith's ring, but this was different. He mirrored Kaskin's move. Weuh was sure he didn't need to waste magic on a man. Men were too easily filled with hate. "Why? Surely you know that is suicide. Or maybe your friends did come, and they abandoned you here to die by my hands." *This man is no different from any other.*

*   *   *   *

Yia watched what was going on by using the Scrying Rituals. As far as she knew, no witch of her age was able to do this for a long period of time; the distance was too great. Most witches couldn't perform more magic while they were performing the rituals. Sweat was streaming off her. Yia knew she would be exhausted later.

Yia made a caldron appear next to her. She poured a purple liquid into it. *I'll see what happens during the fight before it actually happens.* Yia watched the fight unblinkingly. Kaskin was doing pretty well, considering that he wasn't a wizard himself. But what she saw at the end shocked her so much that she gasped. Her concentration was broken, and that affected things that were happening at that very moment.

*   *   *   *

Weuh turned around, shocked, at the sound of a sword being slammed against the barrier protecting the morith. *Why didn't I know he was there!?* Weuh made a move towards Satreih, but didn't get far.

Kaskin slashed his sword across Weuh's back. "I thought someone like you would know to never leave his back unprotected." He blocked and parried one of Weuh's attacks. The parry was successful. But in the split second when Kaskin was preparing to land another attack, Weuh slammed the flat of his blade against the side of Kaskin's head.

Satreih continued to strike the barrier with the fire sword. The barrier was showing tremendous resistance, but Satreih knew it would give way very soon. He was right. The barrier collapsed and turned to dust.

Weuh took advantage of Kaskin's slight dizziness and ran towards Satreih with his sword raised.

Kaskin knew, or guessed, what was going to happen. That knowledge gave him a burst of adrenaline, and he ran between Weuh and Satreih before Weuh struck.

Weuh had aimed well. His sword was sticking in Kaskin's heart.

BATTLE FOR DOMINATION

Rasnir huddled in his corner, watching the steel door with a mixture of fear and surprise. It was glowing white-hot. The heat was getting close to unbearable. Something from outside was slamming against it, occasionally bellowing with anger.

Razij clung to Rasnir's shoulder.

Rasnir asked, "W-What is outside that thing?"

Remember annoying dragon I told you about?

"The one named after Satreih's mother?"

Razij nodded. *She try to break down door.*

With one last slam, the door shattered. Chikara tumbled into the room.

Have fun with door, dragon?

Chikara growled in response. *C'mon, get on.*

Razij immediately jumped down from Rasnir's shoulder and climbed onto Chikara's back. Rasnir didn't move. Fear and awe had paralyzed him in place.

Chikara leaned down and grabbed the back of Rasnir's shirt, although it was more like a rag.

Rasnir protested, "Hey!"

Chikara put him on her back. *I can take you to Satreih!*

*   *   *   *

Weuh took a threatening step towards Satreih, with his sword pointed at him. "So, my misguided friend, what's it going to be? Have you lost your sights since your friend's tragic death?" He nodded to Kaskin, who had fallen into Satreih's arms. "He was just a man, after all. They are not capable of great deeds. They only care about themselves."

Satreih was in shock, not moving an inch from where he stood for awhile. Finally, he got his mind around what had happened. Anger and hatred started tearing at his chest. Satreih gently placed Kaskin on the ground. He picked up the fire sword which he had dropped in shock. He killed Weuh with a single slice.

An overwhelming sadness dissolved the anger and hatred. It was almost as bad as when he had "killed" Makue.

"Kaskin ..." There was no chance to stop the steady flow of tears. *T-That's right. The sword has healing powers.* Satreih placed the sword across Kaskin's wound.

Kaskin's body glowed for a second, then turned back to normal.

It didn't seem to do much—I have to stop the bleeding myself.

Satreih tore off his jacket and shirt. He picked up Kaskin's neglected sword, and used it to cut his shirt into strips. He knew his shirt would burn if he used his fire sword. The bandages he had just made were ready. He tied them around the injury. He wrapped Kaskin in his jacket, trying to keep him warm. He gently moved Kaskin's head onto his lap.

Satreih cried for several minutes, applying more pressure to the wound. After what seemed like a lifetime, but was actually a few minutes, Satreih heard a barely audible, strained voice. Though weak, the voice didn't show any hint of a stutter.

"What did I say about the first move?"

"N-Never make it." Satreih somehow managed a small smile through his tears. "Why did you do that? I'm the only one with armor on."

Kaskin was having trouble focusing. "He still would have killed you. He is a wizard." He made a weak movement for his sword.

Satreih handed the sword to him.

Even though it was a weak stab, it utterly destroyed the morith. The cave collapsed, but the fire sword formed a protective barrier around them.

Kaskin said softly, "I don't regret my actions. Leave me here; Chikara will find me. Go kill Verteq." He said in a somewhat stronger voice, "I'm proud to have known you as my best friend." Kaskin closed his eyes.

Satreih hesitated for a few seconds. He had no more tears to shed. The anger had returned. He gently moved Kaskin off him and stood up. Satreih started walking to the crater of Mt. Ogick. Somehow, he knew Verteq was there waiting for him.

✻   ✻   ✻   ✻

Rasnir sniffed the air. He nearly gagged. "This blood scent is overwhelming."

Razij scoffed, *Scent worse for us.*

"Yeah. You probably have stronger noses than I do."

There's that. And we also know the blood scent. A friend has been fatally wounded. Satreih just told me. Chikara flew lower to the ground.

"Shouldn't we be up a little higher? We're in range of their archers."

I'm not worried about that. There! Chikara landed next to Kaskin; her flank up against him. She was making mourning sounds. She growled softly when she smelled Weuh's stench on Kaskin. She knew the wizard put a spell on him so she wouldn't be able to heal him. She tried anyway, but, as she expected, there was no effect.

Rasnir leaned over, shocked. *What happened here? The scents are confusing, they're all jumbled up.* Rasnir jumped. He numbly reached up for the fallen stranger. Chikara had picked him up with the neck of Satreih's jacket in her mouth.

Rasnir held the stranger to Chikara's back, so he wouldn't fall off when she flew.

In a few seconds, Chikara had taken herself and her riders across the gates of Mosiania. She was flying as fast as she could.

Where we goin'?

Chikara gave a simple answer: *Help is in Meikosa.*

✻   ✻   ✻   ✻

The volcano's crater wasn't what Satreih expected. The crater was enclosed, exposing only a small entrance.

Verteq stood on a narrow rock that jutted precariously over the bubbling magma below. His hood was off. Verteq had a small patch of dirty, black hair on his head; his face was deathly pale; his nostrils were slits. Wounds from battle had marred the entire right side of Verteq's face; along with the battle scars were the marks of a dragon's talons. One eye looked like it was painfully shut, but Satreih got the weird feeling that Verteq was still looking at him through it. Verteq's other red eye had no pupil. It blazed with a fierce and powerful evil that existed only within him. The ash from the volcano that swirled around him made him appear even more demonic. Behind him were five cascades of magma that poured into the crater's abyss.

"Y-O-U—!" Satreih ran at Verteq with his sword raised high and clutched tightly in his hand.

Verteq placed the tips of two fingers on the hilt of his fire sword. A barrier appeared out of nowhere, blocking and repelling Satreih's attack.

Satreih flew backwards. He quickly got back on his feet.

Verteq seethed, "Your mind is only filled with hate and vengeance, is it not?"

Satreih replied coldly, "The hate and vengeance of those that you and your people have killed."

"Don't lie. Those emotions have been within you ever since you learned that I had killed your family. They have only intensified since Kaskin's murder."

Satreih growled, "Was Kaskin's death part of your plan?"

Verteq shrugged, unconcerned. "Men are relatively weak. Think of it this way: it is like squashing bugs."

Satreih replied, with his distaste for Verteq clearly showing in his voice, "But if you kill enough of them, it causes problems."

Verteq chuckled knowingly. He raised his arm.

Satreih took a few running steps toward Verteq, expecting him to attack. The attack never came. Instead, Satreih heard Verteq's army moving. "What?" Satreih looked behind himself, watching the crater's entrance. Shadows were moving past.

"Your friends will not be alive much longer. Nor will anyone else around them."

*   *   *   *

"King Thuoj!" Yia called, breathlessly. "You must prepare your elves for battle!"

"What has happened?" he asked.

Yia panted, "Verteq just sent an army to attack."

"How do you know this?"

"I am a witch."

King Thuoj nodded. "How much time do we have?"

"A week at the most. Verteq sent all of his minions. Moving that many takes a while."

King Thuoj ran off to ready his elves.

Yia made sure nobody was watching. She transformed into a cat. She rested her head down on her paws. *A little sleep before the fight would help. This way I can smell Chikara when she comes.* Yia sighed and glanced up at the sky. It started to rain. A cat's thought came into her mind. She hissed. The cat's mind was sometimes annoying. *Damn! I tried everything I could to prevent Kaskin's fate. I probably stopped Weuh's blade from going all the way through, but still…*

Another unpleasant thought wove its way into her mind. Yia stood up suddenly, but forced herself back down. *Satreih will be fine. He has the sword. He doesn't want me to help fight anyway. If I keep thinking like this, I'm not going to get to sleep. I won't even be able to lift the dagger!*

Yia! Verteq sent—

Yia opened her eyes and transformed back into her normal self. As soon as her body would let her speak English, she said, "An army. I know. I was watching."

Yia! Razij jumped up onto Yia's shoulder, purring. His purring didn't last long. He growled. *Kaskin*—He didn't finish his sentence.

Yia nodded sadly. "I know. There wasn't much I could do to prevent that from happening. Especially against a wizard."

Chikara gently took Kaskin from Rasnir and placed him in Yia's outstretched arms.

Rasnir slid down from Chikara's back. He wasn't graceful about it; the continuing downpour was making her back slick. His legs were also weak from lack of use.

Yia was already using magic to heal Kaskin. She was also undoing Weuh's spells, which was extremely difficult. If Kaskin survived, she knew his recovery would be a long one. Yia said warmly to Rasnir, "Looks like somebody's finally out of that disgusting cell."

Rasnir nodded. He had never seen someone so close to death before. His son had died while he was at work; Satreih's mother was already dead by the time he had gotten there.

Yia gently laid Kaskin on the bed. They were in the same room where Yia had woken up after fighting the spy.

"Is there anything I can do?" Rasnir noticed that the other injuries Kaskin acquired during the battle were also healing.

"I don't think so." Yia gave Rasnir a quick glance. A plate of food appeared in front of him. "Don't eat too fast. Your system's not used to it."

"Easier said than done," Rasnir said between inhaled mouthfuls. He forced himself to slow down.

Yia chuckled and concentrated on Kaskin. *Poor Kaskin. He's already stiff.* She thought back to when Satreih had laid the fire sword on Kaskin's heart. Her eyes widened in shock. *I bet Satreih has no idea what he did. I thought that part of the sword's powers was just a myth!*

✶   ✶   ✶   ✶

"It's over, Verteq. You're out of moriths and nearly out of power. I've come to kill you." Satreih's surprise from seeing the army moving so quickly was gone. He faked a swing to Verteq's chest, then went for his head.

Verteq didn't fall for the fake. Instead, he blocked the head-shot and made a successful counterattack. "You will regret fighting only with hate and vengeance."

Even though the fight had just begun, Satreih suddenly felt drained. He looked up in surprise. A big, angry cloud hovered above Verteq. Satreih's sword instantly erected a barrier around him as the cloud attacked. To Satreih's shock, the barrier shattered, and he felt immense pain.

Verteq smiled evilly. "That gives another meaning to the saying 'feeling drained of emotion.' You should have listened to Kaskin when he was trying to teach you the art of swordsmanship."

Rasnir and Razij sniffed the air at the same time, but Rasnir beat the werecat to the comment. "They're almost here."

Yia looked up and nodded. "Will you guys watch Kaskin?"

Both of them nodded.

Where you goin'?

"I've done all I can for him. It's time for me to help the Meikosans in battle." Yia formed a purplish dagger that hovered above her outstretched hands. "Catch." She tossed it to Rasnir.

✶   ✶   ✶   ✶

To Yia's surprise, King Thuoj was sitting on Chikara's back.

Are you ready?

Yia nodded and climbed on in front of the king.

Chikara flew, perching on one of the palace's highest towers. Right below them—minus the women and children—was every elf in Meikosa.

King Thuoj explained, "I've gathered everyone I could. Kings Lathik and Castelo are on their way with their people."

I'd suggest that you cover your ears! Chikara bellowed long and loud. The bellow was more like a combination of a roar and a screech.

After she finished bellowing, Yia cautiously lowered her hands from her ears. "What did you bellow like that for?"

To get help from the other dragons, and from the one overseas.

"You mean, Auburn would have heard that? Even though he's all the way in the other land?"

He should have.

*   *   *   *

Itimei was watching the guards play a sport of theirs during their break. In the distance, she heard a roar. She could barely hear it, since it was so far off. To her, it sounded like Chikara. She tried to contact Kaskin with mind-speech to ask if that was Chikara or not. Even though she did manage to get through to him, his words were barely heard and strained. He only said a couple of words before he slipped out of her grasp.

None of the guards heard the roar. They were too intent on their game.

Itimei saw something red streaking toward the other land. *That might be the dragon in this land. Isn't his name Auburn, or something like that?* "Auburn!"

The red thing paused, but then it started to head her way.

The guards looked up in fear. They were used to Chikara, but not this dragon.

"Don't attack!" Itimei looked up at Auburn and asked, "Was that Chikara who just roared?"

Auburn nodded. He blew red fire. The fire landed on the steps of the palace. It formed into Verteq's image.

"They're fighting?"

Auburn nodded again as Verteq's image disappeared.

"How many men can you take?"

Auburn pointed to a painting inside the palace.

Itimei counted the number of men in the painting quickly. "You can take a hundred?"

Auburn nodded. It was one of the few ways that he could communicate with the Race of Men.

Itimei used mind-speech to tell King Stephenson what was going on. Out of all the people in her land, she and her father were the only ones who could use mind-speech. She had taught him.

*   *   *   *

Satreih did his best to ignore the intensifying pain and hunger. He gained control over his emotions. He realized what a huge difference it made in fighting. Now that he was thinking clearly, he was making more successful attacks and more efficient blocks. But the battle was so fast that he couldn't tell if he was making the first move or not. There wasn't enough time for thought.

Verteq was now bleeding. In the past, the only two people who had managed to injure him were the Satreih before him and Meithoko.

Verteq made another sword appear with magic, and drew it across Satreih's chest.

Satreih looked at the sword warily. Breathing was suddenly much harder. He knew that Verteq had ruptured a lung. He was expecting Verteq's fire sword to attack him, not this one. The new sword looked equally nasty in terms of its ability to cause damage. Satreih knew it was a magical blade.

For some reason, the ophilla wasn't really helping. He might as well be fighting bare-chested.

Verteq hissed with malice, "Interesting blade, isn't it? You will most likely never heal from the injuries it gives you."

Both Satreih and Verteq were bleeding heavily.

*   *   *   *

Rasnir stood up and turned sideways. He held out the magical dagger that Yia had given him. The Spies had stolen and broken his bow and arrows. Rasnir pointed the dagger at the Wi'oks that had just entered the room. Rasnir asked, "W-What brings them here?"

Razij jumped onto Kaskin's chest, protecting him. He hissed. *They attracted to those near death.* His ears were flattened against his head and his fur was standing on end.

"Aii!" Rasnir barely dodged an attack. He stabbed the Wi'ok with the dagger. It instantly turned to gray dust. "Wow. This is easier to use than a regular dagger."

A Wi'ok brought its sword down near Kaskin. Razij hissed. He jumped up at the Wi'ok, biting it multiple times.

Razij felt the Wi'ok's bony hands wrap around his neck. *Rasnir!*

Rasnir acted quickly, slashing the dagger down the Wi'ok's back.

*   *   *   *

Chikara reared up in order to avoid an attack from a Spy. King Thuoj and Yia had jumped off of her back to help the others in battle.

A dozen arrows were neatly lodged into the Spy's back. It fell.

As men clambered down from Auburn's back, Itimei yelled, "More are on the way!"

The other dragons, the centaurs, and the dwarfs had also arrived.

Chikara grinned. She combined her fire with Auburn's, making a plethora of Verteq's minions fall.

Itimei shot a pig creature with some arrows. "Where are the others?"

Satreih's fighting Verteq; Yia is somewhere else fighting, helping the Meikosans. Kaskin is unconscious in a separate room.

"What happened to him? He said only a couple of strained, incomprehensible words when I tried to contact him with mind-speech." Itimei slashed at a darkish cloud with a dagger that had been strapped to her ankle. The cloud of evil was too close to her liking.

He was critically wounded. Chikara growled. *Some Wi'oks have managed to get into his room. They're overpowering Rasnir and Razij!*

"Where's the room? I'll go help!"

Chikara nodded in the direction.

"Did you … truly think … that you could … defeat us?"

Rasnir looked up at the Wi'ok that was sitting on his chest. He said indignantly, "I'm *not* going back into that cell again."

"No … problem. Master … told us to kill … you. Your … death … has waited … long enough."

The Wi'ok raised its sword.

Razij heard a familiar and welcome voice. "I don't think so."

An arrow lodged itself in the Wi'ok's back. It instantly turned to gray dust.

Itimei attacked the other Wi'oks before they had time to recover.

*   *   *   *

"Damn!" Satreih's sword flew from his hand, landing on a rock that protruded out of the magma. The magma completely surrounded it.

Satreih dodged Verteq's attack and rolled around him, closer to the edge. He popped back up and slammed the fire sword's empty scabbard against Verteq's head to buy some time.

Satreih ran down the rock's side. Without stopping to think, Satreih leapt for the pillar of rock that his sword was on. He scrambled on top, with the sword clutched in his left hand. *Argh! I trapped myself!*

*   *   *   *

Yia used her magic to help herself and the other elves, dwarfs, and centaurs around her. She made sure that her allies' attacks never missed. She was also forcing most of Verteq's army back, preparing for a finishing blow.

Yia felt pain on the back of her head. She slashed the dagger at her attacker's chest.

"Remember me?"

Yia gasped. The attacker was the Spy that had beaten her so badly. Satreih and his friends were the only reason why she had survived. "It will not end the same way as it did last time."

The Spy hissed, "You're right. It won't. I will kill you this time."

Yia backed away to give herself more room. She knew her eyes were not betraying the fear that she felt. Yia dropped the dagger.

"You're not even putting up a fight this time? How sad. I wanted to have some fun."

Yia grinned. The Spy assumed she was giving up. Yia formed a red energy ball between her hands. It was the same spell that she had performed when Satreih had first seen her use magic. The only difference was that this time, it was much, much more powerful.

The spell began to suck in the elements of the storm. It was getting hard to hold. Yia flung her arms out, releasing the spell. All of Verteq's army instantly fell.

AFTER THE BATTLE

Yia woke. Chikara, Auburn, and all of the other dragons were leaning up against her.

Chikara grinned once she realized Yia was awake. *That was amazing, Yia! Verteq's army was totally obliterated!*

Yia asked softly, "Was it?" She coughed. It was painful to breathe. She felt like she was going to fall back into unconsciousness any second. "Where's Satreih?"

Still fighting Verteq, I'm guessing. But by the time he gets back, the elves probably won't let him be alone with us.

"Why not?"

King Thuoj's life was taken during the battle. Meikosa is without a king. There is no heir to the throne. The other elves are saying that they want Satreih to take over.

*　　　　*　　　　*　　　　*

Satreih was having a hard time keeping his balance, due to the staggering amount of blood loss. *We've been fighting for nearly two weeks ...*

He and Verteq were fighting on the rock where Satreih's sword had fallen. The fight had slowed as weariness gradually began to take its toll on both of them, but it was still very violent.

Suddenly, Verteq disappeared.

Satreih stuck his sword in the ground and leaned on it, panting, slightly confused but thankful for the break. He looked up, sensing that he was not alone. In front of him, hovering over the magma, were his parents. Behind them were other spirits that seemed somewhat familiar.

Chikara and Airon said in unison, "We will give you strength."

Satreih's parents and the spirits behind them disappeared.

Verteq returned.

Satreih felt as much strength as he had possessed at the beginning of the fight. Without hesitating, he stabbed Verteq, knowing the death match was nearly over and about to sway in his favor.

The fire sword, too, seemed to realize what was happening. It flamed brightly, manipulating the magma. Unwillingly, the magma obliged. It roared up with demonic speed, enveloping both Satreih and Verteq.

Satreih knew fighting against the relentless surge would have been useless if the sword hadn't protected him from it. Verteq's scream of infinite hatred cut through him.

Desperate to make one more attack, Verteq's magical blade made a weak—though still vicious—successful attempt to cut Satreih's neck. But any further attempts to murder Satreih were halted as the magma claimed the sword's master.

Satreih's fire sword seemed unwilling to claim its twin along with its master. Verteq's fire sword was left at Satreih's side.

Satreih collapsed in exhaustion as the magma returned to the bowels of the crater. The energy that he had felt was gone. Just as he let the blackness of sleep claim his mind and body, he heard a familiar, welcome roar right outside the cavern.

✳   ✳   ✳   ✳

Satreih woke and twisted around in Chikara's talons. Meikosa was coming into view. He concentrated on clearing his lungs. The fresh air was a blessing after breathing in smoke and ash from the volcano.

Are you all right?

"Not really."

I would be surprised if you were. Don't worry. We'll reach Meikosa in a few minutes. Yia will help you.

Chikara gently placed Satreih on the ground, helping him get his footing. Satreih noticed that Meikosa was badly damaged. People from both lands worked together to rebuild. The elves and the dwarfs were getting along. Even King

Lathik was doing his best to help. He was even shouting encouragement to every-one.

Yia ran up to Satreih and gave him a "welcome back" kiss.

Satreih kissed her back, happy to be with her. "Sorry about the blood."

Yia gently pushed Satreih's head back. "Is that from Verteq's magical blade?" She asked softly, referring to the new scar on his neck.

Satreih nodded. An unpleasant thought came into his mind. He pulled away from her and asked, "Where's Kaskin?"

Yia didn't answer. She wrapped an arm around Satreih's waist. She began to lead him to Kaskin's room.

Satreih looked around, watching things progress. He noticed that the elves were looking at him with longing expressions. He asked Yia, "Why are they look-ing at me like that?"

Yia replied softly, "I'll tell you later, after you get some rest."

*   *   *   *

Razij leapt up onto Satreih's shoulder and began to purr loudly.

Satreih grinned. "Hey. Long time no see." His statement wasn't directed to the werecat. It was directed to the person sitting next to Kaskin's bed.

Rasnir turned around and smiled. "Yeah, it has been a while." He glanced out the window. The sun was just starting to rise. He looked back at Satreih and asked, "Somebody kill Verteq by any chance?"

Satreih nodded vigorously. "Do you want proof?"

"I already have some." Rasnir motioned to the window.

"I have more." Satreih held out the two fire swords.

"Cool."

"That's one way of putting it."

Yia made two extra chairs and a plate of food for Satreih appear with magic.

Satreih sat in the chair and looked worriedly at Kaskin, only nibbling at his food. He had suddenly lost his appetite. He asked softly, "Has he been uncon-scious the entire time I was fighting?"

Rasnir nodded. "Razij, Yia, or I have been with him the entire time. Chikara has been directly outside most of the time. Kaskin will survive. Itimei was here at the beginning, but she had to return home, since she's the princess and has much to attend to. The men from that land will be leaving shortly." After hesitating, he asked slyly, "How long have you had Chikara?"

"About two years. Remember when I found mother's grave?"

"Yeah."

"I found Chikara's egg in the same clearing. She hatched pretty much as soon as I got there."

Rasnir thought for a bit. "Hmm. Dragons have healing powers. So *that's* why you were suddenly healed after falling down the hill with the thorns. And you said that elves heal more quickly than men."

"We do. But it would have taken longer than that to heal from that many cuts." Satreih could feel his injuries being healed by magic. Breathing was easier. "To tell you the truth, you could have heard her. Chikara squeaked inside my coat pocket, but you were too intent on eating your food."

"Guilty."

Yia said, "Satreih, you probably should get some rest soon. I doubt that you've had any sleep during the past two weeks."

Satreih looked at Kaskin. He could feel Yia's eyes on him.

"If you don't get some sleep willingly, I'm going to put that sleeping spell on you again."

Satreih sighed. "Fine. You win."

Rasnir laughed. "Not even going to put up a fight, eh?"

"I've done enough fighting. Besides, I won't win. I think I've only won against her brain once."

Rasnir offered, "I'll wake you if he does." He nodded in Kaskin's direction.

Yia had just finished preparing a potion. "Here. Drink this. It'll help you sleep. You won't have any dreams."

Satreih muttered, "Dreams are the last thing I need." He gratefully drank the potion and made his way to the bed. He was asleep before his head hit the pillow.

Yia was also exhausted. She laid down next to him and went to sleep herself, with a hand on his scar.

Yia was fighting someone she didn't know. She felt sick and queasy, but she did her best to ignore those feelings. Two unpleasant emotions swelled inside of her. Sadness and desperation. Yia looked around the battlefield, while keeping an eye on her opponent.

Using one of the fire swords, Kaskin was fighting Weuh's spirit. He was also using a powerful, wizard-like power that Yia didn't know he had in him. She admired the mastery of spells that he was using. He was successful in disintegrating Weuh's spirit.

Chikara was fighting another golden dragon, but she was hesitant to attack him. Most of their battle was in the air. They were seldom seen.

Satreih also seemed hesitant to attack Verteq. He was bleeding much more than his foe was. Verteq kept taunting him, goading him to attack. Verteq thrust his two magical blades forward, piercing Satreih through his lungs and back.

Yia felt herself cry out as she rushed to Satreih's side, forgetting about her opponent. She pulled him closer to her, cradling his dying body and sobbing uncontrollably.

Verteq backed off, grinning evilly. The grin fell off his face and formed into a confused frown. He felt for sure that when he killed Satreih, his friends would attack him like an angry swarm of bees. They didn't attack.

Kaskin withdrew his fire sword. He knew that it had healing powers, even better than the ones he had.

Satreih looked up. "No thanks, Kaskin. You know that it is for the best." He looked to Chikara. She had just flown down from the sky. Satreih asked her, referring to everyone, "Take care of them, will you?"

Satreih said to Yia, "Remember what I told you." With a last, dying breath, Satreih added, "Ikasi ... Erastos ..."

Yia felt herself cry out in anguish once again.

*   *   *   *

Satreih slowly woke. Yia's arms were wrapped around his shoulders. She had cried out a couple of times during her sleep. She looked like she was having a bad dream.

Satreih shook Yia awake. "What's wrong?"

Yia stared at him in confusion. She shook her head, trying to rid herself of the images. "N-Nothing ... just ... just a nightmare." *That dream was so vivid.*

"Maybe you should've had the sleeping potion as well."

"I should have." She thought for a bit. "Who are Ikasi and Erastos?" *They sounded like names.*

Satreih gave her a confused look. "Who are who?"

Yia shook her head. "Never mind." She tried to slow her racing heart. She asked, trying to change the subject, "Do you know why the elves were looking at you like that?"

Satreih shook his head.

"King Thuoj died during the battle."

He blinked in surprise. "And?"

"The elves want you to take over."

"What? There's not an heir to the throne?"

"No." Yia stood, offering him a hand. "C'mon, let's go back to Kaskin's room."

*   *   *   *

Kaskin opened his eyes slightly. Razij and a man he didn't recognize were sitting next to the bed. "Nnn?"

Kaskin! Razij jumped onto his stomach and began to purr loudly in complete bliss. *War over! Verteq dead!*

"It is?" Kaskin looked at Rasnir. "Who are you?"

"My name is Rasnir. I'm Satreih's father." Rasnir held a canteen to Kaskin's lips.

Kaskin lifted his head off the pillow a little and took a grateful sip. The water felt good against his cracked lips.

"Kaskin! You're awake!"

Kaskin let his head fall back onto the pillow. It had taken a lot of energy just to lift it. "Hi, you two."

Satreih and Yia had just walked in. Satreih asked, concerned, "Are you all right?"

"I could be better." Kaskin remembered something and sat up, causing a bolt of intense pain to shoot through his body. Kaskin winced and looked down, fumbling to remove the bandages. Once the somewhat stained gauze fell away, he noticed that there was a huge scar over his heart. He felt Yia sit on the bed next to him.

Yia placed a hand on Kaskin's shoulder. She said softly, "There wasn't much I could do to heal that."

Kaskin was shocked. *I knew I was seriously wounded, but ...* "Both of you probably saved my life. Thank you."

Satreih said quickly, "You don't need to thank us. We're friends."

Yia nodded in agreement.

Rasnir said, "I'll let you guys be alone for a while."

*   *   *   *

Chikara inquired, *Is Kaskin awake yet?*

"Yes he is. I left so Satreih and Yia could spend time with him alone." Something was bothering him. Rasnir voiced his thoughts softly, "Most men wouldn't survive an attack like that."

I was thinking the same thing. Chikara looked at the ground. *The attacker was a wizard. Don't you think he would have used a spell or something to make sure things go as planned?*

Rasnir pointed out, "But Kaskin had Yia on his side."

Weuh has many more years of experience at magic than Yia does. Something is going to happen because Kaskin was almost murdered. I can feel it.

COURAGE AND
REJECTION

In Meikosa there was a party that lasted a week to celebrate the end of the war. Kaskin stayed in bed for most of it as he continued to recover. Satreih, Yia, Razij, and Rasnir stayed with him. Kaskin kept insisting that they didn't have to wait for him, but they wouldn't listen. Chikara stayed right outside the room.

Kaskin was able to get out of bed on the last night of the party.

✳   ✳   ✳   ✳

Satreih waited for Yia to come out of her room.

Yia opened the door and asked, "How do I look?"

Satreih's mouth dropped open. Yia's hair was completely loose and brushed. She was wearing a silky, deep purple dress with long sleeves. She had done something to make her eyes stand out even more. She was wearing diamond earrings, and a beautiful headpiece.

Satreih gasped, "Beautiful. I thought you didn't like dresses."

"They get in the way most of the time, but not tonight." Yia grinned. "C'mon, let's go. We don't want to be late!" She started walking towards the sound of the music that was playing. On her way, Yia shut Satreih's mouth for him, laughing as he comically chased her.

After the small chase, Satreih finally noticed that Yia was holding something. "What are you carrying?" The "something" was in a bag, so Satreih couldn't see what it truly was.

Yia winked at him. She said playfully, "You'll see."

Satreih made a wild guess. "Fireworks by any chance?"

How did he know? "Maybe. Maybe not." *I don't want to spoil the surprise.*

Chikara asked, curiously, *What's in the bag?*

Satreih exclaimed, "That's what I want to know!"

Satreih and Yia arrived at the party. Chikara, Kaskin, Rasnir, and the werecat were already there.

Yia emptied the bag's contents onto the grass.

"Hah! I was right!"

Yia asked, "How did you guess?"

Satreih grinned. "My blood-related father said that your family made the best fireworks." He called, "Oi! Kaskin! Father! Come over here!"

Razij jumped onto Chikara's head. For once, Chikara didn't growl at his appearance. *I no invited?*

"You, too."

"What?" Kaskin and Rasnir came over. It hurt for Kaskin to walk, but he ignored the pain.

Satreih took out Verteq's fire sword. He asked Yia, "May I?"

"Light away." Yia quickly put a spell that blocked fire on the trees, to prevent them from burning.

As Satreih slashed the fire sword above a couple of fireworks, they instantly ignited. Gold, green, and blue streaks were launched into the sky.

The streaks transformed into a chimera and sea serpent. The chimera roared as the sea serpent swam across the night sky. They exploded, sending a wave of harmless blue and golden specks to the people below. The chimera and sea serpent were followed by excited cheers.

Satreih laughed. "He wasn't lying!"

Chikara grinned. *My turn!* She blew fire on her selected fireworks.

Yia sat on the soft grass and watched the dueling wizards above. The grass had almost instantly popped up after Verteq's demise. "For some reason, I don't think the fireworks are going to last that long."

Satreih had a big smile on his face. "What gives you that idea?"

"Oh I don't know." Yia spotted a couple of children taking off with their prize of stolen fireworks. "Hey!" The fireworks flew from their greedy arms.

The children made disappointed noises and ran off.

Yia's prediction was right. The fireworks were gone in no time. There was tremendous applause when the display of fireworks ended.

There was still plenty to do after the fireworks.

*   *   *   *

Satreih looked to the east. It was just getting light. He stood to the side, watching everyone have fun. He arrived at a couple of decisions. One was that Kaskin was a bad dancer—not that he was any better. The other one was that it was time to ask for Yia's hand in marriage.

Satreih had already asked Rasnir about this decision, and he already knew that his parents approved.

Satreih approached Yia. "Do you have a moment?"

He led her to the beautiful chasm on the outskirts of Meikosa.

"What's on your mind?"

"I probably would never have made it as far as I did without your help."

Yia said quickly, "We all played our parts."

Satreih smiled. Yia was modest. "It would have been much more difficult to complete our tasks without magic."

"What are you trying to say?"

"You know that I love you." Satreih hesitated a little, but then brought out the ring he had bought. "Will you marry me?"

Yia looked at the ring for a while. She said softly, "No."

Satreih was crushed. "Why? Because I'm younger than you? Because I'm not a wizard?"

Yia pulled him into a tight hug. Satreih hugged her back, but not as tightly.

She said softly, "I do love you, Satreih. But the time isn't right for marriage."

"Why not? The war is over."

"It's not." Yia pulled away from him and walked to the rim of the chasm.

"What do you mean? Verteq is dead."

"No, he's not. As usual, he survived by using dark magic." Yia sighed. "You don't know what you did when you laid the sword across Kaskin's heart, do you?"

Satreih didn't answer.

"You brought him back to life."

"Wha?"

"An attack like that would kill any man."

"B-But how do you know that I brought him back to life?" Satreih was shocked.

"It is one of the sword's powers. The legend said that if the owner of the fire sword lays it across a recently deceased person's heart, the sword will resurrect them."

"Does Weuh somehow factor into this?"

"Unfortunately. Did you kill him with a vengeance?"

"How could I not? I thought he had killed Kaskin." Satreih added darkly, "Turns out I was right."

Yia placed a hand against her forehead. "That's why the war is not over. It is complicated magic. I don't fully understand it. Because you killed him with a vengeance, Weuh is able to come back as a spirit, but more powerful than ever. Verteq was sheltering some of his power within Weuh, hence the reason why he's not dead."

Satreih asked, horrified, "There was another morith?"

"No. As I said, I don't know how this works. But I do know this: you will not be the one to disintegrate Weuh's spirit."

"Oh? Who will?"

Yia looked him directly in the eye. "Kaskin."

978-0-595-47625-1
0-595-47625-2